**Please check all items for damages
before leaving the Library.
Thereafter you will bc held
responsible for all injuries
to items beyond reasonable wear.**

Helen M. Plum Memorial Library

Lombard, Illinois

A daily fine will be charged for
overdue materials.

MAY   2009

APPASSIONATA

APPASSIONATA

EVA HOFFMAN

OTHER PRESS • NEW YORK

Copyright © 2008 Eva Hoffman
First published as *Illuminations* by Harvill Secker in the UK in 2008

Other Press edition 2009

Production Editor: Yvonne E. Cárdenas

This book was set in Garamond.

10 9 8 7 6 5 4 3 2 1

Library of Congress Cataloging-in-Publication Data

Hoffman, Eva, 1945-
[Illuminations]
Appassionata / Eva Hoffman.
265p. cm.
Previously published as: Illuminations.
ISBN 978-1-59051-319-4
1. Women pianists--Fiction. 2. Political refugees--
Fiction. 3. Arts and society--Fiction. I. Title.
PR6108.O34I45 2009
823'.92--dc22
2008042015

APPASSIONATA

. . . See her there, among the perpetual crowd, moving through the routines of check-in, security control, departure lounge. She's an attractive woman, with her stylishly cropped, reddish-brown hair, her clearly delineated features, and large, nearly transparent green eyes. She cuts her way through the airport's bland spaces with some impatience, her slim tall figure clad in jeans and short leather jacket, her head bent slightly as if to avoid notice. But there's something about her that attracts notice nevertheless: perhaps it is a certain concentration of expression, or of being; perhaps it is the pale, light-absorbing eyes. What cannot be seen, as she pauses to buy her bottled water, or look around some insipid airport shop, is that she's filled with a force of expressive meaning, a power of significant sound that enlarges the space within her to an immeasurable degree. Intimations of Schumann and Beethoven are always just below the surface of her mind and at the tips of her fingers, ready to emerge. She's trailing a comet's tail of music, a repertory of beauty and shaped feeling and strenuous human effort. She's barely conscious of it, this lived history of the soul; but it is always within her reach, almost audible in the stray motifs, rhythms, musical suggestions that inform her movements, and speak to her as eloquently as any sentences.

What she cannot see fully is herself, as she cuts her way through the old-new world, or as that world cuts through her. She does not discern the vectors of power within which she is held, or the currents of strife and change that may pass through her too, for good or ill. After all, the world through which she travels doesn't yet have a shape, and she is a new kind of creature in it. The forces pressing on her from within blur her own outline to her vision. She doesn't yet know what the music inside her is driving her toward; she is on the border of herself, of the present.

She closes the book on her lap, and thinks, this is only a transitional passage. The passage one hardly hears, the neutral arpeggio meant to get you from one theme to the next. She straps herself into her seat, wills herself into a kind of inner immobility. She thinks, only seven hours . . . The great machine rumbles and churns, and then crescendoes into unnatural speed. Even through the shield of the airplane, something runs down her spine like the uncanny: a power of velocity and sound that could crush her in a mini-second. Then the stunning artifice of lift-off; the swoop above Long Island Sound; and as they leave it behind, the unending expanse of the resistless sky. She stares at it for a while, the vast blue space with no shape or horizon. Somewhere beneath the white noise of the airplane, phrases of Schubert rise up from within, with their lovely, fluent motion. Scraps of music, scraps of thought. To anchor herself, she reaches for her briefcase—the touch of sleek leather is a kind of reassurance; she is, among other things, a person with a sleek leather briefcase—and looks through the folder with her schedule. An anticipatory excitement simmers, the lit-up excitement of the tour ahead. A string of city names extends itself on the page with a still glittering allure: Paris, Sofia, Berlin, Brussels, Vienna, Stockholm, Budapest, Barcelona . . . Magical metropolises, her generation's fantasy of worldliness; of adventure. What is Sofia doing in that awkward place, though, and why didn't Anders get her Moscow or Rome? She thinks, how strangely arbitrary, and does it mean she is slipping, that the big cities will stop wanting her. That might happen, she knows, through some imperceptible elision, one never knows how or when. She peruses the file for the name of her Paris minder, and notes that it is Rougement. Well, that's nice. He has been around forever; he will cushion the first moments. There are some publicity materials in the folder, and she looks at a photo of herself briefly and with some dissatisfaction. It was taken three years ago, and she didn't like it in the first place, its staged pose or the smooth fake flow of her hair on which the publicity people insisted.

She feels the attention of the man in the next seat turning in her direction. He is corpulent in a forceful, packed way, and he is staring at her quite intently.

"Excuse me," he finally brings out, with a careful respect. "I just couldn't help noticing . . . You're Isabel Merton, aren't you? I mean, I know it's strange to recognize a person from a photo, but I've seen you on posters, you see, or maybe in the newspapers."

She says yes, she is, and smiles politely, though not too encouragingly. She isn't sure she wants to get into a long conversation. "Well, I can't tell you how much I've admired your recordings. Especially your Schumann, the *Davidsbündlertänze* . . . So mercurial, so . . . true. True to the music," he adds, as if to assure her he doesn't mean anything trivial. He's speaking in a diffident rush. "You've given me so much pleasure, you see. In fact, I just got you on CD." His large, not unintelligent eyes look moony. He's face to face with one of Them, the veiled ones, an Artist.

"Oh, thank you," she says, and smiles more openly this time, sensing his difficulty, as well as her own. She has emerged from behind the veil, from the impersonal closeness of recorded sound, into this pseudo-intimacy of an airplane seat. It's undoubtedly disconcerting, this disjunction between her rather tired, embodied self, and the brilliant, disembodied sound by which he has known her.

"Are you going to be playing in Paris?" the man asks. "You see, I've listened to you so much, but I've never been to one of your concerts."

"Well, yes, I am scheduled at the Champs-Elysées on Saturday," she tells him.

"Ah, that's wonderful," he says with enthusiasm. "I was going to go to Périgord for the weekend, but I'll stay to hear you, what a great coincidence."

"My heavens, that seems rather extreme," Isabel says, feeling oddly small in the face of such dramatic appreciation. She isn't sure she wants to be responsible for his change of plans.

"Oh no, I wouldn't miss it for the world," he declares with obvious sincerity. "Especially now that I've met you."

But she must have somehow reinstalled the remote look in her eyes, because he looks rebuffed. He says, "It must be very hard, all this touring and airplanes . . ."

She says yes, sometimes it's quite hard, and after a few more polite sentences mutters, "Please excuse me, I need to read this before . . ." and opens Ernst Wolfe's *Journal of a Summer*. "Oh, I'm sorry, please, don't let me . . ." the corpulent man says in a flattened tone, and unfolds his *Financial Times*.

She tries to read, but is still too restless, too distracted. Images skivvy through her mind in no particular sequence. A lesson with Wolfe all those years ago . . . This morning's hurried preparations, the long room of her downtown loft, covering up the Steinway against the sun, and Peter, picking her up to take her to the airport, from his apartment, from their old home. She can envision him exactly, waking up in the high-ceilinged, dusky bedroom, with its fraying Turkish carpet. Still, by now she doesn't know: was he alone before he came to collect her, and would she mind if he wasn't . . . Sotto voce, she admits she would, even though she has no right to, none at all . . . She couldn't ask, of course, it would have been too unfair . . . As it wasn't entirely fair to accept the endless ride to Kennedy this morning. Ahead, the aleatory sequence of the cities, and the absolute glow of the music. A hard life, the man said . . . It's a formulation, a view. Though how can her life be hard, by what possible standards? She does what she most loves. She's free, free as a woman has ever been. Freedom is the element through which she moves, and she peers into it as into a milky fog, trying to discern what she is moving toward, what she so restlessly, so keenly desires. And yet maybe the man is right, maybe there's something hard about her life, in its deluxe late-capitalist way. She thinks of the stages she will have to cross before reaching the piano, the interviews she'll have to give, the dinners she's promised to attend. Bourgeois heroism is what Peter calls it, the acrobatics of being in so many places practically at once, and doing so many amazing things in one day, and then conversing over dinner with unflagging energy. She'll have to be on the qui vive, it is expected. You must never be tired. You Must Love Your Life.

The carefully calibrated one-third of a Valium is beginning to take its effect, and Isabel submits to it gratefully. She'll figure it out another time . . . She takes a measure of her encapsulation, and adjusts the seat for a simulacrum of comfort. A vague thought drifts through her mind that the man next to her might be disillusioned to see her asleep; then she dozes off.

She sleeps through dinner and a movie, and is woken by the pilot's voice announcing landing. Familiar aridity, discomfort of squeezed bones. Her left wrist is hurting, and she massages it deftly, working out the strain; fortunately, nothing is badly cramped. The man next to her clears his throat tactfully to warn her of his presence, and says he's been thinking about it and will definitely stay in Paris for her concert. Could he come and see her backstage afterward? She says yes, of course, and he hands her his card, "just so you know who I am—it's only fair, no?" She looks at it briefly, noting that his name is Louis McElvoy, and that he apparently works at the State Department, though she can't immediately make out what he does there. They sit silently through the physical tension of the landing and lose track of each other shortly after getting off the plane.

Neither East nor West, nor North nor South. The eerily quiet corridors of Charles de Gaulle pulse softly with fluorescent images, emanating from no visible source. A liminal space, a traveler's limbo, and as in limbo, she lets herself be conveyed along passively, an item to be processed.

She thinks, just another hour, it's all right. Outside, the mid-morning gray, the minute, precise drizzle (staccato, moderato), immediately recognizable as Paris. She steps into a taxi, falls into a doze again through the long approach to the city; comes awake to the city itself. Ah. The archetypal city still. "St. Regis," she says again, in case the driver has forgotten. He nods impassively. The hotel is on a quiet street not far from the Champs-Elysées. That's good, she can walk to the concert hall in the morning. She pays the driver, notes the white-canopied balconies on the hotel's upper floors, the after-rain glisten of the street. On automatic still, she lets the concierge take her suitcase up to her room; manages, with some effort, to hang up her concert gowns; then curls up on the bed and falls asleep.

Paris

She takes a few minutes to reorient herself when she wakes up, registers the low gleam of the digital clock on the side table, the long white drapes. She used to be thrown by these moments, before she could place herself in yet another anonymous room or even figure out how her body was stretched on the bed. Now she has rituals for such transitions. She draws the curtains open and looks out into the full, and now sunny afternoon. That's better. She takes a few more things out of her suitcase, and turns on the gilded tap to run herself a bath. She stretches in the hot water and sponges herself vigorously. Fragments of the Schubert keep rising up in her mind; she's almost ready to receive them. The

6

internal cells are rearranging themselves in the hot water, as if by some crystallizing process. After an interval, she gets out of the bath, feeling something like coherence, a calm.

She takes out Wolfe's *Journal*, contemplates the cover. The white trunks of birches in a pristine West Virginia setting; against them, his tall, gaunt figure, his sensitive, highly etched face. Published posthumously. She wonders if he would have wished it. He would have said no, of course, as he said no to anything that threatened the absolute purity of his privacy, and his dedication. But perhaps there was another side, other desires. Who doesn't want to be known, as completely as possible, precisely in the most private places . . . She knew Wolfe only through the music. That is, she knew him perhaps in the most essential way; but not in any of the other ways that also count. She feels some suspense as she begins to read.

Roanoke, West Virginia
July 2, 1982

Last night, a dream—a nightmare—of a sound. Nothing more than a sound, and yet it had all awe, all terror in it. It was not so much loud, as super-heavy, super-condensed. Heavy water, plutonium. A kind of absolute sound, its mass expressing something of the cosmos. Its weight threatened to crush me and everything in its path. But it had a kind of beauty in it, the beauty of the ineffable which cannot be grasped. Even if the ineffable is composed of pure menace.

Perhaps my composition should be just that sound. Infinitely extended and minimally wavering within. A condensed black hole of sonic matter, within which the particles and waves of former life can still be obscurely sensed.

It is twelve years to the day since I began the Requiem. Perhaps that is why I had the dream. Twelve years of labor condensed into one, all-encompassing sound. That would be a kind of triumph. Reduce. Distil. That is what our age demands. After all the excesses, after everything which happened. We come after, that is what I must never forget. We come after. Therefore, distil absolutely. Distil to an absolute.

I must work hard. They come soon, the youths of this summer.

She wakes up the next morning knowing only that she has a task ahead of her. She puts on her khaki slacks and a loose shirt for practicing, and walks out into a crisp fall day and the sharp clarity of Paris. The enchanting round garden, with its precise iron grisaille framing the flowering trees, themselves pruned to a precision; the spiff and polish of chrome and glass windows in the overpriced shops; the amusingly neat movements of waiters rushing about at the outdoor cafés; a lucid city music. She sits down for a quick croissant and her morning dose of coffee. Focus. A gathering of forces. She sees pleasure and expectation in people's faces. Strange, she thinks, this returning of vision, this alteration of mood on which so much depends.

She walks over to the Champs-Elysées, responds to the nod of recognition from the doorman at the artists' entrance and makes her way through the familiar maze of corridors and cubicles, into Rougement's office. He comes out from behind his desk to give her a peck on both cheeks and a careful squeeze of her elbow. Mustn't damage the pianist's hand. He is dressed as always in an impeccable gray suit which sets off his salt-and-pepper hair, every one of his gestures courteous and calm.

"We have a new piano," he says, as he takes her by the arm

to lead her toward the stage. "Did you know? The most mellow bass I've ever heard. Bosendorfer still can't be beat for the bass, don't you think? Even Rothman couldn't find anything wrong with it, and we know how he loves to complain, like all prima donnas. Let me know what you think of it, OK? We're all so excited about this evening."

Left alone with the big, beautifully curved beast of the piano, she wonders if there was even a quaver of excitement in Rougement's voice, if he's still capable of feeling anticipation before a concert, after all that music pouring out over him evening after evening, after he's been witness to such quantities of proficiency, and excellence, and sometimes peerless perfection. What can she do that has not been done before . . . Like so many things in the world, music is old, she thinks, and there is too much of it. No longer conceivably a scandal, as when *The Rite of Spring* was first performed here; no longer a shock.

But as soon as she touches the piano, doubts evaporate. She adjusts the leather stool to the right height, plays some warm-up arpeggios in C and C-sharp major. Instantly, she feels a jolt of satisfaction. The piano has responded like some sensitive living creature. The sound produced by her fingers is startlingly good: full, round, clear, but without the hard edge of less refined instruments. She begins the Schubert slowly, luxuriating in the tone, the piano's even temper, the way the keys react to the slightest nuance of her intention, movement of wrist, pressure of fingertip.

She plays through the Sonata, testing the tonal range while keeping it a measure reined in. She mustn't let herself go just yet, must preserve her energies for later. The full glory of the music lies within, waiting to be uncoiled. The Chopin Ballade, without the full fortes, sotto voce. Then the Ravel. Passages in the "Jeux d'eau" still require an effort and she goes over them several times, gearing up the tempo, till they begin to slide off her fingers like butter, like water.

On the way out, she stops in Rougement's office to go over the evening's arrangements. The piano will be tuned later in the afternoon; the car will be sent to the hotel at seven. He holds her hand for a moment, as if to say thank you. "I overheard parts of the Schubert," he tells her. "You understand him so well. I mean, how much his lovely melodies tell us. How it isn't all smooth and easy." She smiles gratefully. On the way back to the hotel, she thinks, yes, perhaps there is something she understands. It is the winding of human longing as it reaches and extends itself into heavenly lengths, as it submits gradually to perfect symmetries. When she is playing Schubert, she understands something of that.

Time to get ready. Her hair has to be washed. Snippets of the "Jeux d'eau" float through her mind, pianissimo, and she goes over them mentally, finger by finger, note by note. Room service: soup and salad, a chocolate dessert for extra energy. She takes out the book she brought as a relaxant, a comic novel about academia. Characters make clever remarks, flirt, converse. Then a funny joke, some twist of rhythm, or of paradox. She laughs, taken by surprise. Good sign, that. If she can laugh, the nerves are not too bad. Get dressed. Deodorant, talcum powder, a very light bra. She moves her arms upward, to make sure nothing inhibits her movements. Brief moment of resentment: Rothman doesn't have to worry about this. But then, he has his tuxedo, although, these days, maybe he has given up on that. Passages from a Bach Partita peregrinate through her mind, steady and ceremonious. She steps into her dress, brushes her hair. Long mirror, in which she contemplates herself impartially. It works well, the glistening green of the silk flowing down along her body, the sharp diagonal of the low V-neck echoing the slant of her cheekbones. She wonders briefly what she looks like to them, from out there, under the lights, then flicks the question away superstitiously. If she for a moment considers herself as an object up there onstage, all is lost. If for a moment she tries to court the audience's attention or admiration, all is lost. Still, she allows herself a moment of satisfaction. There is a kind of elegance in her, a distinctness and flow to her gestures. She senses briefly but clearly that the element which impels her movements is made of the same stuff, same sap, as the thing that moves Schubert's phrases. Or anyone's movements, if they know anything of grace. The principle of beauty is within us. Then the intuition vanishes. She puts on her coat, makes sure that the scores are in her briefcase, even though she won't use them, and takes the lift down to wait for Rougement's car.

Rougement leads her to the Green Room, where she'll spend the next half-hour. His manner is perfectly calibrated for such occasions: attentive, but not so solicitous as to suggest that she might be feeling unsure or nervous. He keeps up a gentle stream of remarks, which fortunately demand no response. Did she know that the new Opéra was an acoustic disaster, though that popinjay of a culture minister has claimed it as a triumph for the government, but then what can you expect from politicians, especially from *soi-disant* socialists who insist on behaving as if they were de Gaulle? In the Green Room, he surveys the surroundings calmly. He is one of those Frenchmen about whom there is an unflagging expectation of order, built into his very bones. He makes sure that the bottle of Perrier and the blanket with which she likes to wrap herself at intermission are in place, and takes her hands in his. "Warm and dry," he comments approvingly. "As I remember, you like some time on your own?"

"If you don't mind," Isabel says, half apologetically.

"Of course," he says, and closes the door carefully behind him. A half-hour of focused blankness, then he's back, nodding that it is time. She follows him through the backstage messiness, over some wooden plank. Her stomach lurches, horribly, practically turning over. She wants desperately to turn back; she would give anything to be able to turn back. Then the threshold between dark and light, and she's out there, in the flood of light. She calms instantly, as if shot through by a powerful chemical, or a starry bolt from the spotlights. Her body straightens as if in response to a summons, her step slows. She should know by now about this effect, but it's always a surprise. Her consciousness has hid somewhere, folded away, with its jangling questions; in its place, another alertness unfolds, wide and bright. Applause, from out there, from the dark. She lets it come at her impersonally, like a shaman's touch. She and they are participating in the same ritual, a rite of preparation, the preparation of an instrument.

At the piano, she lowers her head briefly to listen to the rhythm of the Mazurka she has chosen as the opening piece. Her hands place themselves on the right keys. With the first bar, the delicate, definite mood imposes itself. The wistful dance motif, with its syncopations, carrying in itself sadness and stubborn defiance; then the release of the middle part, the stomping, proud peasant chords; and back to the beginning, more accepting the second time, infused with everything which had gone before. A microcosm in three minutes.

Two more Mazurkas. The applause comes at her with believable warmth, stoking her for the next, larger effort. The fingers are looser by now, the instrument has been oiled. She lowers her hands again on the dreamy, distant opening line of the First Ballade. Somewhere in the dark, she senses the audience, falling into quietness, altering its collective breath with her, with the long breath of the music.

. . . ah, listen, thinks Louis McElvoy, Row N, Seat 5, the beauty of that line, honestly she's good, the technique, fantastic the same woman, strange / she was crumpled on the airplane sort of withdrawn / but listen, the distinctness of the notes, the lift of the arm, the way she comes down on the keys, those chords must be difficult / power like a commander, a general, where does it come from / ah, that melody quiet distant magic why does it move me like that / a sort of charisma / glad I came not disappointed, glad I came // . . . ah, thinks Fernand Mercier, the melody, weaving meandering, lyrical, ah, the sheer beauty / Chopin, incomparable / it's in me, weaving through me, she's poured it into me / directly, into the veins, the soul / what is it we exchange / the Exchange early morning, must read the figures damn it bloody figures, must catch up / ah, that modulation, where are we, C-sharp minor, the snag on the soul / the economics of the soul // . . . just listen, thinks Sister Jeanne, the turbulence the passion, passion of Christ, no, no, sacrilege / beautiful but not like Bach, so serene, rest in God / Chopin, was he doing it for God / no, there was that woman / and yet, the music / he was very ill, here in Paris, far away from his country / consumption, consumed by the flame / divine flame, divine spark / human passion but divine / is it sacrilege // . . . ah, listen, thinks Ricardo Lopez, chromatic delicate like powder / all senses at once / Alicia / yes, I wanted her in that room, the powder, the gesture of her hand coming up to her face, the musk of her body and then / how could they do it, her wrist, broken, shattered / how could they / cold metal the pain how much pain did she feel / ah, listen, that phrase, the elegance, grandeur, the grand arc / the bend of her neck, the curve of her arm Alicia / her wrist, broken, the cruelty, where is the music for that! / the torment of it always // . . . oh, thinks Marie Briand, how graceful, her hands, her confidence / I stayed hidden, hidden beauty what's the point, but yet I knew / he knew / that quiet afternoon oh it is there, here, that afternoon, forever, he is bringing his body down toward me, he saw the beauty, hidden beauty / those grace notes, light, like a soufflé . . . I will die. Stage Four. Incurable. No. Impossible. I do not accept. / ah, but it hurts, the sadness the beauty, it will still be there when I / no cannot be / but it will still be there //. . . who is she, thinks Anzor Islikhanov, Row N, Seat 6, those chords, the harmonies / sublime, yes, the fire, the passion / head thrown back / why does she speak as if to me, it enters, the music, the melancholy / who is she, beautiful woman, no, not for you / she would disdain me, they all do, I see it, their condescension, their tight-lipped smiles / let me not forget! / mad Chechen mad country, I see it in their eyes / ah, but look, her hair over her face, the quickening the rush, from her fingers, like wild mountain streams oh God yes the cold streams, my country / it pierces she pierces / my country, destroyed, the bastards the thugs / I hate them it grows in me it will burn me, let it burn! / Chopin knew, hated the Russians the tyrants the thugs / ah, listen, that line chromatic into the distance, from a distance, transporting, she transports me / must meet her, MUST, McElvoy will introduce me / he won't want to mad Chechen, primitive, savage, don't contaminate her / I will make him, he must / ah, those chords, rising, swelling, the fierceness yes like Chechnya, my longing, Chopin's longing, beauty and violence all combined . . .

The applause comes with a shock, separating her from the audience, whose silent breath she has felt almost as part of the music, moving through the Ballade with her. During intermission, she wraps herself up in the blanket left there by Rougement, and sits curled on the sofa, garnering warmth, gathering her forces. By the time Rougement knocks on the door to take her back out, she feels energy flowing again.

The "Jeux d'eau," frisky and watery; then the Schubert. The first, extended movement of the sonata is nearly unbearable to play; she fears, at times, that she cannot contain its modulated intensities, its melodic beauty. Her breath draws in almost painfully; then finds some deeper runnel. The music emerging from under her hands has an eloquence of a child's song, but one proceeding from an angelic source. Her head bends back, her mouth opens slightly to receive it. Someone, something, is speaking to her and through her. By the end of the great sonata, an enormous and gentle panorama has been traversed; a complex geometry of silent thought has been outlined and has come to its completion. Something in her locks into place. She feels, as her hands come off the keyboard of their own accord, a spacious joy.

She takes her bows with a more than perfunctory gratitude. She has been given something; something impalpable and essential has been exchanged. The sonata would not be complete without the anonymous listeners out there, receiving it, moving through it with her. The bravos are insistent enough to demand an encore; and, with a little pleased nod of encouragement from Rougement, she goes out again and plays an amusing Satie piece, to finish things off on a lighter note. Then she is backstage again and Rougement takes her arm to lead her back to the Green Room. He is murmuring something she can't quite make out; the music hasn't subsided yet, it's hard to hear him through it. She tries to adjust her breath back to its ordinary pace, as people begin to trickle in. Well-dressed French people, some of whom she vaguely recognizes, probably from previous Parisian concerts. A music producer whom she does recognize gives her a thumbs up from a distance and then backs out the door, with an apologetic must-go, can't-help-it gesture. Nice of him to come, though. Then the man from the plane is there. His corpulent body has a certain grace in his good suit, and his face is flushed with excitement. "Wonderful," he says. "Unforgettable. I wouldn't have missed it for the world." He introduces a man standing next to him, saying, "Another fan." Isabel doesn't catch his name, but it sounds vaguely Slavic, or Balkan. He looks somehow Slavic too, with his longish face and dark eyes. He gives a quick, rather formal bow, then looks at her with a curious intentness. She looks back, baffled; she isn't sure what he's trying to convey. "The Ballade," he brings out. "I cannot tell you what it meant to me. Or perhaps you do know." He speaks with a surprisingly British accent. "It is a wonderful piece," she says, perplexed still. "Yes, but that's not what I mean . . ." he begins. She waits for him to continue, but he gives a small shrug, as if conscious he is not going to be given more time. "I hope sometime I will be able to tell you," he says, sounding almost offended. "Perhaps my friend here"—he indicates McElvoy—"will be kind enough to bring us together." "Thank you," she says, because she doesn't know what else to say. He gives a small bow again and turns abruptly to leave. The man from the plane raises his eyebrows in ironic apology, and indicates that he must follow, saying in an undertone, "I hope we'll meet again."

There are a few more people who've been waiting to speak to her, and whom Rougement discreetly hurries along. Then he brings her coat, and helps her put it on quite gently. "Wonderful," he says. "Believe me, you were very good. And I hear a lot of concerts." She feels a warm candle lick of satisfaction. A task accomplished, a labor in beauty. "You're sure you don't want to come to dinner with us?" Rougement asks.

"Perhaps next time," she says, feeling apologetic again. She's not ready for the comedown into dinnertime conversation. The engines have been going full blast, it's hard to brake so abruptly.

She changes into slacks and sneakers after the others leave, and on the way back, tells the driver to stop a few blocks short of the hotel. She walks along the Seine at a brisk pace, hardly looking at the glittering night vistas on the other bank. She is still wrought up, currents racing through her head and body. She circles back, through the narrow streets around the Madeleine. People at café tables look up at her with some surprise as she walks by, drawn perhaps by her agitation, the tension of the condensed time frame in which she is enclosed. It's like being on a hallucinatory drug, or drunk among sober people. She thinks she'll sit down and have a coffee, then changes her mind. She's beginning to feel a familiar desolation coming on, the arid ghost of the performance. She has been in plenitude, and has been rapidly ejected and she feels she's walking through deoxygenated air. Her breath, emerging from its depths, is short and narrow. She'll call Peter, even though it isn't completely fair. She no longer has the right to assume he'll be there, or will want to talk to her, or help her through her descent from intoxication. But she also knows he won't mind; doesn't mind. At least, she's pretty sure.

In the hotel, she changes into a terry-cloth robe, and dials Peter's number.

"Ah, it's you," he says his voice terse, slightly hoarse, familiar in every quarter-tone shift. "I take it this is post-concert?"

"Yes," she says somewhat sheepishly, because he knows so well why she's called. Because this used to be their routine. Then she stops, because she's suddenly unsure what she wants herself.

"Well?" he asks. There may be a shade of annoyance in the question.

"How was your day?" she asks.

"Oh, you know, the usual. Robertson is being headhunted by Yale, so he is strutting around like a goddamn peacock." She hears him take a sip of coffee, mentally supplies the little round table placed next to his easy chair at just the right height, the legal periodicals strewn about on the floor. "One of my students asked whether I thought the principle of contracts is universal," he tells her. "I think that was the high point of my day."

"Well, is it?" she asks.

"Is it what?"

"Universal."

He sighs, humorously. "In principle, yes. If you really want to know."

"I do," she says, stretching on the bed more comfortably. She wants to be distracted from the susurrus of the music, to step into his crisp, logical world.

He sighs again, heaving himself into a mock-pedagogic explanation. This used to be part of the comedy of their relationship; her almost childish enjoyment, after the exertions of a performance, of the nicely contained, orderly progression of an argument. He is willing, it seems, to humor her still.

"What I told the student," he says, "was that the idea of contracts enters human relations as soon as we differentiate ourselves from the primal horde. As soon as we notice that others don't necessarily have our best interests at heart. That they can grab something away from us. Unless we make a compact. I was improvising, of course."

He pauses, waits a beat. "How are you?" he asks, dropping into a different register.

"Oh, you know. I'm post-concert."

"Is anything wrong."

"No . . ." She pauses, tries to figure out how to put it. "It's the . . . comedown, I suppose. The contrast. Or maybe just the tension. And then the decompression."

"Just don't forget that you actually added something to the general scheme of things this evening," he says quickly. "You don't feel like this for nothing. What's been taken out has been added. First law of thermodynamics, I believe."

"Do you really think so?" she says.

"I do," he says.

"Yes, maybe," she agrees. "Though I wonder . . . Do you know how many concerts there are in any given week? In Paris?

Or in Cleveland?"

"But how did it go?" he asks. "Were you good?"

"I think I was, you know," she says.

"How did the audience take it?"

"Oh, the audience took it lying down," she says, and giggles. He's cheering her up, after all. "But you know how audiences are. So eager to be . . . pleased. To . . . forget themselves." Her voice recedes again. "Or else they just like to have some soothing sounds washing over them in the evening. It probably doesn't mean anything more than that."

"Look," he says more firmly, more seriously. "Don't elevate a mood into some . . . philosophical problem. This is post-concert, you know that. Or maybe post-partum."

"I suppose so," she says, and there's another pause. "There was a man on the plane," she then resumes, inconsequentially. She's feeling pleasantly tired.

"Yeah?" Peter asks. He doesn't sound exactly pleased.

"Yes," she says, and sleepily tells him about the conversation, and the man's reappearance after the concert.

"There you are then," Peter says, tersely. "He was apparently satisfied."

"I suppose so," she repeats, dozily. She's coming back to herself. If that is what it is. She's never sure. Up there on the stage, as she leaves herself, she feels she is never more—herself; or at least, filled with being.

"Well then, stop brooding," he says. "Go get some sleep. Oh, and by the way," he adds, his voice turning more terse, "you know I don't have your schedule this time. So if you want to talk . . ."

"Right," she says, also more tersely, because she is both grateful and oddly, unjustly, irritated. Her old irritation, at how good he is, how calm, how unfailingly, almost immovably tolerant. "Thanks."

"Goodnight then," he says, and she detects a fraction of sadness in his voice.

"Goodnight."

In Between

The melancholy of travel. On the TGV to Lyons, she stares at the golden landscape moving past in blurred, reiterative motion. Yellow stubble of wheat; azure sky. Nature has the best color combinations. Through the reverie of the fallow fields and hypnotic haystacks, she returns to last night's conversation with Peter, and the mood space of the large, comfortable Upper West Side apartment where they spent their few years together, and which she still can't help but think of as home. They were lucky to get it, through Peter's teaching job at Columbia. The white-painted high-ceilinged rooms, into which the sun entered in the afternoon, the motes of dust on the elongated shafts of light, the quietness permeated with the pulse, the urban surf of the street . . . The apartment was never entirely protected from the pugilistic honking of cars during the day, or the monotonous beat of disco music at night, or the loud metallic rattling of garbage trucks at dawn. She'd wake up for their passage, and suffer it like some social duty, then go back to sleep, duty done. In the morning, the moment of small passage, into the piano room, which was sound-insulated and just big enough to contain the Steinway and some shelves. A dip into a different space, different state: she can still feel the pleasure of it, stepping away from the street's perpetual agitation, and into her musical cave and subsiding into a denser, more viscous element.

At the end of the afternoon, the distance between the rooms was sometimes hard to cross. There was the time, early on, when she emerged from her cave just as Peter was opening the front door. He stopped mid-movement, as if disturbed by something in her appearance. "Why are you blinking?" he asked. She had just been practicing some unearthly Schoenberg pieces, and was standing in the hallway in a state of half-absence. On the threshold. "You look as if you weren't expecting me," he added.

"I am, I am," she said vaguely, trying to snap out of it, feeling slightly dazed. He moved toward her and kissed her on the forehead, as if to see if she had a temperature, or was slightly ill. Peter . . . He never seemed to suffer such transitions; he was equally himself whatever he was doing, moving at an even pace, somehow evenly distributed in his packed, solid body. It wouldn't have occurred to him that he should speed up or slow down, or otherwise modify himself for anyone, or anything.

Her blinking became a running joke between them for a while; then he started ignoring it altogether. If he found her in her border state on coming in, he simply went over to the liquor cabinet to pour them both a drink. He never attempted to pull her out of her dazes forcibly, or draw her toward him. From within the well-defined boundaries of his person, he did not attempt to cross hers. Or anyone's. She sees him, taking off his jacket and lowering his tall, well-built frame into a large leather chair and placing the whisky and soda on the small glass table—that's where he sat last night, as they talked—and taking a few sips before glancing at her again to see if she was back, if she was with him. Then he'd ask her about her day. Or tell her about his. He had already started his rise through the professorial ranks at the Columbia Law School, at a rather precocious age. She'd watched him, progressing steadily from one advance to another without ever losing his footing, or his composure. Others told tales of all-night marathons, with amphetamines to get them through before exams. Peter never lost a night's sleep . . . Then there were those papers on the links between law and justice she

21

could never quite read, but which soon added up to a hefty tome that came to be referred to as "definitive." But then, he was doing exactly what he wanted; what he was meant to do. He had that calm . . . that particular kind of pleasant confidence which in her mind went with the pleasant setting of his childhood home, the unpretentious, tree-surrounded house in Illinois, where nothing ever seemed to go very wrong. Peter didn't have to strain or reach beyond his grasp to get where he wanted. He'd simply come into his own. The phrase seemed made for him; it fitted him like a glove. Anyway, the idea of excessive ambition would have seemed slightly histrionic to him; slightly vulgar.

It was safety that permeated Peter's body so evenly, like a good-smelling substance. Was she happy then, without noticing? Did she simply not notice, did she not know what contentment looked like, its weight or shape . . . Her own early career, Peter had joked, progressed through some form of punctuated equilibrium, rather than a more gradualist version of the evolutionary process. There were lengthy periods during which nothing happened, except for punishing invitations to multiple-use halls in mid-sized Midwestern towns. Then the programming director of a prestigious festival happened to hear her in Wisconsin, and offered her a prime spot in his recital series. That was when she seemed to leap to another level, like those organisms in the prehistoric eras which, without warning or seeming transition, all of a sudden developed new organs or assumed another morphological form. All of a sudden, she was visible; desirable; a rising star.

. . . the sun-shafts in the Manhattan apartment, the close warmth of the piano room. When did it change . . . She isn't sure when she began to feel Peter's presence in his study not as an anchor to which her mind turned for quick reassurance, but as a sort of chafing. He listened to a lot of baroque music as he read, and even that began to irritate her, out of all reason. All those endless tonal permutations, as background. At some point, his very calm made her restless. Not fair, she knows, not fair. When did she stop wanting an antidote to the restlessness, and start wanting to pursue the restlessness itself? She sits back in her train seat and remembers the concert at Alice Tully Hall. It was one of those evenings when the adrenaline coursing through her veins worked to stoke all her deeper energies, rather than inhibit them. There was an atmosphere of excitement in the auditorium. Afterward, she was almost painfully excited herself; she might as well have been on cocaine. When Peter came into the Green Room, she expected—well, what? A matching excitement, she now supposes, a glow, a heightened alacrity. But of course, it was not he who had just given a concert, not he who felt the effects of extra electricity in his body. He came up to her and held her against the satisfyingly large expanse of his chest, looking at her from under his already somewhat craggy eyebrows with equable approval. "Well, kiddo," he said, "you were just excellent. Your best yet." And then he moved away to make room for the rest of the well-wishers who were lining up behind him. He left before the end of the celebratory dinner, because he had an early class to teach.

There were other moments . . . With a twinge of embarrassment, she remembers the party in SoHo. It went on till all hours, coming after the music, out of their making music together, so that they danced afterward and held each other close as if it was a natural culmination, a cadenza, a coda. By the time she entered the apartment in the gray dawn, she felt diminished with exhaustion and obscure shame, and not a little alarmed. Peter was sitting up in his bathrobe and pajamas.

"What happened?" he asked, observing her carefully.

She shivered a little. "I'm so tired," she said. "I want to go to sleep."

"Then you can tell me about it tomorrow," he said. "If you want to."

She never did tell him anything, and he didn't ask again. Peter was quite an expert on contracts, and this was his understanding of the agreement between them: that they were both autonomous agents and that, however they wished to treat each other, they would do so of their own free will; and that, if their intentions toward the other, or their feelings, changed, the other was obliged to accept that. It was as clean, as pure as that. He is a man of principle, Peter. Or perhaps, she now ruefully thinks, perhaps he knew something she didn't; that when it came to the basics, you couldn't change anyone. Not unless you wanted to exert power over them. And he didn't. That was what he had decided to give up, when their implicit contract was drawn. And yet he had a kind of power over her, of course; she feels it still, the power he exercises precisely through not exercising it, as if there was no need to make a point of it; as if he had enough to spare. It is complicated, she thinks, even this simple story is complicated . . . Through the window of the train, she can feel the warmth of the ripening afternoon and of the zenith sun. She opens Wolfe's *Journal*.

July 5, 1982

The first student of the summer. Her name is Isabel Merton. She's very young, but with a peculiar seriousness, which makes her seem older. Quite attractive, it must be admitted. She is tall, but there's something delicate about her, and skittish, as if she were a small alert animal which has come out of the forest, but might at any moment retreat. Or as if she didn't quite trust the world. Well, there is much about the world that ought not to be trusted. I should know.

I wasn't anticipating much when she sat down at the piano. She didn't look as if she had the necessary strength for the music. But the storm she unleashed with the Chopin Scherzo took me by surprise. Very fierce, almost wild. She needs to learn much more control. But she has the flair for emotional extremity that, if it is disciplined, may perhaps make her an interesting performer. She throws everything she has into each and every passage. Further study of composition is necessary, to show her the great laws of structure which enable the music to reveal itself. To be what it is.

At the end of the lesson, I asked what brought her to the Retreat; why she wanted to study music. She said it was the only element in which she feels she is fully alive. She then looked up at me with a certain timid surprise, as if she had not expected to say those words. Or to be understood. But I understood, of course. I understood her very well, although I could not tell her so. I do not want them to think that they will get confessions from me, or any *sharing*. Let them get that from their other, incontinent pedagogues. The very idea disgusts me. What I have to teach them is impersonal. Or, for those who can recognize it, more than personal. This must be made clear from the beginning.

The train is passing a perfectly picturesque village, moving past in Muybridge motion. A fragment of a rap song incongruously spikes up from some portable radio. *Baby, gimme what I want, all you gotta is your cunt* . . . At least that's what she thinks the lyrics are unbelievably saying as the aggressive pounding rhythm comes nearer and then recedes. She cringes, feels oddly unprotected. Without Peter, without her shield . . . She sometimes folded herself into his tall frame like a child seeking succour; and she felt sometimes that he looked at her, from his measured distance, as if she were a child, needing to be kindly understood. He took her measure, and enfolded all her agitations in his calm acceptance: her anxieties, her euphorias, her entranced states. Her Saint Teresa syndrome, as he called it.

When she told him she wanted to leave, there was no false emotion, or emotional blackmail of any kind. There was only that moment, the silent exchange. The door to his study was half open, and through it, she could see him, sitting at his desk with his feet up, uncharacteristically idle, seemingly just looking out the window, or into space. She came in behind him, softly. She knew he'd heard her, but he didn't look round or move. She put her hands on his shoulders; still he said nothing. She pressed down slightly, and felt a kind of resignation in the way he submitted to her gesture, which he knew to be one of apology, and a kind of consolation. For what she was going to do; for what she apparently had to do. After a moment, he pressed his cheek against her hand, as though acknowledging that he'd been wounded, that consolation was needed. Neither of them said anything; after a few moments, she simply left the room.

"Aren't you curious to know why I'm leaving?" she finally asked, in a kind of desperation. "Don't you want to know?"

"The reasons you'd give me wouldn't be the real ones anyway," he said, evenly.

He was right; she hardly knew the reasons herself.

A few days before she was due to move out, he asked, "What do you want to do about the piano? Do you still want to use the practice room?" She nodded, humbled by his generosity, wrenched with ambivalence. But she did, in her utterly selfish way she wanted to use the room, which by now was filled with her musical karma like some ritual cave, not the philosopher's cave from which one tries to see the truth, but one into which a warrior or a priest retreats to invoke and commune with the gods.

"I think you're making a mistake," Peter said then. It was the one statement of that kind he allowed himself. "I'm not trying to stop you, I'm just saying." She quivered with a sort of fear at this, the fear of making a mistake; and, also, the sense that he understood more than he let on. That maybe he was seeing something about her that she couldn't possibly see. They were standing in the hallway, and she wanted to go up to him and embrace him wordlessly, to express somehow the excruciation of the moment. But it was she who was leaving; it seemed wrong to be the one who was more upset; and he didn't make the gesture of insistence, of last-minute persuasion, which might just have stopped her in her tracks after all.

But of course he wasn't going to exert pressure, not even then. That was the basic principle. Did he let her go through sheer rectitude? Though there's just a chance that he has some calculations of his own. What is she pursuing, anyway . . . She hardly knows, except that it's something *more*, something for which contracts don't apply, in which how much is given or taken doesn't count, because one gives and takes everything. In which one relinquishes all power and thereby exercises it absolutely. Isn't that the only possible contract? she mentally asks Peter; and she imagines him looking at her with his steady, intelligent eyes, and saying, no. The answer to that is no.

Lyons

In Lyons, a brief stop at the hotel, then the concert. A venerable nineteenth-century hall, a relaxed, attentive audience. She plays Bach's First Partita to begin with. It seems fitting, somehow, in this dignified old town, to be contained within Bach's serene symmetries. It is a deep satisfaction to progress through the propellent, *perpetuum mobile* progressions, through the even, irrefutable logic which itself adds up to a kind of joy. The Schubert; some Brahms Capriccios and Intermezzos; and at the end, Bartók's Suite. Another kind of propellent motion, more motoric, more fierce.

Dinner afterward with her local minders, at an unusually good restaurant. Unhurried conversation, connoisseurs' remarks on the music and the food. She feels a mild glow of pleasure at the salubriousness of the arrangements, the starched white table-cloths, the mellow wine.

Back at the hotel, she stares at the room for a while, trying to fix her location, and herself within it. Her internal compass oscillates slightly. The spectre of the music threatens. Is that all, is this what she works for, strives for, yearns for? This mild satisfaction, this modest completion? Long drapes on the tall white-framed windows, a writing desk; a luxury of anaesthetic bathroom fittings. The new Europe, it seems, can provide comfort in all its corners. Well, that's nice, isn't it? Isn't that what everyone wants, the culmination of decent, moderate wishes?

She puts on a terry-cloth robe, picks up Wolfe's *Journal*.

July 6, 1982

I woke up this morning knowing I had been dreaming of that day in Berlin, when I had—no, received—the first intimation of my composition. All through the morning, I was back there, in the gray, drumming rain, even though, outside my window, it was sunny and fresh. Perhaps it was the phrase Isabel Merton uttered that brought the day back to awareness, from where it always lies, dormant. I was once again walking near the Wall, in a drizzle, trying to avoid the glum, low-lying rubble nearby. The last rubble in West Berlin. The city was cleaned up quickly. Not like Warsaw, which I had just visited and which was still lying in ruins. I felt the injustice of it with a bitterness that was almost bilious. I saw two men making some monetary exchange, with that peculiar, sensual expression that accompanies such transactions. One of them was counting the bills, licking his fingers to ease the sticking. I wanted to kick him in the shins. I wanted to scream at my countrymen, to spit at them, to take everything away from them, out of their bellies which were growing fat again, out of their pockets which they were again filling with lucre, with gluttonous, single-minded lust. Their Mercedes-Benzes and their sausages, that is all they cared about. Berlin, the betraying city. The shelter with its awful fear was still at the surface of my consciousness and the corpses on the streets, the anonymous bloodied, haphazardly splayed corpses. I had loved the city as a child. Now I hated it with the bitter hatred that grows from within the emptied husk of love.

Then the church. I walked in for the warmth. It was filthy cold that day, wind piercing to the bone. And there was the Requiem. I should write that in worshipful calligraphic letters, in special luminous ink. The sublime, the most profoundly moving of all compositions. Moving at such a depth as to create calm at the center of being. As to lay the heart prone under its divine moving hand. Movement, moving . . . Mozart. What exactly is it that touches his tonal sequences with the breath of divinity, when other composers' sequences, made up of seemingly similar elements, do not possess it? This is the mystery.

I walked out of that church shivering with questions. How does one pierce the soul as Mozart did in our joyless, jagged, murderous age? I have spent twelve years trying to find a musical language that would do justice to that day, that would capture its double truth. The Angel of History was still hovering in the city, with its black, bat-like wings. Until you understand the Angel of History, you understand nothing. But then you must go beyond it, to some source or force from which the Angel emerges. I need a musical language so pure and distilled that it can bore to the dark core of menace and through it to its own kind of beauty. For when you get to the heart of things, you always come upon beauty. This I continue to believe. A requiem to catch the spirit of the age. It has to be condensed beyond anything Mozart imagined, to a dark mass from which one can only sense an emanation of light.

Paris

Back at the St. Regis, there is a message from Marcel. She feels a small fizz of surprise, of pleasure. She hasn't seen Marcel in a long time; but he resurfaces once in a while, here and there; has done so, with reliable irregularity, since his year at Columbia, when he was in some classes with Peter, and they all met for long coffees at the Upper West Side Cafe, and inevitably ended up going to the movies afterward. How many movies did they manage to see in those days, how many hours did they spend in those dream caves?

She calls him, gets his precise *allo*. "It's Isabel," she says.

"Ah, our distinguished visitor," he responds instantly. "Our practically unavoidable visitor."

"So they've been doing some publicity," she says.

"Publicity?" he repeats, with mock incredulity. "It's more like a blitzkrieg. A musical *Anschluss*."

She laughs. Marcel and she are in the habit of amusing each other, as he amused all of them that year at Columbia; but with the added frisson of eroticism, which neither of them, as far as she knows, has ever planned to take further; but which gives their talk the edge of playfulness.

"But as far as I can tell from the *Pariscope*, you're not giving a concert tonight," he says, and tells her he wants to invite her to a reception this evening, at the Foreign Ministry. "So I can see you, of course. But also a person I know has apparently attended your concert, and has practically begged me to bring you along."

"How did this person discover you knew me?"

"Oh, by coincidence. You know how it is. It came up in conversation."

"Sure," she says. "Sure." It will be nice to see Marcel; anyway, she has her free evening.

He says he'll pick her up at the hotel, and she goes out into the afternoon, to shop and stare. She picks up a pleated skirt at the Samaritaine, then finds herself walking down a long narrow street off rue de Rivoli, a glissando into the further past. Urban quietness, punctuated by occasional sounds of a cart wheeled into a courtyard, or the steady beat of a hammer on wood. Work sounds and the chalky smell of the street, with its intimations of patient, orderly lives going on behind the membrane of walls and windows, seemingly unchanged; and behind it, behind her own mind's membrane, she feels that heavier, stickier mood of long childhood days. This is where her mother brought her from Buenos Aires, for reasons which were not clear to the little girl; but which probably, Isabel understands now, had to do with her failing marriage. Her mother, an avant-garde nomad, experimenting with her own forms of restlessness. She comes upon a small neat square where Lena used to bring her to play, and sits down on a bench as she did then. Nearby, the great metropolis spews its traffic and human masses; here all is calm and geometry even now. Through her porous skin, she can feel the past's rustling return into the present. The deliciousness of the sun and the pointed shadows playing over the whitish pathways and well-shaved lawn, and a fluffy, ridiculously puffed-up poodle she used to pet, and its sharp, sudden yup. Toffee time, sweet and stretchy. There's something else within the distended moment, a penumbra, a shadow; the shadow of Lena behind her, on the bench where she is now sitting, Lena reading a book and letting it fall open and inert in her lap. The little girl drawing lines with a stick in the resistant ground, her braids bobbing as she stooped, and sensing, through the sun, that her mother's eyes are no longer on her, that her gaze has abandoned her . . . Isabel was already afraid of her mother's lassitude, her hands falling useless, her eyes filming over. She didn't look up or turn toward her mother, she didn't have to. The change was as palpable as a shift of tonality, the deepening or lengthening of a shadow . . .

The wholeness of the past. She gets up, walks toward the Marais and into its warren of old, crooked streets. Andante. Dolce. She came for her first piano lessons here, with Mme Hortesz, a Hungarian émigré, who mostly taught children of fellow exiles to tide herself over her difficult time. Isabel recognizes the house, with its low, squared-off wooden doorway, standing at a slight diagonal just where the street angles toward its next jag. Mme Hortesz herself is probably long gone . . . Isabel remembers a poorer, shabbier version of the neighborhood, less white-washed, less locked up. She thinks, all my madeleines have to do with shabbiness. Now the Marais is finished to a sheen, with polished wood and cute boutiques. She pushes the door, but it doesn't give; the house now has an entrance code. Still, she remembers its protracted aged creak, as its heavy weight gave way to her child's hand; the small echoing courtyard; the dark staircase with its smooth wooden banister; and then Mme Hortesz, large and soft, beckoning her into the dusky flat, with its small rooms and frayed carpets and its melodiously curved baby grand. There it is, in its enchanted wholeness.

"Here, darling, come in and show me what you've done," Mme Hortesz would say, pushing her gently toward the piano. "I always like hearing you, you've such a nice little talent . . ." Then she'd pick up her large, lazy angora cat and place it in her lap, where she stroked it as she listened to Isabel play.

Isabel doesn't know whether Mme Hortesz discerned talent, or whether she took her on because she knew Lena, had been part of the same "milieu," as she called it in her soft Hungarian accent. Even then, Isabel half understood that she was a recipient of benevolence, rather than a properly paying student; but still, the half-hour lessons were a charmed interval. Afterward, there would be tea with *confitures* and a little chat, which was probably the real point of the visits.

"How's your mamma?" Mme Hortesz would ask, looking at her not so much with concern as a sort of alert inquisitiveness; and Isabel would say in a very small voice that her mother was fine, "except she had to stay in bed a lot."

"Ah, don't worry about her so much, little one," Mme Hortesz would say, inclining her large head with a bird-like sharpness, as if she wanted to gauge from Isabel's face or tone of voice exactly how bad things were. "Don't worry, she'll recover soon enough, poor thing." Isabel remembers how Mme Hortesz ran her hand over her hair, firmly and soothingly, though she was probably inspecting it for lice at the same time. "And if anything is wrong, just come to me, yes?" she would conclude. "Just come over and tell me what's going on."

Isabel in the meantime was listening for undertones as well, trying to gather from Mme Hortesz's voice whether her mother was very ill, whether she would be soon orphaned, or had been orphaned already; whether she should think of herself as motherless. Then her mother's belly began to swell, and then there was Kolya. She walks, through some unconscious mnemonics, toward a small café—yes it is still there—where Gyorgi, Mme Hortesz's husband, started bringing her shortly after Kolya's birth, to conduct his lessons in general humanism over small cups of coffee, and with many cigarette butts squashed into the ashtray while he discoursed on pictures he had sent her to see in the Louvre, or the ethical ideas of Aristotle. There was a wonderfully illustrated book about Greek myths, and she remembers being impressed and worried by the free and ruthless behavior of the Greek gods. She had shyly asked Gyorgi whether Athena was a good goddess; whether she was nice. "Perhaps nice-ness isn't the point of a goddess," Gyorgi answered. "Perhaps it isn't even the most important thing in the world." He contem-plated her with a sort of whimsical affection. "If I were you, I would try not to be too excessively nice when you grow up," he said. "It's bound to get you in trouble." His lips made a *put put put* sound on his cigarette. "But the great thing about the Greek gods," he went on, clearly for his own benefit as much as for hers, "is that there are so many. Not just one god, who decides everything for everyone; but lots of gods, hashing it out among themselves. Fighting it out, because they love and hate. Because they have passions. Just remember," he said, raising his index finger to notify her he was going to say something important, "a power struggle is always better than absolute power."

And she does remember. She can see Gyorgi's impish look when he was pleased with one of his bons mots, and the precision with which he stubbed out a cigarette, as if to under-line that he'd hit the nail on the head, and herself smiling up at him to show she appreciated his cleverness, even if she didn't really understand, and the way she leapt up from her chair, as he said, "Come on, let's take a little walk." Then their stroll back to the flat, Gyorgi talking all the way; and the cluttered, dusky room with the piano and Mme Hortesz, large and soft, stroking her large, fluffy cat. The wholeness of the past. That's where it started, really, where it all began to matter: the music, the glimpses of grown-up play; and her trembling keenness to extend herself beyond her own small frame.

The fortuitousness of the present. Marcel comes to pick her up punctually at six, and strolls into her room as if they'd only parted this morning. "Ah, Isabel," he says, and gives her a casual peck on both cheeks, "it has been too long."

"But whose fault is it?" she states, adjusting easily to their accustomed banter. She feels instantly amused at seeing his well-chiseled, habitually amused face, the unforced nonchalance of his movements, as if he's already told a joke. The lightness of Marcel.

He inspects the room, with its long white curtains and imitation antique desk, appraisingly. "But you've clearly been doing well, yes?" he concludes. "Career graph going up?"

"Well, you know how it is with those graphs," she replies. "They seem to zigzag and wobble rather a lot."

"I'm a good reader of graphs," he assures her suavely, "and believe me, yours is showing a nice, steady upward movement. Nothing too violent," he expands, "but we wouldn't want that. Rapid rise too often precedes . . ." He shifts gears and looks at her appraisingly in turn. His eyes, behind the camouflage of irony, hold a deeper, tougher intelligence.

"It's good to see you, you know," he says, putting some seriousness into his words this time. "So much has happened . . . in the meantime." She knows he means Peter. She doesn't know how much he knows.

In the taxi, he tells her that the reception is in honor of some new legislation on the European currency. "It's the kind of event

I must attend these days," he says, shrugging expressively. "You know, in my work." As far as she can tell, he works for some European agency which regulates flows of currency, or its exchanges, or comparative quantities. She's never been able to grasp more than that. She imagines a somnolent gray bureaucracy, although she knows Marcel would never lend himself to something entirely unglamorous.

It's glamour that reigns in the crowded reception room. A glittering setting, sparkling chandeliers, the flickering interest of elegantly clad figures, of faces she'll never see again. She adjusts the silk shawl around her shoulders. "You look fine," Marcel murmurs reassuringly. "You look great." A few years earlier, she would have felt impressed to find herself in such a room; now she's used to being a nomad of the social scale, moving up and down its reaches, though always slightly on the outside. Somewhere between the Artist and a traveling artiste. Marcel looks around, raises his hand to a figure he spots across the room, squeezes her shoulder slightly to signal he'll be back soon, but is detained by someone approaching them, smiling jovially. It's the man from the plane. He is accompanied this time by a tall woman in a long satin dress, with bouncy black hair, and a bright, open smile.

"Hello, old fellow," the man says, extending his hand to Marcel and shaking it vigorously. "Well done, you got her to come."

Isabel blinks, in an effort to jog the automatic association mechanism into place; then it clicks.

"So you're the friend whom Marcel mentioned," she says. His name is McElvoy, she remembers now.

"Didn't Marcel tell you?" he asks, rather baffled in turn. He is dressed in a black-tie suit, and huffing a little; beads of sweat are showing around the collar. He looks at Marcel reproachfully. Marcel spreads his hands in a half-apologetic gesture, and gives an unapologetic shrug.

"Excuse me," he says with a suddenly absent look. "I'll be

right back." She watches him move across the room with deliberation; then making his movements more casual as he nears his goal. A person who clearly matters to him.

McElvoy introduces his companion as Margarita Peters, a dear friend from Washington.

"You have no idea how excited he was about that concert you gave," Margarita tells her cheerfully. She speaks with a genial Southern drawl. "He listens to music all the time, you know, he knows the whole piano repertory. Recognizes all the pieces, it's amazing. And he's just nuts about you."

McElvoy looks at his companion half gratefully, half reproachfully. "But it was so much better to hear you live," he says, "especially after meeting you like that—" He interrupts himself to greet a short, plump woman who has approached them in the meantime.

"*Zdrastvuyte*," McElvoy pronounces heartily, half bowing from his portly chest. "I thought you might be here." He introduces the woman as Katrina Marinskaya, and says in a gallant tone that she works at the Russian Embassy, but is really a poetess.

"Ah, poetess," Katrina repeats, pronouncing the word with a prolonging lilt. She has large blue eyes which remain disconcertingly wide open as she talks, and an aureole of blond hair framing her round, porcelain-skinned face. "I'm not sure I like that word. In Russian you can say it and not sound like you're a lady writer in the nineteenth century. In English I believe you cannot." Her soft Russian accent is nicely spiked by the droll intonations.

"What do you prefer to be called?" Isabel asks.

"To tell you the truth, I don't really care what I'm called," Katrina answers. "I prefer to be read. But that is of course too much to ask, for a . . . poetess."

McElvoy raises his index finger to hush them. A discreet clink of a glass summoning the guests to silence is produced from the small podium. The minister is about to speak. She has noticed him before, has followed the darting glances leading, always, to him. He seems, from this distance, perfectly quiet, perfectly composed, as only the powerful can be composed. He isn't even trying to give the impression of geniality; he doesn't have to. He doesn't have to do anything. Others in the room are scattered, half their attention directed toward him. He seems to gather their attention like a magnet gathering scattered filings. She can sense the condensation of energy within his stocky, not very tall body. In a way, she understands this state, recognizes it. He too, after all, is on a stage.

He begins to speak, with an unapologetic seriousness. He asserts that this is a period of unprecedented peace and prosperity for Europe. Perhaps for the world. Of course, there are problems. There is Kosovo, where the embers are still dying down from the fires of war. We must make sure they do not flame up again. Still, he continues after the briefest caesura, we are deeply convinced that we can preserve the stability which has been so hard won in the second half of this century—and the legislation we are celebrating is going to ensure that it lasts well into the next.

He goes on to explain the legislation, in intricate detail. She cannot follow, strains to hear some modulations in his uninflected sentences, a rise of rhetoric to eloquence, or drama. But the minister sticks unswervingly to his muzak plainness. What is at stake here, what is it that matters . . . The others look at the speaker with rapt attentiveness. What is it she is missing, is it the music . . . or is this the famous dullness of democracy, which according to Peter, she should relish? He used to hold forth about it; but her eyes glazed over when he did. She wonders, vaguely, if Wolfe's Angel of History is present anywhere in the glittering room; if so, it is surely hovering somewhere in a corner, with becalmed, folded wings. She stops trying to follow; her fingers move against her wine glass over phrases of a Brahms Intermezzo.

The speech comes to its end; light bulbs flash. There's applause and raised glasses. Marcel reappears, and says, "Our undertaker. The one presiding over our slow embalming."

"But he has such . . . gravitas," McElvoy protests.

"Oh honestly, Louis, you're such a sucker for authority," Margarita scolds him unexpectedly.

"Better an embalming than a burning," Katrina pronounces rather cryptically.

McElvoy looks at her disapprovingly, and asks Isabel where she's going next on her tour. "Sofia," she says. "Another flight."

"Ah, you poor thing," he says. "I could tell you don't like being on an airplane."

But Margarita suddenly exclaims, "Isn't Anzor going to be there? Wouldn't he just love to see her?"

"Yes, I think so," McElvoy says uncertainly. "He's the man who came with me to your concert," he explains.

"He's a great guy," Margarita says enthusiastically. "And you'll be all by yourself . . . It must get lonely . . . We'll let him know to come to your concert, won't we, Louis? You'd enjoy seeing him, I'm sure of it. He's just so . . . cultured."

Isabel notices that Katrina's eyebrows go up a fraction.

"I'm sure I would . . ." she says vaguely. She doesn't really remember the man who came with McElvoy, except for some ambivalent after-image, a trace of an expression or gesture.

"Please excuse us," Marcel says, taking her by the elbow, "I have an early meeting tomorrow . . ." He has ascertained through a silent query that she doesn't mind leaving.

"Well, that was interesting," she says neutrally, as they walk down the curved staircase.

"Was it?" he asks sharply. He doesn't seem to be in a good mood.

"Who is that man, exactly?" Isabel asks, about McElvoy.

"Ah, exactly," Marcel repeats. "Nobody is anything exactly these days." He gives a small shrug. "He's a retired diplomat. Knows everyone in Washington. One of those." Something did not go well for Marcel at the grand reception. He shrugs again, and speaks less irritably. "Well, maybe not retired. He ran around Yugoslavia a lot, trying to make everyone talk to each other. Not a bad man. He has good intentions. Though how he can approve of that dull apparatchik or his trivial policies . . ."

"You didn't like the speech."

"Ah, I'm sorry, Isabel," he says, "I'm not a very good, how do you say, companion this evening. But this is actually a moment of crisis for me."

At the bar of her hotel, where they sit down for a drink, he explains that the crisis has something to do with the shared economic infrastructure for the new members of the European Union, which in turn follows from the legislation approved by the maddening undertaker. "If I advocate lower interest rates, the French will be pissed," Marcel says. "And if I don't, the Germans will veto my promotion." He raises his eyebrows in a kind of sardonic QED. "I don't know which is worse."

"Shouldn't you think about what's best objectively?" Isabel asks, feeling sanctimonious even as she poses the question.

"Objectively best for whom?" he retorts sharply. "It's not so simple anymore. If it ever was. Somebody always loses, no matter what. Though they don't lose very much, that's how things are different now. We're good at lowering the stakes, it's our specialty. Of course, nobody ever seems to win," he continues, gaining steam on the momentum of his own logic. "But that's all right. At least nobody goes to war over it. Nobody gets killed. Not over interest rates. Not in Europe. That's our great improvement." He looks at her directly. "But in the meantime," he says, "I would like to get my promotion. Soon."

"Aren't you making yourself out to be even more of a cad than you really are?" she says, half jokingly. She thinks, everyone wants power after all. There must have been fierce tension in that room, had she only known how to read it.

"Ah, no, that's exactly how much of a cad I am," he replies, idly. His eyes, looking at her over his brandy, are acute and cool. She knows he's basically uninsultable; that was part of his charm when he was at Columbia, his distinctiveness. His moral dispassion was so confident, that it made him almost equally indifferent to praise and opprobrium.

"What would you like to do, then?" she asks.

"What I'd really like is to *run* something, for God's sake," he says with surprising vehemence. "Something large and inter-national. It's about time . . . And I would be good at it, too. I am already good at it. Negotiating different interests, playing them off against each other till they fit. I just want to do it on a larger scale."

"No matter what."

"No matter what." He looks ill-humored again. "I don't care which organization I run. As long as it's important or big. Or both, preferably. Very preferably."

"Is there nothing you really care about?" she asks, feeling horribly earnest again.

"My dear Isabel," he responds, "I'm a worker in the, how to explain it, the *superstructure*." The precision of his pronunciation makes the word sound almost sexy. "It is not our business to care. It is to see the whole picture. To have the overview."

He continues, in answer to her unspoken objections. "All right, I am a bureaucrat. I don't mind being called that. That's what we need these days, the best bureaucrats possible. People who are objective. Who don't get all gooey or sentimental about some . . . small precious nation. Or some desperately important issue *du jour*. People who care so much about one bloody thing as to unbalance the whole . . . structure." He raises an amused eyebrow. "That's why we need a strong superstructure," he concludes with satisfaction.

"So there's nothing really . . . important in all of this," she says, uncertainly.

"Ah, you and your meaning bug," he says, looking at her amiably again. "You've always had it. You're such an innocent, really. Dear Isabel."

As he escorts her to the elevator, he places his hand on the back of her neck lightly, but with unmistakable intention. Without turning round, she shakes her head no. "Is it Peter?" he asks, and she shakes her head again. "Ah, well, then I'm even more disappointed," he says, as if offering a gallantry.

"By the way," she asks, as they wait for the elevator to come down, "who was that Russian woman?"

"You mean the poetess?" He shrugs, as if it didn't much matter. "She's worked at the Russian Embassy for a long time. Pre-perestroika, which is unusual. Mostly, they've revised their personnel fairly thoroughly since then. Which means she must be doing something right. Or wrong."

The elevator door opens, and Isabel turns to him to say goodbye. "I hope you get that position you want," she says, with sincerity. "Whatever it is, exactly."

"Ah, yes," he says. "Whatever. Isn't that how you say it nowadays? Whatever." He kisses her on the cheek, and holds the elevator door open for her as she gets in.

In Between

The long corridors of Charles de Gaulle, the soundless escalators, the indecipherable human figures erased as soon as they are seen, the strange blank comfort of a space which demands nothing, in which everything is deleted as soon as it happens. She thinks, I'm free as a bird, and I skim against the surfaces of the world. Surfaces and episodes. On the plane, she takes out her schedule, tries to fix Sofia on the mental map. She no longer remembers why she agreed to go there, what trace of scruple, or curiosity moved her to say yes, she would make this absurd detour and play for a funny fee in Sofia's main concert hall. She has a vague sense that Bulgaria has been through hard times, has been brave about it, was struggling still. Sometimes, in her hard, indulged life, she likes to feel that she's doing something for a good cause. Something Good. It may have been this that prompted her hand to sign the contract which Anders had routinely faxed through for her approval.

Sofia

She is oddly cheered, though, by Sofia's quaint little airport, the juddering Lada which takes her to her hotel, bouncing insouciantly over the deep and numerous potholes, the general uncombed shabbiness of the streets. She checks into the hotel, goes out for a walk. A fresh breeze, sound of doves cooing through the plane trees, the unhurried steps of the passersby, the low-built streets, the pungent smells . . . Europe eddying into something else, somewhere else, something earlier, an elsewhere. A muezzin's cry pierces the subsiding light from a slim, barely visible minaret. She stops to listen to the sinuous musical line, weaving itself through the dusk and slow air. She falls into a slower tempo in response, feels a sloughing off of her habitual tension. No need to be on the qui vive here.

In the evening, she goes to hear the Bulgarian women sing. They've become famous recently, after having done some recordings in the West. They come out in their folk costumes, a colorful group. Then the music begins, and she sits up because she feels she is in the Presence. It is music, but hardly yet music. What emanates from the women's throats is closer to unmediated emanations, raw whoops, fierce shouts. Wild calls, so piercing that she wants to call in response. It's close to sounds wolves might make, or powerfully throated birds . . . A sort of pre-music, in which violence is not yet distinguished from pleasure, or aggression from wild love . . . Is that what the libido is like, she wonders, this pure, unmediated vitality. The voices go through her body like whipping winds, and she's almost frightened by her pure response. If she were in a circle of Bacchantes, making these sounds, who knows what frenzy she might be capable of, what orgiastic dancing or tearing of flesh.

July 9, 1982

A lesson with Isabel Merton. She played the "Waldstein" quite convincingly. She is learning about discipline, about grasping the structure of the whole, so that each passage can fall into the right proportions within it. So that the form can reveal the meaning. I talked to her about the architectural exfoliation of Beethoven's sonatas, and she listened with full absorption. She has that sort of love, the art-hunger. I felt as though my mind, my ideas, were pouring into hers. Sometimes I am full of wonder that this business of musical transmission still continues. An ancient knowledge, passed from mind to mind, hand to hand.

She played the first movement again, and looked up at me with her transparent eyes when she finished. I felt

44

an urge to reach toward her cheek and caress it. My
hand could have almost done it on its own. I didn't, of
course. Of course, I did not. Instead, I told her she was
improving. There must have been something in my
voice, however, because she gave me a startled, enquiring
look. There was a silence between us; then she broke
into a sudden, almost capricious, utterly feminine smile.
She is, after all, a very young woman who doesn't seem
to comb her hair, and wears blue jeans. But when I
speak to her, she seems to understand. Her receptivity is
almost disturbing. It is a form of innocence, but also of
knowing. She seems to take everything in through her
senses, and to absorb it like some heliotropic plant.
I wonder if she has the strength to become an artist. The
terrible, ruthless dedication. She would need to
unwoman herself, to become harder. I wonder if anyone
should wish such a fate on her.

Unwoman . . . What a strange word. Lying back against the
fluffy pillow in her hotel room, she sees Wolfe's gaunt figure
striding across the Retreat, his sensitive face with deeply set grey
eyes, his chest receding into a concave arc in some ineffable act
of withdrawal. They called him the Great Refuser, the snarky
young who came each summer, secretly to worship him, and
among themselves, to mock him. No late-night carousing, no
joking, no drink, seemingly no sex. Practically no possessions, as
far as anyone could see. So much refusal, in greedy prosperous
counter-cultural America, was practically exotic; and it added to
his cult status, his austere glamour. He was an enigma, in the face
of which they tried to maintain their ironic cool. And anyway,
how could they guess what he was refusing; where his steely rig-
ors came from. She could not, herself . . . Very little was known
about him, except the rumors: that he had been an almost Major

Figure in his native Germany; and that he left, in some obscure act of flight. Perhaps he had committed a crime, or was running away from a broken love affair . . . Although none of them could imagine Wolfe in love. She sees him striding into his white-washed cottage at the end of the day, and into his complete, his uncompromising solitude. A riddling icon, incongruous in the pristine Appalachian setting, like some Easter Island statue found improbably in a South American jungle. She wishes she could have come up to him at the end of that lesson and put her hand on his shoulder, looked directly into his eyes . . . That she could have broken through his solitude. But that was what he chose: the art monk, art sacrifice. Unwomaned, entirely. Was he right to wonder if she had the kidney for it, the necessary strength.

She sighs. Sometimes she feels like a half-blind creature, groping her way through the maze of her own self . . . She checks the next day's schedule, gets ready for bed. The Bulgarian women's singing comes back to her, with its raw erotic calls; desire without shame, asserted as fiercest strength.

Next morning, she practices Chopin's Second Scherzo, which she hasn't played for a while. The enigmatic opening rolls out from under her fingers elastically, followed by the grand proud chords, which leap into the shape of a martial mazurka, as if they were always within her hand. She feels an uninhibited, almost wild joy as the piece opens out into its expansive melody, emerging from her fingers with a fluent, lyrical motion. Like the movement of fleeting thought . . . Then the alteration to another mini-mazurka, ineffable in its melancholy . . . The miraculous capriciousness of Chopin's motifs, turned into a miraculous necessity. How does this happen, she wonders yet again, how did he convert his mercurial fancies into seeming absoluteness? She thinks of Chopin's house which she'd seen once in Warsaw, and the romantic park with sloping lawns and low dreamy horizon, a dark pond and weeping willows, and the puffy clouds moving overhead with a fluent motion of their own. All of it in the music . . . Chopin standing outside peasant cottages in the evenings, listening to raw, wistful songs. In the music too, transformed it into the most exquisite elegance . . . Through the weaving lines of the Scherzo, she remembers a childhood moment, in another landscape. Ah yes, she can almost feel the sun on her neck and shoulders back then, as she stepped out of the hacienda and on to the pampas, with its expanse of ruffled grasses, and a gentle breeze lifting her little white nightie and bending the grass like a great breath, in a sweeping melodious motion . . . Her father coming out behind her and stroking her hair, and before her, the play of light and shadow, and the intimation of a harmonious motion, the inward music of things . . . She continues with the Scherzo, not quite knowing any longer whether she is summoning the music from under her fingers, or whether it is guiding her hand through its musings, just beyond the horizon of her thoughts, her longings.

Longing and loneliness. Back in her hotel room, the longing, left on its own, gapes, gasps, wells, surges. I have chosen this, she thinks, somehow I have chosen it. It always comes upon her before a concert, this visitor, this pure news from herself. Let it ride, let it ride, this horse of the Apocalypse. She has her routines for this too, she knows she has to let It do with her as it will, let it have its way with her. She handles herself carefully, since she is almost in physical pain. She lies down on the bed, waiting for it to course through her. She is an athlete who can't count on dying young; she has to treat herself with professional care. It's nothing, she thinks, nothing, a mood, a vapor. It's nothing, you're nothing, this doesn't matter. This too shall pass. The throb of silence, and then the throb of her own self. She can feel the beast removing its claws, lifting, leaving. The Female Beast is how she thinks of it, the Saint Teresa syndrome in its other aspect. She doubts that Rothman is prone to such states. And yet, as she gets up and composes herself for the task ahead, she feels that this danger is close to the source, the source of strength; that there, her soul recharges its being.

She plays with a fine, unforced elan that evening; and the audience responds with enthusiastic warmth. A reception afterward at the American Embassy. The ambassadress, a handsome woman in a four-square suit, expounds energetically and amiably on the country to which she is an emissary, on the nature, the very character of Bulgaria. Countries seem to have acquired personalities these days, Isabel has noticed, complete with characteristic features, virtues and vices. More character than most people are given credit for. But the ambassadress extols the virtues: the vivacity of the people, their generosity and cleverness. Does Isabel know about the Bulgarian computer geniuses? She's doing her best to entertain the visiting artist, not to let a blank, uncivilized silence fall; and Isabel tries to go along, to keep alert and interested. There is something, in fact, that intrigues her about the country where she happens to have found herself; something she has sensed in the singing of the women, the rhythms of the streets, in the air. The economy though, the ambassadress continues, is a disappointment. She had thought Bulgaria would take well to free enterprise, but it hasn't, it is lagging behind some of its neighbors . . . She stops, turning toward a man who has come up to them, and is making a small bow. Isabel has seen him before, she knows that, though she remembers not so much him, as the gesture he has just made, the small, rather courtly bow; and also, something oddly intense about his expression. Then she realizes: it's the man from Paris, the one who came to the Green Room with McElvoy. Didn't McElvoy say something about his being in Sofia? Or that woman did, at the reception. The man is looking at her out of his long, narrow face, with the same puzzling intentness which had thrown her off guard before. The ambassadress introduces him as Anzor Islikhanov. This time she catches the name.

"My friend Margarita fortunately told me that you would be giving a concert here," Islikhanov says. "So of course I came. I think you have met Margarita?"

"Yes," she says, "I think she mentioned . . . Do you live in Sofia, then?"

"No, no," he says, and makes a self-deprecating gesture with his hands, as if to say it is of no interest where he lives, and it's difficult to explain. "I am here in transit."

The ambassadress excuses herself. Islikhanov pauses, as if uncertain whether to go on, whether more information from him would be welcome. "I travel a lot, you see," he says.

She looks at him queryingly. "It's because of my job," he clarifies. "As a representative of the Chechen government."

She must look baffled, because he adds, "I thought perhaps Margarita told you. Or perhaps Mr. McElvoy."

"No," she says, trying to recall whether anything had been said about Chechnya. "They didn't."

She sees a quaver of surprise, or annoyance on his face, but it disappears quickly. "No reason they should have," he says urbanely. "No reason why it should be of interest. It is just one of those . . . trouble spots. You may know that my country has a lot of problems."

She nods, uncertainly. She's seen images of a ruined city on television, and refugees moving among the rubble of buildings and abandoned streets. She has a sense it has been going on for a long time, whatever it is. A war against the Russians, but she doesn't know why or for what. One of the remote, blurry horrors.

Islikhanov is watching her closely. "No reason you should know very much," he repeats. "It's not as though Chechnya is of any . . . importance. Except of course to us. To us, it is of the greatest importance. But to the rest of the world, if I may say so, we're just one of those . . . hellish places." His voice has migrated from polite irony to a darker sarcasm. Then he spreads his palms again, in a gesture of humorous resignation. She notices that his hands are surprisingly long-fingered and delicate. He has a narrow, olive-skinned face. He speaks very good, British-accented English. She wonders why.

"But you don't live in Chechnya?" she begins, and doesn't know how to complete the sentence.

"No, no," he leaps in quickly as if to reassure her. "That is out of the question. To tell you the truth, I hardly live anywhere."

"But . . ." she begins.

"The only way I can help my country is from here," he explains. "You may not know that the government of Chechnya doesn't exist anymore. I mean, the legitimate government, of which I am a representative. So I must represent it from abroad. It is a kind of . . . virtual situation."

"And where do you live?"

"Not anywhere, really," he says urbanely. "I am a sort of non-person. Or an itinerant person. Isn't that what it is called?"

"Yes," she says. "Itinerant. That's how I think of myself . . . sometimes. Although, of course—" She stops herself short. Her condition undoubtedly cannot be compared to his. Or vice versa. Though he doesn't look . . . like anything she'd expect. Not, in any way, a personification of calamity.

"So it is perhaps right that our paths should cross," he says with emphasis. She half wishes she could end the conversation right there, get away from the peculiar pressure of his attention. Still: she is intrigued. Here is an actual person who has stepped out from behind the news images, from that other, impossible

50

reality, and he is talking to her in this rather normal way. She is curious, and in some odd way, flattered.

"Is there . . . fighting going on right now in Chechnya?" she asks, but he waves the question away. "No, I should not bother you with such gloomy matters," he says. "I should tell you instead what the Chopin Ballade meant to me. In Paris. And the Scherzo this evening." Someone passes by with refreshments, and Islikhanov indicates he wants his wine glass refilled, with a graceful, surprisingly authoritative gesture. She follows the movement with interest, and he catches her gaze; and pauses on it.

"Do you particularly love Chopin?" she begins, but the ambassadress is again at her side, wanting to introduce her to someone, and Anzor Islikhanov, making his courteous bow, moves off.

He keeps her in his sight lines, though, she's sure of it. She can sense it out of the corner of her eye, is half expecting him to rejoin her and resume their conversation. He comes up as the party is thinning out, and says he would like to show her something of interest while she's here; to give her something in return for what she's given him; all of them. Would she like to see one of Bulgaria's old monasteries tomorrow? The drive is not too long, and he thinks she would find it worth a visit. She calculates whether she needs to practice before the following day's concert, and decides it is not strictly necessary. Surely, she can break her regimen once in a while. She says yes, she would like to go.

The drive toward the monastery takes them up a steep mountainous road. Anzor Islikhanov navigates his tiny Fiat smoothly over the winding ascent, slim hand turning the wheel with a steady sureness. Not a pianist's hand, it is too narrow for that; but the fingers are long and mobile. Not the hands of hardship either, or of violent wreckage. He seems less intent on engaging her attention than yesterday, or perhaps more comfortably in charge; and she feels herself relaxing into the snug capsule, into a suspended mood. She gazes at the landscape, and gives herself over to the sheer interest of the unexpected, of not knowing what will happen next. Is it her illusion that the landscape here has a freshness and craggy vigor that is also expressed in the robust yet elegant silhouettes she has seen all around her, in the lively Bulgarian faces? Some morphology of the place, reiterated in its human inhabitants. The deep evergreens mass into a dense forest. Anzor tells her he loves this mountainous country because it reminds him of his childhood. He grew up in Grozny, the now ruined city; but his grandparents lived in a mountain village, and he visited them there often—a landscape like this, except more vast, more austere.

"We used to play games of calling out echoes when we were kids," he says, and briefly turns to her. "I really felt sometimes I heard spirits speak. I thought the mountains were inhabited by strange creatures—everywhere, just out of sight. Now there's literally almost no one there. Now the villages really are inhabited by ghosts."

The car swerves round a sharp turn and jolts her forward; but Anzor regains control almost instantly. He puts a protective arm against her, and his hand grips the wheel more tightly. They stay silent for a while.

"Do you miss Chechnya very much?" she asks, once her balance is recovered. She doesn't know how to talk about such things, doesn't want to commit an indelicacy. What does the remote country mean to the man next to her . . . ? She ponders his face, as if she could penetrate to the landscape through him. The mountains of the Caucasus, high ridges; eagles; a sparse population. And now the ruins, the refugees, the rubble . . .

"One always misses a country which has been . . . wounded,"

Anzor says. "And my country has been very hurt. Very damaged." An odd expression crosses his face, a setting of the jaw, a hooding of the eyes, as if to fend off vulnerability, or a private anger. She feels as if in the very hooding of his eyes, something has been unmasked.

"Not that I didn't want to leave when I was young," he resumes. "Or at least to travel. I felt so . . . restricted. To tell you the truth, I was almost excited when I was forced to leave. I was going to see the world."

"And now?" she asks.

"Now I've seen it," he says tersely. "Now I only think about my country. My mission."

She is taken aback by the unadorned earnestness of his tone. "And what is that? I mean, your . . . mission?" She hesitates before the word. She's afraid it will sound unnatural in her mouth; she doesn't really have the right to it.

"It is to help my people in their struggle," he answers reluctantly, almost churlishly. Perhaps he has sensed her hesitation. "I am called upon to do . . . what I can. As the situation arises."

She isn't sure whether the occasional oddities of his syntax have to do with his English, or some unfamiliar angle of vision. She looks at him questioningly; but he is turned away from her, and his eyes are hooded again. She stays on his face, wanting to know more. Something about this stranger has adhered to her imagination, like an overheard motif that bores itself into the mind and keeps turning itself over . . . She wants to ask him more about what he does, but they've reached the monastery. It sits atop a flat ridge, a long wooden and stone structure that has elements of a rustic country house, and a fortress. Inside, there's a small jewel of a chapel, its walls entirely covered with visages of saints, gleaming, in their golds and red and blues, with a rich, dark light. Two-dimensional faces, uncompromisingly flat, except for the eyes, which emit deep, solemn zeal. In a wooden, high-backed pew a solitary priest sits very still in his black robe with a tasseled belt. His face is a perfect icon too, with its long beard and black eyes. The eyes should be burning as in the images around him, but instead, they are staring vacantly into space. He sits, immobile and seemingly unexpectant; as though he intends to remain in his pose for a long time. But perhaps as he feels her eyes on him, he gets up and shuffles toward the altar as slowly as if movement were a reluctant variation on stillness; as if time did not exist. She notices that his hair at the back of the neck is matted, and his collar dirty. "He is probably only a deacon," Anzor says, and turns her gently toward a famous icon. But her attention is drawn back to the priest, who, in another almost imperceptible variation, comes to a standstill. She follows the line of his lethargic vision, and sees a figure— a woman's figure, dressed in black—prostrate on the stone floor. She makes an instinctive gesture of recoil, and Anzor puts a staying hand on her shoulder. "But . . ." Isabel says, and then sees that the figure is beginning to move, levering herself along the stone mosaic with her arms, toward the priest. It is moving laboriously, the black-clad prostrate body, head facing the stone floor in consummate abnegation. The priest waits till it comes close, and the supplicant, reaching out to lift the hem of his robe, kisses it reverently. He makes the sign of the cross over her; then returns to his imperturbable posture.

Isabel feels she's watching the scene through a long, distorting funnel which turns nearby reality surreal. She is slightly dizzy, as if she's been swung around too abruptly. She has wandered into some strange dimension, which yet has about it something ambiguously, distantly familiar. The prostrate figure of the unseen woman, now lying utterly still, as if in mimicry of death . . . It is disturbing in a way she cannot identify, as if it posed some personal danger. Anzor puts his hand lightly on the small of her back, steering her toward the exit.

She wants to ask him about what they have witnessed, but restrains the question; she realizes she has no idea how he might react to such a scene.

But as soon as they step out on a stone patio, he says, "It's an old tradition. You mustn't think she finds it humiliating." He is speaking carefully, as if wanting to soften the shock, for Isabel, of what they'd seen. "She probably finds a kind of . . . satisfaction in it. A release."

"Release from what?"

"From her problems. Her burdens. She probably has a hard life. This lifts her up. Takes her out of herself. It's a kind of . . . trance."

Again, a twist of dizziness, of fascination. Of curiosity. She's wandered into a strange dimension, and feels all of her usual judgments giving way. Anzor asks her if she'd like to stroll around the monastery grounds. There's a wind, and she feels the bounce of her own mussed hair with sensuous relief, as if it had been released from the prostrate figure's black scarf. Anzor tells her that the mountainous fortresses were centers of resistance against the Turks, when the region was governed by the Ottomans. The monks here fired cannon balls at Turkish armies, and gave refuge to peasant partisans. "These holy men were resistance fighters," he says. "But you know, mountains are always places of resistance. Mountain people love freedom. They do not give it up . . . ever."

The fresh lawn elides into a wilder mountain brush, leading out to the edge of a narrow ravine, a foaming river running deep below, its ceaseless whoosh reaching them as an echo of watery turbulence. They listen to the sound quietly for a while; then Anzor, as if looking at a different landscape in his mind's eye, tells her about the austere beauty of the gray stone towers, built as strategic lookouts in Chechnya's mountains. And about his parents and grandparents, who had to leave their village during the great deportation, when the entire population of Chechnya was stuffed into cattle cars, or if they were lucky and in favor with the regime, into passenger trains, and herded off, like a population of cows or elks, into refugee camps in Central Asia.

"All of them?" Isabel asks incredulously.

Anzor confirms, his eyes clouding. "Actually, I was born there . . . although I hardly remember anything of it, except the red earth, and the horsemen." But the Chechens came back in the great, sad return, when the Soviets finally allowed it, and the grandparents rebuilt their house exactly on the same spot where it had been before. "That was the one spot on earth which meant something to them. Which they understood and loved," Anzor says. "To them, everything else was alien. Unimportant. Godless land. The light was wrong everywhere else, the air was wrong. They were still like that, you see. There was only one place which was real to them. Where they could truly live. And now the village is gone."

His eyes become remote again, his mouth set. He turns away from her, and picks up a jagged stone and throws it, with surprising force, down into the small ravine. A faint sound reaches them, mixed with the unvarying, gurgling water. She follows the movement of his torso, as he turns effortlessly with the extension of the throwing arm. Line of beauty, she thinks, line of grace . . . The casual arc of the throwing arm seems to slow into a timelessness; and suddenly, as if in concert with the elongated curve, she feels a surge of longing so sudden and powerful that she's afraid she'll fall from it; that her chest will cave in as from a blow.

Anzor's eyes return to her, still occluded, still looking into another distance; then they gather toward a more focused light. His face is for a moment fully unmasked, and he directs at her a stare that takes her in with a kind of encompassing ferocity. She stares back. He is very near and at a great distance. She knows nothing about this man, except the sudden power of his presence. A line of attraction and danger seems to vibrate between them in a tense ostinato. She feels she could travel a long way along that line, beyond the dark glow of his gaze, and into whatever lies within. For a moment, their eyes lock.

Then the moment is over, and they start walking back to the car. On the way down the winding road, they talk politely, as people who are getting acquainted talk. She asks him how he has come to know so much about the technique of the paintings in the monastery, and he tells her he once went to an art school in Moscow for a year. Many people in Chechnya went to school in Moscow, it was necessary if you wanted to get professional credentials. But while he had great ambitions, he tells her with some bemusement, he had no talent whatsoever. "I probably could have come up with some gimmick and deluded myself it was art," he says. "Painting over portraits of Lenin or Stalin to make them look grotesque in some way. Or desecrating some religious imagery. One of my friends got very famous painting various Russian and Soviet symbols in weird ways. I mean, famous in the West." There's a sudden sharpness to his tone, a bite of old rivalry, perhaps; or of genuine disdain. Then he shrugs, as if to dispel the brusqueness with which he's spoken. "Anyway, art is not so important in my country," he says. "We have to win our independence first. Then we can have a few extras, like pictures."

She asks him what he did instead and he says, ruefully, that it was nothing useful after all. He studied linguistic philosophy, even though his father had wanted him to become an engineer. He'd been an engineer himself. "That would have been a better thing to do," Anzor says. "Then at least I could have built bridges. My country needs bridges. Especially after they get destroyed, which happens regularly. But you know how it is with fathers and sons."

She nods. She knows, at least, what it is like with mothers and daughters, though she isn't going to disclose this to Anzor. She isn't going to say much about herself; somehow, that would be out of place. This seems to be the subliminal compact between them: it is his to disclose, and hers to listen and appraise. And yet, she feels his candor as a form of gratifying approval. Across all their barriers, he trusts her to understand . . .

"But what I really love," he brings out suddenly, and then brakes back his tone in some embarrassment: "What I really . . . admire . . . is . . . your art. This great music you play. It reminds me of freedom. Or the love of freedom. If we ever achieve a revolutionary victory in my poor country, I hope it will be to the sounds of Chopin."

"A revolutionary victory . . ." she repeats.

As if to defuse the fervor with which he's spoken, Anzor adds in a lighter tone, "These days, of course, each soldier could choose his own victory music. Earphones under the helmets. It would probably be heavy metal for most." Incongruously, she thinks of Schumann's phrase for Chopin's melodies: flower-covered guns.

They drive silently for a while, along the barely visible road, framed by the looming, dense forest. Has anything passed between them, back there, over the small ravine? A ghost of a gaze, that's all. She contemplates the deepening dark, returns to Anzor's lean hand on the steering wheel. It pleases her, the suppleness of his wrist, the calm with which he maneuvers the small Fiat over the difficult road. There's quietness now in his face and posture, and the composure gives him a kind of natural force. Simple presence . . . There seems to be no need to speak. No need to keep the ball rolling, to keep it up . . . Silence. Unstrained silence, of the kind she hardly remembers . . . Which is hardly possible in her world, where a pause in the conversation bespeaks a failure of ingenuity as well as of politeness. In the intimate, smoothly moving capsule, she feels herself relax, watch the rhythmically passing shadows. No need to be on the qui vive. Is it, she thinks, because the man beside her is from . . . there?

But they chat again, politely, once they enter the better lit city. "I think there is a big exhibition of Russian art in London," Anzor tells her. "Are you going there as part of your tour?"

She says yes, she is scheduled to play in London in about ten days. She'll look out for the exhibition. At the hotel where he drops her off, he says good-bye with a courteous incline of the head, and takes her hand briefly between his. In his eyes, as he raises them to her face, there is the merest allusion to what happened on the edge of the ravine. He says he hopes to see her again. Since they are both itinerants, perhaps their paths will again fortuitously cross. He'll look out for her concerts; perhaps he will come backstage if he can attend one. She wouldn't mind that, would she? She says no, of course not. It would be nice if he did.

In Between

In the air, in no place. Her fingers flex almost unconsciously over the arm of her seat, moving through basic exercises. She peers into the confined space, trying to discern something within it. Did it matter, that line of tension between them near the ravine . . . or the pinpoint light of Anzor's eyes . . . Where's she going, where is her restlessness taking her . . . Sometimes she feels she can almost grasp it, the aim of her yearnings, the shape of her strange, free condition. This is the illusion of flight: that she can gain a bird's-eye view of her situation, of herself. But in this resistless space, her thoughts are too resistless themselves. Nothing to hold her, except the borders of her own body. She can almost feel her bird-like thoughts beating against the walls of her mind. She wonders where Anzor may be now. She didn't ask him where he was going next. He may also be somewhere in mid-space, in flight. She probably won't see him again; it was another brief encounter, that's all. She reaches for her steady companion, Wolfe's *Journal.*

July 10, 1982

A lesson with Isabel Merton. A strange avatar, this young girl with her naive expressions. She played Schubert's Impromptus, then Schoenberg. She is learning, drinking in every suggestion. Once again, I felt the temptation to tell her . . . everything. Perhaps she would understand why I have chosen this life. The renunciation of this solitude. Perhaps her understanding would assuage my loneliness, which sometimes I can hardly bear. But of course, I stopped myself. What would I have said to her, anyway? What do I say to myself, except that I was born into a contaminated world, a contaminated country. And that, for a while, I wanted to sweep the decks clean. Or to pour my rage over everything like purifying fiery water over a bloodied deck. Just one burst, one bomb, one Molotov cocktail, one explosive sound, so that I could consider myself a moral being.

Then of course I realized it cannot be done. The decks can never be swept clean. The Augean stables of history can never be emptied of disorder and filth. Even if these pristine woods seem remote from all filth and danger. And yet, my boyhood keeps coming back to me this summer, and I cannot deny that sometimes I long for Berlin, the betraying city. Berlin of my childhood. Perhaps there is something about these woods that reminds me of the wooded parks where I roamed with my pals, in all kinds of weather. I can still hear our voices calling out to each other, enlivened by our boyish affection and all we knew of each other's curiosity, our appetite for the world. The appetite which was already being perverted by the Führer. For we were also strangely susceptible to his menacing appeal. I can still feel—hear—our tussles as our vigor got the better of us and threatened to spill into God knows what. One day, I made them listen to one of my compositions. I think it was some imitation of Mozart's Turkish March, almost the same thing; but they sat through it abashed, and then made embarrassed noises of appreciation.

Our further histories do not bear thinking about. There were those who murdered, and those who were murdered. Those who did worse than murder, those who were worse than murdered. The horror of it, the utter horror. It sometimes threatens to explode within me, tear my body apart. My human frame can hardly contain that much horror, that much rage. Then I have to retreat to my whitewashed cottage and my composition. Reduce everything to my distilled sound. It is the only way I can continue. The only way I can live.

No, I have no right to burden Isabel Merton with any of this. In any case, I doubt, after all, that she would understand. She seems to perceive the world musically, in its affective-sensuous aspect. But like all of them, she is innocent of the past; the vileness that is history.

So I stopped myself. I let her gather up her scores and leave. I think she realized I was leaving something unsaid. She looked back at me from the door, pausing, as if to give me a chance. But I let her leave, as I do each time. As I am fated to do. That too is my atonement. My penance.

. . . See him there, in his not completely clean T-shirt and two days' stubble, pacing up and down his small room as if it were a cage. Not quite his room, not quite a cage. He moves from one such space to another, they're prepared for him by his comrades. His brothers. This one has a bad smell in it, probably of vermin poison. See him sitting down at the portable computer, to look at information coming out of his country. The news is bad. The news is shockingly bad. A familiar name catches his attention, someone who's been wounded, and something snags at his throat, his chest. Fury. A sad, sad ache. An ache surging into a rage so bitter that he could . . . kill. Or leap out of his skin, his situation, get out of it once and for all, leave it, forget it. Forget his country and his comrades. He wasn't meant for this. He could have been an artist, or a scholar. He could have lived a studious life, contemplating the migration of languages, or the transmigration of the soul. But that is not to be. This is what he is becoming; this is now his fate. See him there, getting out of the stuffy room, shutting the door roughly behind him, striding across the darkened street in nothing but his jeans and T-shirt. A lean, fast-moving man with gloom-darkened eyes. What you cannot see is that he carries in his mind the long history of his country, a history so bitter and so violent that only new violence, he knows, can do it justice. More violence, till justice is done . . . Till the bitter end. The history pursues him as he strides down the quiet street, like a massed black cloud moving across mountains. It is a heavy, coal-black darkness. Ahead of him, he imagines Isabel like a Renaissance angel, in winged flight. She's sailing through the air, as she sailed on the music, her reddish hair streaming with streaked light. Onstage, she was a vision. The power of her art is such that it matches the violence within him. In her translucent eyes, he has seen something that meets his yearning. Something entranced.

See him walk faster, hunched now against the cold, as if he wanted to get away from what's trailing him, the massed darkness. As if he wanted to catch up with her instead. He wants to seize her, hold her, fuck her. To see desire in her eyes. He's seen it already, the lighting of a spark. Desire for him. Esteem for him. From a woman like that, one of the precious creatures. He wonders briefly if he'll cause her trouble, if this is fair. Then he pushes the thought away, shaking with inward protest. Fair: a dim bloodless word he's picked up in their bland, tepid countries. A word which has nothing to do with justice. Or passion. For justice rises out of passion, out of love and hate, not out of their petty reasoning, their on the one hand and on the other. He must watch out, mustn't get infected by their blanched, weak words. He's studied philosophy enough to know that language can infect you with ideas. His resentment rises till he could hit out at something from the twisting bitterness of it, hit out at the trivial flat world he's found himself in and his utter impotence within it. He's seen their eyes, has seen them glaze because they were talking to an inferior, has seen them narrow with suspicion because they were talking to a barbarian.

See him turn back, slow down his step, thinking of her. He wants to take her shining hair in his hand and push it back from her face, and light her eyes with the fierceness he has seen when she plays. He will make her come to him. He doesn't want to hurt her, no. But he deserves . . . He must have her, before his life ends. For he will die soon, he's sure of it. That is now his destiny, and he is only its instrument. He sees that with startling clarity and feels relief at the thought. Death will be a lovely release. From his anger, his impotence, his sad, sad ache. He doesn't know how he will meet it, but he wants to travel toward it as toward a dark light. He must not be diverted by their shallow pleasures, their trivial arguments.

What he cannot see is the spaciousness of the world outside his dedication, his suffering country. There is nothing outside. His thoughts have their own absoluteness, straight like an arrow moving along its appointed path till it meets its target. His mind is its own black box, and the information it contains will not be unloaded till later.

Berlin

She doesn't expect to see him again. But she does, or she thinks she does. She thinks she glimpses him in east Berlin, in a half-renovated, atmospherically lit courtyard flanked by some art galleries. This is in the old East, which is trying to retain some traces of being East still: discreetly ravaged, discreetly picturesque. In the yellow half-light of street lanterns, she thinks she sees him in an open space across the courtyard. She stares at the man who might be Anzor, but he is in profile, and she can't see him clearly. He seems to be contemplating an installation she has just rather fruitlessly scrutinized, consisting of a long nylon string, stretched as if for hanging laundry, but hung instead with large, dangling, variously broken and twisted dolls. His hands are in the pockets of a long coat, and the slight forward tilt of the lean silhouette seems to be Anzor's. But the silhouette is mostly turned away, and before she can ascertain whether it is him, he walks into a passageway on the other side of the courtyard. She has an odd sensation of a perceptual warp, as if a dim electronic sound had bent itself in an unexpected way, though its source is impossible to discern.

She thinks she sees him again in west Berlin, in a bar she haphazardly walks into, to slake her thirst. The place is again badly lit, and crowded. She begins to look for a table, then realizes there are only men there. Men of all ages and colors and manner of dress, though leather jackets predominate. They look at her not with hostility, and not even with surprise—other women before her must have made this mistake—but she understands from those looks that she shouldn't be there. She stops short in the crowded space, uncertain what to do next, and as she looks across the room—she doesn't want to appear unnerved, or hounded out—she thinks she sees Anzor in the back of the bar. He's engaged in what is clearly a very private conversation with a short, leather-jacketed man, of Middle Eastern appearance. They stand close to each other, and the short man gesticulates angrily, his index finger jabbing out at his interlocutor. His Adam's apple, even from this distance, seems to be bobbing. The taller man shrugs contemptuously, in a gesture she thinks she recognizes. But again, she thinks she must have made a mistake. The man is not facing her, and in this dusky interior, with her embarrassment about having walked into the wrong place, everything blurs and her vision turns anxiously hazy.

There's a sense of a déjà vu about the whole scene, though maybe that is because she's seen something like that in the movies, or has stepped into such a place before. She walks out of the bar quickly, trying to shake off a slight eeriness. She knows this sensation from childhood, a ghostly tingle at the back of her neck, as if something hidden within the real were about to make its appearance.

Outside, a stolid street, ordinary light. Wolfe's betraying city, Europe's euphoric site. The Wall goes up, the Wall comes down. She's seen the images, exalted, collective, of people dancing on the gloomy old barrier. Now there is nothing but the concrete day, the stodgy suited men hurrying along with their suitcases, the prosperous shops, the banal business beat of a Central European city. But why is she having these Anzor phantasms all the time? Though this is also something that happens in her kind of life, the sudden emergence of an uncannily familiar face, fragment of a smile, gesture, or turn of mouth, emerging from the crowd, and disappearing again. We're all each other's morphs.

Or is she, somewhere beneath consciousness, imagining a Pursuit, the man hurrying after her, to seize her, lift her up, vanquish her resistance? Ludicrous old images, rising up from some cinematic trove, some obsolescent basement of the imagination. It's her itinerant life, that's the problem; she might as well be moving along some sort of endlessly running, endlessly reiterating Philip Glass loop. Perhaps she should go back to the bar; ascertain whether it was or was not Anzor. Get a grip. She stops in her tracks, doesn't know which way to turn. A brief vertigo of disorientation; she can't get her coordinates straight.

Then she remembers the task awaiting her in the evening and starts walking back to her hotel. She must prepare, must compose herself. Must step into the really real of her life.

She plays Mozart's No. 24 with the Berlin Philharmonic that evening; and afterward, stays to hear Beethoven's Ninth—a rare event. The conductor is a young Englishman with a cherubic face and an aureole of curly white hair, who guides the orchestra with his baton as if he were both lightning rod and magus. From her observation point behind the stage entrance, she is close enough to see the detail of his hands, which are a da Vinci drawing come to mobile life. Or Michelangelo's hands, igniting the orchestra with a pointed finger, and being reignited by the life thus awakened in turn. God and Adam, all in one. The music surges in power like a great engine churning, like an airplane gathering speed. More than human power; and she wonders how one mind could have summoned it, one man's frame contained it. She thinks of Beethoven, hurling himself down on the ground, thrashing about in paroxysms of rage. He thought his deafness was brought on by such a tantrum, his eardrum broken, perhaps, by a force of fury in excess of what the blood vessels could bear. The music grows through its symmetrical progressions, surely the way plants grow, as well as cathedrals, the way great oak trees make their way up through accumulating sequences, up and out from the tiny motif of the acorn. The force of the music accumulates till she feels almost endangered by its massed power, and the simultaneous knowledge that she can never sustain such a vision, can never live within it. Only intimations, only glimpses. Of what? Is it nature's force, or human libido increased to its nth power; or the impersonal whirling of particles and spheres, generating the world through their patterns? Or is this human desire, intuiting more than it can attain? Desire seeks eternity: Friedrich Nietzsche. The majestic lines and great chordal combinations gather toward each other and vastly intertwine, in terraced orders, in tiers of ascending harmonies which demand that she ascend with them or be torn in twain. Oh, so beyond the border of the possible, beyond the grasp. The conductor's hands rise up to the choir, striking it to life. The music grows in beauty till beauty itself becomes a more than human force. She thinks, I live in paltry arbitrariness, and yet I live in this. The music breaks through its own urgency and ascends to a dimension where all is calm; and Isabel, without knowing why, and without worrying about the guard standing nearby and observing her closely, cries.

*

July 10, 1982

It must have been the silence at the end of the lesson
that brought back, like an increase in air pressure, those
five days in Warsaw, so many years ago. Five days in that
simple room, with its own silence and its dense atmosphere. Oh that silence, in which everything was contained. The speaking pause. And Renata. I still do not
know why she summoned me to that room, and why I
followed. The festival was called Warsaw Autumn, and
everything in Poland seemed autumnal, all grays and
shabby clothing and the muted gold of the fallen leaves.
And the still fresh ruins. The Poles were beginning to
compose in their expressive post-war vein. They had the
right to the tragic mood. As I did not. I hardly felt I had
the right to make music. I spent my days there walking
around with a bowed head. So when she summoned me
. . . Of course I followed. I was almost crazed with wanting to compensate for something, to show one human
being that I was not like that. A German, but not like
that. Though I was of course also following *her*. Her
lovely face with the high cheekbones, the hair uncompromisingly tied back, the unswerving eyes. There was
nothing she seemed to want from me, except the trans-
portation of those documents to the West. But that was
at the beginning, she didn't need to invite me to her
apartment once I agreed, night after night, day after day.
Perhaps she wanted to confront me in some way. Or to
deposit her sadness with me, to show me how much she
had been hurt. By us. The Germans. Perhaps she wanted

to touch a man who stood for men who had visited destruction on her country. There were only those five wordless days. She knew only a few phrases of German, and I none of Polish. Oh, how it comes back. The way we stood at the window of her apartment, looking down at the melancholy street below. I want to write it down, yes, I want to know that it actually happened. That I have had that experience. We ran our hands over each other's bodies, again and again, slowly and meticulously, as if learning a new terrain. Mapping it, molding it, molding ourselves into the other's body. There was nothing else, just time and us, the barely furnished room and us. A sort of eternity. At the end, I asked her to come with me. Because by that time, I—yes, I loved her. I did not see how I would live without her. But that was not what she wanted. I did not see how I could leave, how I could pull away. I was crazed with pain. By the end, we were part of each other; we had exchanged everything. But I had to go back, of course. I knew I had just lived through the happiest—no, the fullest—no, the most profoundly meaningful—days of my life. And that they would have to last me forever. I would not find anything like love again. I did not deserve it, and therefore I would have to refuse it. At least I owed her that act of contrition, that penance.

Strapped into her seat, Isabel feels herself bending forward, as if to reach the Warsaw room, plunging into its scene of silent passion as into a well. Wolfe's Passion. Is such intensity possible only in the past, in its chiaroscuro depth; its compelling wholeness?

*

The flatness of the present. Touchdown, airport; a drive into the city, through the no-man's-land, everywhere the same, everywhere a nowhere. In Brussels, a drizzle again, falling differently than in Paris, onto the more stolid stone. The hotel clerks, the waiters and bellboys avoid her gaze. One could begin to feel despondent from so many averted, lightless eyes. In the hotel room, comfort and meaninglessness. To think "how nice," to think anything at all, is to raise the decibel of meaninglessness still higher. Once, in Cincinnati, she came into such a room, in which someone had left a large bowl of fruit for her, and she thought "how nice," and smiled into the room, as if someone were watching, and then felt she could leap out of her skin, or had leapt out already. For who was she smiling at, who was watching, who providing the commentary? Now she knows how to ward off such thoughts. She retrieves her newly pressed gown from the concierge, gives herself over to an interval of concentration. She's playing at the Beaux Arts this time, a step up from the smaller halls where she's performed before; and she's pleased and nervous.

She feels fragile as she comes out onstage, fragile and lonely in the grand elegant space. Can she fill this palace of art with her presence? She tries; but as she faces her audience after the first half to take her bow, she thinks she sees people in the front rows coming out of a doze. She is thrown. Had she been that dull?

In the second half, propelled by a sort of vengefulness, she plays with mellifluous facility. Liszt's *Transcendental Études* emerge in all their gorgeous richness, bravura passages ascending and descending in seemingly effortless cascades. Whatever adrenaline is coursing through her seems to fuel her technique to a fine fluency, and she navigates the keyboard with a kind of I'll-show-you insouciance. At the end, the "Jeux d'eau" slides off her fingers like butter; like water. The applause is quite convincing; quite satisfactory.

At the sponsors' reception, a blonde, perfectly coiffed woman comes up to her, with a polite smile. She is wearing an Armani suit, pale pink and smooth as chocolate.

"We always love it when you come to Brussels," she declares. "We are so pleased to have booked you into the Beaux Arts this time."

"Thank you."

"We don't have enough . . . real culture," the woman continues in a sincere voice. "Especially where I live. You know, I came in just for the concert."

"Did you really?"

"Well, you know, I'm on the board of trustees of an arts fund . . . I feel it is so important to support this kind of thing."

Isabel smiles and says that's wonderful, the arts would not survive without people like her, classical music would not survive. She knows this is true; feels some proper gratitude. But later, when she is alone in her room at last, she wonders why on earth it's important to the perfectly dressed woman to come to yet another recital, why it's important for anyone. It's the post-concert ghost coming upon her again. She stops herself from calling Peter. It's not fair; she needs to find ways to cheer herself up without him.

The ghost is still there when she wakes up the next morning, pitching her into a state of irritable disaffection. What can culture mean, she wonders as she sets out on her morning walk, in a city where it is so ubiquitous. We're fat with culture, she thinks, like bees overfed with pollen. Fat and lethargic. No *Rite of Spring* to awaken us into astonishment. She wanders through the old Austrian quarter, her steps slowing from a sort of tourist boredom. It's an ordinary old quarter of a big European city, with grand architecture and wide avenues, and a surround of concert halls and museums. Does anything *happen* anymore . . . No horizon, nothing beyond the epidermis of stone. Things are what they are, it's no use trying to peer beyond the ostensible. She is walking through a disenchanted world. She enters the grand national museum, feels stifled, turns right back to go out on the street. The city is museum enough, becalmed and perfectly maintained, perfectly finished and glossed. Almost asking for destruction, an upheaval, an overturning; for what else could happen next?

In her restlessness, a susurrus of music tugs at her from within, and she remembers a crowded train in Russia, years ago, taking her to Odessa from some proximate city. A heated compartment filled with sweaty Russian youths, disheveled, sloppy, rowdy . . . She was a bit afraid. Then they took up their guitars and harmonicas, and started singing songs from the steppes. Music which was nothing but shaped yearning, fierceness, lament, praise, lust. Blood, sweat and tears. They passed a bottle of vodka from one to the next, and to her as well, and poured it down their throats without ceasing to play. She loved them for that hour or so, the disheveled boys, traveled on the pure raw lines of their songs as if she were at one with them. The guitarist threw his head back, and his pale, pasty face opened up to the music as to a fresh large wind across a large sky. The others joined in as if they were carried on the same vast, gusty breezes, the same galloping horses, the same rolling, spacious melody.

She continues to wander through the placid streets without particular aim, finds herself somehow in another old quarter where men with linked arms walk along the echoing cobblestones, their expressions hardening slightly as they pass her. Women with covered faces appear in high windows, only their eyes visible, and unreadable. Quiet, it is very quiet here; a veiled, puzzling hush, different from the calm of Brussels's burgher heart. She begins to feel nervous. She is the alien here, she cannot read any of the signals; and she retraces her steps to get back to the more familiar regions.

It is as she pauses at a street crossing that she sees him, waiting on the other side for the light to change. This time there's no doubt: it is Anzor. He sees her too, and waves at her, signaling that she should stay where she is; he'll come toward her. She stops, doubly disoriented because, in a way, he's been present in her mind. She feels as if she has conjured him out of her thoughts, or the air; out of what she now recognizes as her wishes. She keeps him in the line of her sight as he crosses the street with a light, long stride. She has always been moved by human beauty. She takes in his unstrained movements, his well-defined face, with a sort of inward assent.

"Isabel," he says simply, having reached her, "I am so glad to see you." There is nothing desultory or playful about his tone, no formal bow this time, or concession to the improbability, the sheer capriciousness of their meeting. His earnestness adds to her confusion.

"How did this happen?" she nevertheless asks, and then realizing that even this holds too much of an assumption, rephrases: "I mean, what are you doing in Brussels?"

"Oh, it is my job," he says dismissively, as if this were irrelevant. "There's a conference we've been invited to by the European Union . . ." Then he interrupts himself and says, with a quiet emphasis, "I was thinking about you very much."

She is taken aback by the directness of it. What is he assuming? But the pressure of his words carries its own conviction; and she says, "I thought of you too." He asks whether he could accompany her to wherever she's going, and she feels a background tremolo of anxiety. What is going to happen next? She could pull back; perhaps she should. But after the restless morning in an alien city, Anzor seems very vivid to her; very alive. She says she's going to her hotel, not very far from where they are. He accompanies her, talking inconsequentially. Their strides adjust easily to each other as they walk. The tremolo strengthens into a steadier excitement as she takes in the pleasure of his presence; his unqualified presentness.

At the hotel, he asks her if she would like to come to a reception which caps off the conference he is attending. It is on the minorities in Europe, or something of the sort. "But that's not the point," he says. "I just don't want to say good-bye yet. To be truthful, I was hoping we would meet again. In our travels." This time, the pressure of his words seems less incongruous. She says yes, she will come. "Good," he says, and nods, as if something has been confirmed. He grasps her by both shoulders and pauses to look at her, into her. She looks back. Anzor Islikhanov is as arbitrary as all the other people she brushes up against in her nomadic drifts; but somehow, he is gaining a kind of inevitability. Like a Chopin motif, she silently thinks, starting with a mere wisp of suggestion . . . She sighs, and relaxes more deeply into his gaze. They stay still for a moment, in a sort of promise. Then he turns abruptly, as if his allotted time were running out—yes, that was the gesture she's tried to place—and walks away.

The reception to which Anzor has invited her takes place on the top floor of a European Union building, in a low-ceilinged space whose windows, ranged into a wall of glass, reflect the city's jeweled nighttime glitter. The building gleams too, though in a muted way, glass and chrome mingling with blond wood and unostentatious spaces. A becoming modesty, probably achieved at great cost. A graceful sculpture, made of delicate metal rods, cascades down several floors, into the well of a curving, conch-shaped staircase. She takes in the nicely dressed crowd, the sanitized hubbub of restrained conversation, the sideways glances. When it's not a concert, the world is, apparently, a conference.

Anzor is nowhere in sight. Instead, another familiar face manifests itself out of the scattered groups. It is the Russian poetess introduced to her by that man in Paris—she'll remember his name later—and she is hurrying toward Isabel as if they were old friends. Isabel restrains a gesture of slightly alarmed surprise. What is the Russian woman doing here, how come she is surfacing again in this unexpected setting? She was exhaustingly clever, Isabel recollects; and Katrina—yes, that is her name—instantly confirms this by launching into some playful disquisition in lieu of a greeting—something about the thickening of coincidence as a correlative of the increasing density of the modern world.

"But what are you doing here, darling?" she asks, stopping herself midstream. "I didn't know this was your kind of scene!"

Isabel mutters something indistinct about having been invited by someone named Anzor Islikhanov, perhaps Katrina has come across him, he is from Chechnya . . .

"Ah, Anzorichka," Katrina says liltingly, but her eyebrows go up a fraction, and she looks at Isabel with sudden attentiveness. "Good old Anzorichka . . ."

"What do you mean?" Isabel asks in increased confusion, but Katrina has turned toward the window, and is pointing to the view outside. "Isn't this . . . poetic?" she asks, with a rhetorical gesture of her plump arm. "Surely, poets in such a country should have no difficulty finding subjects, don't you think?" Her tone is hard to read, and Isabel isn't sure whether she's being taken into collusive confidence, or included among the objects of Katrina's seemingly ubiquitous mockery.

"Why, do poets in Russia have difficulties finding subjects?" she asks.

"Ah, this Russia where I live," Katrina answers, "it has nothing poetic about it. Except maybe its extreme ugliness, and we've never learned to make poetry out of that. Very backward of us,

75

don't you think? But we Russians, you know, we need our poetry to be misty and ideal."

Katrina is speaking with silver-quick merriment, but she continues to inspect Isabel quite carefully. Then Anzor is suddenly there, and Katrina raises her glass to him with sly complicity. "Isn't that right, Anzorichka? That we all need an ideal, we children of the Soviet Empire?"

They clearly know each other well, Isabel notes, with a small but informative twist in her diaphragm. Jealousy is a possibility even when she has absolutely no rights to it.

"Ah, you're impossible, Katrina," Anzor says, and his gaze travels toward Isabel, in an implicit inquiry. He clearly wants to know what they've been talking about. "Is she bending your ear?" he asks Isabel, in his civil, urbane tone. Not the tone of their few private conversations. Isabel begins to say something polite, but Anzor interrupts. "If you don't watch out, she will confuse you completely. She is our theorist at this conference, as well as our poetess. She has confused most of us already."

"Poet," Katrina corrects him sternly. "You have to keep up."

"Yes, yes," Anzor agrees, as if he's heard this before. Their in-joke, apparently. Just how well do they know each other?

"I was just saying to Isabel," Katrina lilts on, undeterred, "that the new ugliness in Russia is at least more interesting than the old ugliness. Don't you think so, Anzorichka? That's our great improvement, that these days we can afford to be ugly in a really vulgar sort of way. Camp, isn't that what you would call it? I know it's old news in the West, but in the past, we couldn't even afford that. Kitsch is a sign of progress."

"Is that your new theory?" Anzor asks, without a hint of humor. There are undertones in their exchanges that Isabel can't quite catch.

"The newest," Katrina drawls. "You have to keep up. And what interesting conclusions have you gathered from this conference, darling?" she asks, raising her eyebrows again in sly expectation.

"Ah, conclusions . . ." Anzor repeats sardonically. "You know, they invite us, they observe us, they study us. Like noble savages. And we perform for them. We try to prove we are civilized." His tone has traveled from irony toward something darker and more edgy. Katrina gives a brief laugh of appreciation.

"But sometimes it's nice to perform, no? I mean, isn't it more fun than always having this one *identity*?"

Anzor shrugs impatiently. "And there are all these good roles to choose from," she continues, though her tone is again becoming unreadable to Isabel. "For example, you can be noble savage or ignoble savage, or a marginal of the margins, or of the center. . . . Ah, Ahmed," she croons, without missing a beat, and greets a handsome chocolate-skinned man in a cream-colored Nehru shirt who is hovering hesitantly nearby. "Come and talk to us. I'm sure you can explain everything to our guest, can't you? As a marginal, you can't get any more central than Ahmed," she informs Isabel. "Can you, Ahmed?"

She twinkles at Ahmed, as she twines her arm through Anzor's conspiratorially, and leads him away. So they know each other very well. Isabel tries to turn her attention to Ahmed, whose manner and liquid eyes are almost excessively gentle, and who is looking at her with a compassionate, or maybe slightly pitying gaze.

"Katrina likes to mock everything and everyone," he says feelingly, though whether in complaint or compassion, Isabel cannot tell. "I am actually not very important at all." Isabel asks him where he's from, and he says, smiling wistfully, that answers to simple questions are becoming ever more complicated. "But I was born right here," he says, pointing at the floor. "In Brussels." She must look surprised, because he says, "Yes, I know it is unexpected. But it is true. Although, you see, in some other, perhaps truer way, I come from Bangladesh. That's where my ancestors are from. That is the place that draws my soul." He speaks soothingly, as if to soften the effect of his difficult disclosures. "You might say, that is where my soul comes from, even if my body came into the world right here."

"But you live here," Isabel notes, or asks. He smiles even more consolingly. "I no longer have any choice," he says. "I have made my bed in Brussels and must lie in it. I have a responsible job, you see, I could not let people down. But my sons . . . I hope my sons will go back to Bangladesh, to find their true community. I hope their souls will be in better alignment with where they live." He looks at her wistfully, and asks which country she is representing. She explains that she is there under false pretenses, a musician on tour who happened to be invited. A traveling performer, let in through the back door.

"A musician, is it?" he says appreciatively. "Then I think you may understand about having a true home, yes? A soul home." She nods, charmed by his sincerity, his lack of guile. "Sometimes I go to Bangladesh, you see," he continues, "and after several days there, I experience more human warmth than in several years here. I sense that you may understand this. You should go to my country, you would see the hospitality. People make sure things are nice for you, even if they don't have much to give you. Here . . . they don't care very much. It is cold here, isn't it?"

Some embers light up in the soft liquidity of his eyes; Isabel thinks she detects the low burn of resentment, or of disappointment. She is about to respond, but they've been approached by a personage who causes her to stare in some amazement. His likes are known to her only from paintings: of Liszt, or Byron, or other romantic androgynous boys with wild hair and angelic faces. But this one is here and now. She thinks for a moment he might be in costume, but he's much too serious for that. He's wearing a short black cape over a brilliantly white shirt with an upturned collar; and his long black hair is thrown into high relief by his very upright posture. Proud posture, that is the only phrase which will do. As for his eyes, they are black and fiery. The clichés apparently come from somewhere.

"Our guest from Catalonia," Ahmed introduces him, as Isabel makes the effort not to stare too conspicuously. He too seems delighted to learn that she is a pianist, and is soon discoursing on the music of his country, of Catalonia. Does she know it? Yes, she says, she loves it, the mix of sensuousness and Christianity, of pagan rhythms and troubadour love.

"But that music expresses our very own, special character," he asserts, his eyes flashing. Yes, his eyes flash. "That is what we are trying to preserve. Our special spirit. And our *sardanas* and *habaneras* are as important to us as our unique language."

"I'm sure . . ." Isabel begins, but clearly, her tone is insufficient to the occasion, because the Catalonian's posture becomes even more upright, and his voice stiffens with dignity. "It is the genius of the people . . ." he says. Then his mobile phone rings, and he fumbles for it beneath his black cape awkwardly, his posture suffering some impairment in the process.

Isabel briefly wishes she had Katrina at her side to provide the appropriate commentary, but instead, a short, broadly built man in a herringbone suit has come up and shakes hands with Ahmed and the Catalonian energetically. He acknowledges Isabel with a bare nod. Judging by his effect on the others, he must be the host of the gathering, or its director. He focuses their energies the way the minister did at the reception in Paris. The two men adjust their postures toward him. Ahmed's voice shifts from dreaminess to something quite a bit harder. The Catalonian leans forward with an eagerness that almost sacrifices pride. The short man wants to know what the two guests think about some new European policy on immigration; and they volley some acronyms back and forth with speed and precision. She tries to follow out of politeness, but as they pay her no attention, she turns away, and stands uncertainly, trying to spot Anzor somewhere in the room.

But it is Katrina who is again next to her, and who has apparently been observing her for a while. "Ah, the gender problem, it's the same all over the world," she launches in immediately. "They do exactly the same in Kiev and Manhattan. They're extremely rude."

"I don't really mind," Isabel says. "I suppose they have their concerns."

"Ah, but you should mind, darling, you really should," Katrina lilts at her, with a sort of collusiveness which suggests they might have much more to say to each other on the subject. "They shouldn't be allowed to get away with it, it's not . . . nice. They need to be shown how to behave." Isabel smiles. "Even our Anzorichka," Katrina continues, giving her words some odd emphasis. "Yes, even him. He's very smart, of course, the darling. But he shouldn't be taken too seriously, you know? He gets ideas. They all get ideas. That's the problem, it's always the problem."

Isabel tries to follow the curlicues of suggestion in what Katrina is saying. Is she warning her off her own territory, her own lover? Somehow, the tone is wrong for that. She's beginning to feel light-headed from all the placeless chatter. She's been moving through thin air. But a woman standing nearby picks up on Katrina's little speech.

"Well, we *need* ideas," she says. "Or rather, we need an Idea, which is something quite different."

"An idea for what? Another conference?" Katrina asks rather sharply.

"For Europe, if you must know," the woman answers. "Of Europe." She speaks with an enchanting accent, syncopated and soft. She's from Budapest.

Katrina's eyebrows go up above her large blue eyes, but the woman continues earnestly. "I mean, we need an idea for Europe that would include us. I mean, us the marginals. I mean, really include. An idea of Europe which would appreciate us. Take on board what we have to offer."

"Ah, now you're really asking too much," Katrina drawls. "Appreciate? We don't even appreciate ourselves."

"But without us they're lost," the woman says in her soft voice. "We're the last ones to believe in Europe."

"Well, yes, I'm sure they would be thrilled if they realized that," Katrina lilts merrily. "Ah, Anzorichka. Here you are. We're just talking about what's good for Europe. Got any ideas to contribute? I mean, from your very own marginal vantage point?"

"Honestly, Katrina, you're impossible," Anzor says drily, and shoots her a look in which Isabel thinks she discerns real hostility. Katrina cocks her head slightly, and narrows her eyes, as if to diagnose what on earth might have annoyed him.

Isabel feels Anzor's touch on her back. "Come," he says, "I want to show you something. You don't get to see it very often."

He steers her away, and she feels, at the touch of his palm at her back, something like a drop into a different register, thicker, heavier, closer to herself. The room he leads her into is oblong and light, with another wall of windows giving out on to the urban nightscape, and a curved desk of impressive length at its center. "The President's office," Anzor announces. "The heart of the heart." He observes her for her reaction; but she's surprised more by the lack of pomp in this new nerve center than at finding herself there. No *gloire* or grandeur here, she notes. The world seems to be getting lighter, and more transparent. Anzor puts his hand on the small of her back again, to turn her round. "See?" he says. He's pointing at a large mural, painted in bright, cheerful colors above the doorway. "There you have Katrina's

Europe. There it is." The mural is painted in a style not so much satirical as saucy; but the images belong to the great pan-European iconography. At the top, sunny Apollo surrounded by whimsical, leaping horses; below, sexy Europa insouciantly riding the bull which is about to rape her; on the left, Adam and Eve exiting from Paradise with slightly abashed expressions of adolescents who had stayed out too long at a disco club.

"It is so light-hearted—" she says.

"Exactly," he cuts in, as if she's made his point for him. "Nobody takes this idea of Europe seriously. Not even here." He indicates the President's desk. "This could be a gentlemen's club. They all think it's a sort of . . . enjoyable game."

"Is that good or bad?" she asks.

He smiles at her question, then looks at her appraisingly, as if to see what can be said to her, or how much she can understand. "It is fine if you can afford it," he says, and despite his effort at casualness, she thinks she hears a catch of resentment in his voice. "If you are very safe. In my country, we can't afford to play . . . games. When you're really getting raped . . . Then you take power seriously. You don't make light-hearted jokes about it."

His voice has filled with feeling, and she turns toward him, to see what is thickening it. But the door to the President's room opens, and the compact man in the herringbone suit enters. He pauses when he realizes he's not alone, and takes in the situation with an expressionless look. She sees now that he has a thick, tough face. "Excuse me," he says, addressing himself to Anzor without any change in his expression, "but you should know that only very few people are permitted to come into this room."

Anzor speaks in a light, civil tone. "I thought that as a participant in the conference . . ." he begins, and stops, as if the sentence surely didn't need to be completed. The other man gives him no help. She senses Anzor's breath come faster. "Anyway, the door was open," he picks up, still affecting a sociable carelessness. "After all, we're all colleagues here."

"As I remember, you are not a full participant in the conference," the broad man states curtly. "Only an observer." There's no suggestion of courtesy in his voice.

"I'm sorry," Anzor says. "It was a misunderstanding. Please excuse us."

She hears the agitation of his breathing as he guides her out of the room, and out on to a quiet balcony, overlooking another part of the city. He doesn't look at her for a while. "I'm sorry," he finally says. "That man was very rude."

She senses how much effort it costs him to say this, and begins to say something to dispel the unpleasantness of the small incident. But he puts his hand on hers, interrupting her. "Ah, Isabel," he says, pronouncing her name softly. "Never mind that . . . man. It is not why I invited you this evening. I wanted to . . . see you again." He is looking at her with unqualified seriousness, with sheer assertion. She feels the return of gravity. It is the heaviness of desire, of being held by his desire; his certainty. Grounded, as if an electric current had been run into the earth. Something has passed between them that is more than the sum of the words they have exchanged. She has glimpsed the quickness of his moods, the urgency of his feelings. She doesn't know where they come from, but she senses that something matters to him, matters hard. And she can sense him sensing her . . . Seeking for her, for what is within. As he puts his hands on her shoulders and draws her to him, she looks into his face and, with a kind of relief, as if coming to rest, nods her assent.

In retrospect, this will be in parentheses, an intermezzo. But she doesn't know that yet. For now, it is all-encompassing, without limits or outlines. She trusts the music of it, what else is she to trust? She thinks she's well attuned to it, the tempo of Anzor's gestures as he moves his hands over her body (adagio, sostenuto), as he draws her to himself; the way their limbs and lips travel over each other (accelerando), until the borders between their two bodies vanish, and they each both possess themselves and each other in common. She is porous, that is her weakness and her advantage, and now her consciousness has become a perfect open space, into which she takes his dark eyes, as her skin takes in his long fingers, his lean graceful body. Somehow, his gaze has entered her, and now she has no choice but to keep taking it in, absorbing it more deeply. She gives herself over to the tenor of his movements, a fierceness of need which releases her till she is perfectly present and perfectly lost to herself. Another consciousness awakens, wide and bright.

Anzor's eyes, in the half-dark, look into hers very steadily. "You're so beautiful," he says softly, running his finger over her cheek. "This was so beautiful . . . A beautiful death, isn't that what the poets called it?"

"Not exactly," she says, taken aback. "A small death, surely. Something like that."

"No, not small," he says. He lies on his back, and seems to peer at something in the half-dark. "It's large. Larger than this room. Larger than what is outside. You know, when I was a child," he continues, "I felt this big beauty everywhere. In the mountains. In the streams. In the songs that people sang there. They were wild songs. Raw. They seemed always to come from over the mountain, from far away. Even if people sang them right there. Sometimes I do not know how I can be without it."

She is perplexed by the turn his thoughts have taken. "But don't you find it everywhere?" she asks. "I mean . . . beauty?"

"Not here," he answers calmly. "Not in these crowded cities. You know, this sensation of beauty . . . it needs space. Great space. Where something can breathe. Maybe a kind of spirit. Where you can feel it, moving through the spaces."

She thinks of the spaciousness of Chopin, of Mozart. The breathing of beauty between the sounds, or through them. The motion of something so much vaster than the notes themselves. Is that what Anzor means, what he is trying to speak of in the awkward medium of words . . .

"You miss your country very much, don't you?" she says.

He doesn't answer directly, but she can feel his chest rising and falling. "Did you see how that man treated me?" he blurts out.

She knows what he's alluding to. "I suppose he's some kind of functionary," she says, trying to be soothing. "You know, one of those who follow the rules."

"He is an . . . apparatchik. A bureaucratic *despot*," Anzor says. He pronounces the last word contemptuously, with a Russian inflection. "One of your . . . chilly men." His voice has darkened and tightened. "He invites me to his bloody conference, because he has to. But he thinks I'm . . . primitive. A savage."

"Aren't you exaggerating?" she asks.

"You wouldn't understand," he comes back quickly, sharply. "You've never been treated . . . like an inferior."

She's hurt, even though it's too early to be hurt.

"You're probably right," she says, and her voice comes out muffled and small.

He turns to her in a passion of apology. "I'm sorry," he says, putting his hand softly on her breast. "Sometimes . . . these things come out. But men like him . . . You do not see it, but I know how they see me. How they *think* of me."

She would like to go back to the silence, the wordless language of gaze and moving limbs through which everything can seemingly be said. But Anzor continues, his voice now quiet and even, as if he were not so much talking to her, as looking at something within himself, in his mind.

"Sometimes," he says, "I feel like a traitor. I should be over *there*. I should not have left. I'm a traitor there . . . and a barbarian here."

"But you are working for your country," she says. "You have told me so."

"Working," he says acerbically. "Sure. I do this job. I go around with a begging bowl. I'm lucky if someone throws me a bone. But it has no risk. They are the ones who are taking risks. Who are willing to face . . . the real danger. To sacrifice themselves. I should be with them." His voice breaks a little on the last sentence.

She is as disoriented as if the bed had been turning on its axis, and for a moment, very lonely. It is the stark simplicity of Anzor's words that she cannot grasp. What sort of border has she crossed without noticing . . . She shivers a little.

"It must be so awful," she finally says. "To be at war."

His breathing comes harder. "You see, under the Soviets, nobody could even imagine freedom. Nobody could resist. But this . . . resistance has restored our dignity. You should see how strong people are, strong and alive. They're willing to die, and it gives them a kind of . . . beauty. Yes, beauty."

"Do you have any relatives?"

"They are all relatives," he says almost brusquely. "You may not understand this . . . but we are all together in this. That's what gives us strength. When I think of them, I feel such . . . longing."

His voice has wandered into a far distance, and now she tries to follow its trajectory, to imagine what he is seeing as he speaks, what awful extremity. She thinks, I was not meant for this . . . And yet, a sort of tenderness for Anzor breaks upon her. Why should she doubt the reality of his words. People are dying in his austere country, fighting and dying; and in his voice, she can hear the fierceness of it, and a kind of passion.

"Perhaps I should not speak to you about these things," Anzor says, as if sensing her ambivalence. "But it is what I think about. What is on my mind. If we are going to be . . . like this . . . I want you to know me."

She shivers again, and he pulls the blanket up over her solicitously. Images of the ruined city float through her mind, slow phalanxes of refugees, women with scarves on their heads and bundles on their backs, and fatalistic faces. She turns toward him, and peers into his face through the deepening dark; then embraces him closely, as if to fathom the heft and weight of this world through his body. "I want to know you too," she says, quietly. He gazes at her wordlessly; and they subside into a longer silence.

In Between

July 18, 1982

"My personal feeling is that music conveys a prophetic message revealing a higher form of life toward which mankind evolves. And it is because of this message that music appeals to men of all races and cultures."—Arnold Schoenberg, "Criteria for the Evaluation of Music," 1946.

How I envy him, with his twelve-tone system, his form into which to pour his Belief. Or his hope. Even at that improbable date. He had something to reduce, something to distil, something to think against. To feel against. It is too late for me. I have studied systems, the twelve-tone and the Marxist, and I know where they end. I have also studied death. I come after. After That. I

must begin with that condensed pre-sound I dreamt.
With the shifting of bones and inaudible underworld
murmurs. I was the child who ate death for breakfast.
Only that ground is true, all the rest is ornament.
Whatever sounds of pity and praise I find must rise up,
however improbably, out of that.

July 20, 1982

A lesson with the cellist today. Jane Robbins. Admit it,
old man, these young women pose a challenge to you.
They vex your critical criteria. This one is particularly
provoking. She burst into the studio almost rudely, with
a wide white-toothed smile. Her breasts were bouncing
freely underneath her blouse. There is something
aggravating about the way she picks up her bow, as if it
were a baseball bat. When I pointed this out, she
informed me that she is "a very physical person," and
has played not only baseball but basketball and girls'
hockey in high school. She would have gone on without
any self-consciousness, had I not interrupted. As far as I
can tell, she has no inhibitions. She is like a big happy
child who hasn't yet learned it may not be allowed to do
everything it wants. She hurtled through the first
movement of the Dvořák as if on a roller coaster, from
one burst of excitement to another. Of course, it is an
old warhorse and there was undeniable energy in her
playing. But nothing else. No restraint, no tension, no
wistfulness. Just this unrestrained . . . enthusiasm. I
suppose she is another kind of After. She plays as if
milking an ever-compliant cow. It's very strange.

Isabel feels slightly disconcerted by the advent of Jane in the pages of Wolfe's *Journal*. Absurd, really . . . But Jane is a rival for his attention, even retrospectively. A worthy rival, too, with her gift for happiness, her gift for ease. Enviable ease, even if Isabel didn't entirely admire it . . . She smiles at the thought of Jane's first encounter with Wolfe, looks through the plane's window into the gray nothingness outside, prepares for the descent.

Rotterdam

At the hotel, she opens a window—it's an old-fashioned window, which can actually be opened—and looks out at the street below. A clean, broad avenue, lined with solid mid-century buildings and sturdy, large-leaved plane trees. Comfort and quietness. From the rooftops, from somewhere, she can hear the gentle, vacuous sound of doves cooing; the pan-European sound. She freshens up for the interview, effects a slight shift inside, to a more sociable posture, a more alert pitch of mind for the simulated conversation awaiting her.

The interviewer is a young woman with wispy zigzags of dark hair framing a full face, and a sleek briefcase, from which she pulls out her notebook and tape recorder. She too has a sleek leather briefcase, Isabel notes. Her name is Mariella, and after the obligatory fussing with her equipment, she assumes a look of efficient competence, and proceeds to ask Isabel the usual run of questions: biography, studies, her preferred composers, the influence of Ernst Wolfe on her style. Rather impressively, Mariella seems to know all about Wolfe. Then she looks at her notes, and bites her lip worriedly before posing the next question: Does Isabel think that romantic, nineteenth-century music which forms such a large part of her repertory is still relevant to our times? And doesn't that imply a rather conservative, even a retrograde position? "What I'm asking," she emphasizes, "is whether it isn't arrogant to believe that this very particular manifestation of European culture expresses some timeless or universal values?" The young woman, with her porcelain skin and blackly outlined eyes, looks at Isabel intently. The question is apparently of some import to her, and she's waiting for the answer with heightened and somewhat sceptical interest.

"Why should it be retrograde, if people all over the world want to listen to it?" Isabel retorts rather defensively. "If people everywhere love it? If people play it, as if it were their own?" Mariella's question strikes her as being itself arrogant in some way, and she adds, "I'm not sure that music, of all things, follows our local ideas of what is progressive and what is not."

"Right," the young woman says, writing busily. The tape has come to the end of side one, and she doesn't bother to change it over.

Isabel lets her annoyance pass. "Perhaps we love this music because it speaks to us of desires which we all have," she says, more simply. "And which don't seem to change that much over time. Desires don't follow political lines, after all."

"Oh no?" Mariella intercedes sharply.

"We still recognize them, don't we," Isabel says. "The things that Chopin or Schumann speak of. Even if we no longer speak about them in the same way. We still seem to *want* to experience what these composers bring us. The shape of the emotions. The passions, even. This . . . beautiful vocabulary of the soul. I mean, where else do we find it? That is why we listen to this supposedly retrograde music. Because it speaks of what we are, any time, any place. Something essential about us. Or maybe outside us, too."

"Is that on the record?" Mariella asks oddly. Perhaps Isabel has spoken too seriously, or at least too nakedly. She has let some private perception puncture the buffer zone of media speech.

"Yes, if you like," Isabel says, and Mariella flips the tape over. She consults her notes again, and looks up with a quizzical, an almost whimsical expression.

"Do you think music is fiction or nonfiction?" she asks, and then stops, as if the brevity of the question were part of the joke. Isabel gives a little surprised laugh.

"That's an interesting question," she says, and then stops. She has no idea how she'll answer it. "The problem is," she begins, "that music doesn't refer to anything. Except itself. So it doesn't tell you anything. It doesn't explain anything and it is . . . illumination." The word has slipped out, unwittingly. Mariella's lusciously lipsticked mouth opens slightly with the small shock of the word. "I don't mean anything . . . smarmy by it," Isabel hastens to assure her. "I mean that music reveals rather than tells . . ." Mariella looks confounded again, and Isabel tries to clarify. "Or maybe the word is evokes rather than reveals . . . But it either does this, or it is nothing. Just a bunch of sounds." She pauses to gather her thoughts together. "But the one thing music cannot do is lie . . . The way some fiction can. And nonfiction too." Mariella nods, uncertainly.

"Music is truth, truth music," Isabel sums up, rather pleased with the proposition. "That's all we know and all we need to know."

"Are you quoting something?"

Isabel is about to explain, but there's an energetic knock on the door. It's the photographer, coming in with his importantly bulky equipment and an ebullient hello. A moment later, he's rearranging the furniture, making approving noises as he creates his little stage set. Why are photographers always so pleased with themselves? Isabel has noted this before. It is as if the habit of looking at others through the merciless lens boosted their narcissism, a cheerful sense of their own inviolability.

His eyes narrow to a focus as he appraises Isabel. A different focus from Anzor's. These are the ineffables, and yet she cannot help but notice them.

"Why don't we try you there?" the photographer says, pointing to a plump chair. She sits down, drapes her hand over the armrest, and tries to pour some kind of energy into her smile, as the clicking begins. Another simulated scenario; but she knows that the camera is a ruthless register of karma. If she withholds herself, the photograph will mysteriously lack a sense of life, of a living presence.

"How much longer?" Mariella asks, and then the phone rings again. Isabel picks it up, hears an agitated voice speaking in Dutch, and hands the receiver to Mariella, who looks troubled as she listens. She says something in Dutch to the photographer, who turns his attention abruptly away from Isabel. "*Zeker, zeker,*" he says briskly and begins to fold his equipment.

"There's been some sort of . . . accident near here," Mariella explains to Isabel, in a changed voice. "Some . . . violence. It's my editor. He says we should go there. We should know what it is about. To find out."

"Violence?" Isabel asks.

"A bomb, perhaps. Or an explosion. Most probably." Mariella is speaking with a sort of embarrassment. "Someone has been killed. Or maybe a few."

The photographer gathers his equipment hastily. "I'm sorry," Isabel says. "How terrible." She hesitates, uncertain what to do, then decides to go with them. She has some inchoate sense that it would seem callous if she didn't. Maybe she should know what it is about too.

Whatever it is that has taken place, has happened just minutes away from the hotel, on a quiet side street. By the time they get there, the scene consists mostly of policemen and photographers. Policemen to provide a belated semblance of protection; photographers to provide images suggesting the lack of any protective power. The two groups form a small cordon sanitaire, in the middle of which something—something hideous, something that should not be looked at—is going on. The photographer pushes his way through the outer circle, clicking all the way. She follows, and looks. By now, whatever had happened here has been to some extent managed, covered. Bodies—people?—are blanketed in mercifully opaque plastic. The pools of blood have dried. Nothing virtual about that. Nothing simulated. Whatever has happened here has absolute reality. It doesn't belong in this comfortable, cushioned city, this quiet street. Some medics are bent over one of the camouflaged forms; Isabel sees that they're cutting delicately at bits of substance hanging out of the plastic covering, where the arm should lie. With an upwelling of nausea, she realizes that the covered object next to the injured woman's body is probably the rest of the limb. The familiar thought flickers through her mind that if this happened to her, she wouldn't want to go on living. She couldn't, actually. The real begins and ends here, in the flesh. The combination of relief and empathy—it isn't even pity, she just feels a twitch in her arms, her chest—makes her dizzy. She lowers her head, so that she won't see. Then she looks again. She must look. She mustn't. Both gestures are obscene. Given that this is none of her business, that she doesn't know whom she's looking at, who is suffering, whose life has been taken away or is being destroyed, that she shouldn't have seen this in the first place.

She shouldn't have come out of the hotel. Now that she has . . . a thought of Anzor brushes against her mind. But he is in Brussels, she knows that. He told her he had to stay on to meet with the British ambassador there. The British seem to have better understanding than the Americans of their situation, their cause. "Your cause," she repeated, disconcerted yet again by the forthrightness of his rhetoric, its unabashed simplicity. The photographers are still clicking, with an incessant, monotonous rhythm that spells a certain kind of excitement. Media excitement, she thinks with sudden anger. Paparazzi. The world is ill. She must get away from here, must think about the concert tonight. She cannot play in this nauseous state.

She makes her way out of the circle, tapping the photographer on the shoulder to let him know she's leaving. He turns to her, and must see something on her face, because he looks at her with a startling, naked directness, the way you're not allowed to look at someone who's not your intimate. Except through the camera. She doesn't know what he sees, but he grasps her shoulders as if to bolster her. "I'm sorry we got, how do you say, interrupted," he says. "But I think I have some good photos. Of you, I mean."

She'll have to figure out later why the remark adds to her revulsion. Outside the immediate cluster, Mariella is talking intently to a policeman and taking notes. She turns to Isabel, and must see something as well, because her face furrows with concern. "I'm so sorry," she says. "I mean, that this happened in our city . . ."

"What does he say?" Isabel asks, pointing to the policeman.

Mariella looks embarrassed again. "Nobody knows what it's about," she says. "There've been some secret negotiations with a group from Kosovo somewhere near here, so probably . . . You know, the Serbians . . . But nobody knows. He says it doesn't look like a Middle Eastern job. It is the wrong kind of explosive."

Her face has a slackened, washed-out look. This is not the kind of crisis, Isabel thinks, which makes people rally. Not that she has experience of crises, but she feels the desuetude of the few people left, her own urge to skulk away. Whatever has happened here has demagnetized everything within its radius; nobody will go to a bar together after this, to talk over the meaning of the event.

"I'd better get back," she says to Mariella. She's beginning to shiver. "But thank you . . . for your interesting questions." The incongruity instantly strikes her as indecent. "I mean earlier," she adds, and shakes her head helplessly. That's not what she means either.

"I'm so sorry about this," Mariella says again, indicating the ambulance, and the medics carrying a body into a stretcher. "When you're here to do something so . . . good."

"Yes," Isabel says. "It's just so . . . awful."

Back in her room, she gets into the large bed, and curls into herself till the shivering stops. She tries to locate what she's just seen, what has happened, what has happened to her. She feels shame. Not for the wrecked bodies, but for that naked stare the photographer gave her. And which she returned. What did he see? A widened eye, like his own. An open lens. Don't be so hard on yourself, she directs herself, primly. The homily for murky occasions. Don't be so hard on yourself, don't judge yourself, don't judge . . . The mantras of her generation. Don't judge, try to understand. She wishes Anzor were with her, or Peter, or even the photographer. It's the truth, she'd take anything, anyone, to slake the ambiguous, the pornographic excitement. The camera, that's the problem. That's what is making everyone into voyeurs. Then she thinks of the guillotine, the public hangings. They came to see death in action up close and intimate, more naked than she has seen it today. They wanted full exposure. They flocked from the outer boroughs, to see the wretches hang. She just happened to be in the proximity. It has always been with us, she thinks, this . . . obscenity. Just because she has never come close to it before . . . This is just an accident that follows from her life. Her accidental life. None of her business, really. It's not a part of my life, she thinks. It doesn't count.

On the way to the concert hall, the image of the torn arm jabs at her chest like a sharp object. She thinks about Peter, whom she has hurt, of Kolya, whom she could not save. But no, she's not ready to think about Kolya . . . In the taxi, she doubles over and inwardly keens. She must pull herself together. She doesn't know how she'll get through this evening; she only hopes there'll be no overt fiascos.

And yet, when the moment comes, she plays as confidently, as fluently, as she has ever played. She summons the poetry of Chopin's last Ballade, so shot through with anger and anguish, as if it could heal death and all sorrow. As if it could repair what she'd seen this afternoon. As if, after they've been broken and injured, things could be made whole. As if violence held no dominion over beauty. She feels, with the great arpeggios and chords of the Ballade, a vast spaciousness open up inside her. She feels held in the heart of meaning, safe as if she could never fall out. She feels, only this counts. Only this.

But in her room afterward, images from the Incident float up again, shards of music. A sound-trace of camera clicking, the photographer in his denim jacket, leaning forward into the covered, fleshly pottage with his knee bent, and she suddenly realizes: the photographs he took of her in the hotel room will be next to those of the incident. Someone developing the second roll will go from her oh-so-smoothly posed, her utterly intact body, to the chaos of bloodied limbs and plastic coverings. Her agitation increases, a fibrillation close to pain. Chaos, that's what produces those jagged internal oscillations, that's why she can't find a position in which to rest. No position, no vantage point . . . The photos of the incident won't have focus or structure. The splotches of blood won't direct the viewer's eye toward a border or center.

At 2 a.m., she turns on the bedside light, and dials Peter's number in New York. She has to turn somewhere, talk to someone.

"Did you watch the news tonight?" she asks.

"Yes," he says. "Sort of. I was cooking dinner."

"Did they say anything about what happened in Rotterdam?"

"Ah yes," he affirms after a pause. "There was something. I'm afraid I didn't really catch it."

"Well, I was there. Or here. I'm in Rotterdam. It happened right near me."

"But *what* happened, exactly?" he asks, his voice instantly on the alert. "And how near were you?"

"No, I don't mean I was in any danger," she says, realizing that, somehow, she is making more of the incident than she has the right to. That she might be accused of histrionics. "I just saw it . . . after."

He listens to her description of what she saw in silence. "Well, that certainly sounds horrible," he says, clearing his throat. "I'm sorry you had to see it."

She's suddenly furious at him. He is not taking this seriously enough. His tone does not match the bloody awfulness of what she witnessed. But then, she tells him, a note of entirely unjustifiable accusation entering her voice, he wasn't *there*. He didn't see it. He was probably making himself something nice to eat, she adds in her mind, meanly. Peter likes his food well prepared, even if he's cooking just for himself.

"You're right, I wasn't," he responds curtly. "That's why I'm not offering any commentary. I have no idea what happened there."

She stops herself. "I suppose neither do I, really," she says, feeling a sudden deflation, a drop of moral pressure. What does she actually *feel* about the incident, what sort of emotion is she striving for, except some assurance that she's not callous, that her compassion is adequate, that she's a good person?

"It's just so . . . intolerable," she says.

"What's intolerable?" he asks. "What happened, or the fact that you saw it? Because awful things happen all the time."

97

Anger jolts her again, like electricity. "You just don't care," she says coldly. "Do you?"

"What am I supposed to care about?" he asks, in his most logical tone. "I wasn't there, as you point out. I don't know who was involved. Or who was hurt. OK, I care notionally. I am appalled. Notionally appalled."

"Honestly, you and your legalistic distinctions," she brings out, just avoiding contempt. "This is not some case you're trying."

"Oh, don't give me that," he shoots back. "You sound upset. You called me. I want to know what it is that has upset you. But I am not upset myself." Some sort of steel has entered his voice, and she's almost glad of it.

"Do you mean I shouldn't have called you?" she asks, her voice dipping into a different, more private register. An aside, from the stage of their conversation, to the more intimate listener.

"No," he says, after a pause. "That's not what I mean. I'm . . . glad you called." She can hear him hesitate, before he says the next thing. "You know, I wonder if this has anything to do with Kolya . . ."

She's tigerish in her response. "It has nothing to do with him. Nothing."

"OK," he says soothingly. "I just wondered . . . though what you've seen is horrible enough. I've seen accidents. I know these things can . . . get to you."

"But this wasn't an accident," she says, with a sort of resignation. The moral measure, he's not giving this the right moral measure.

There's a pause in which she hears him take a sip of coffee. "It was an accident that you were there," he then says.

"Maybe that's what's bothering me about it," she picks up. She's trying to make sense of it and failing. "The randomness of it. Of my being there. The way that woman . . . whoever it was under the plastic . . . just happened to be there . . ."

He leaps in energetically. "It's the way we live now, kiddo." He knows she's catching the reference to Trollope, and the fact that it was one of the few books they both loved. One of the few novelists for adults, Peter had said approvingly.

"Well, if that's the way we live now, then Trollope is no guide," she retorts.

"There aren't any guides," he comes back tersely. "Don't you know that?"

She pauses. "I don't know why this got to me so much," she begins again, with a more vulnerable urgency. "Maybe because I had to get through the concert right afterward . . . I just don't know what to make of it."

"I don't see why you have to make anything of it," he says. "You can't be implicated in every goddamn thing that happens to happen in every place on your itinerary."

"So you mean, just forget it," she says. "Forget the whole thing."

"Just stop being so . . . permeable," he says, more intimately. There are layers of allusion behind that word too. Her porousness, her St. Teresa tendencies. "Where're you going to be tomorrow, anyway?"

"Amsterdam," she says. "For two whole days."

"Bound to be an improvement over Rotterdam," he says. "Given everything. Got any plans while you're there?"

"No," she says, suddenly feeling a flush coming up her chest to her neck. "Not really." Now she knows the nagging sensation at the back of the conversation: embarrassment, small hot embarrassment for her petty deception, her failure to mention Anzor.

"Ah well, then maybe you'll even get to be bored."

"Wouldn't that be nice," she says, her voice fading into smallness.

"Take care of yourself."

"Yes," she says. "Thanks. I mean . . . for the concern."

"I know what you mean," he says drily.

There's a silence, not completely comfortable.

"Bloody hell," he then says, "I just realized what time it is in goddamn Rotterdam. Go and get some sleep, will you?"

"Yes," she says. "I will."

He clears his throat, hesitating. "And call me again if you need to," he says. "Remember I don't have your schedule . . . this time."

"Thanks," she says, feeling a sweaty flush come up to her face again. "I hope everything is all right in New York?"

"Yeah, fine."

"Goodnight, then."

"Goodnight."

She paces round the room after they hang up. She mustn't call him again, not as long as she can't tell him . . . isn't willing to tell him . . . She hasn't done anything to violate their current contract; no. He'd be free too . . . and yet . . . she mustn't call him. She thinks of him sitting down to his evening reading, wonders if he suspects. But no, he doesn't. For someone who studies law, Peter is oddly unsuspicious. Or rather, she thinks, the world of deception doesn't interest him. That's what she has admired about him, his particular kind of rationality, which is a form of decency. And this is what she found irritating, she thinks, sotto voce. Peter has no patience for hidden drama, for wiliness, for excess sentiment. It is what is stated, written down, signed and sealed that, for him, counts. What people intend, or are willing to say they intend. He thinks there's no point in bothering about anything else. If people want to lie, or have hidden motives . . . that's their own business. It's not interesting. His respect for the law is profound. His love of law, really. Outside of that is darkness, the meaningless darkness of the lawless chaotic world.

*

But she thinks about Kolya before she falls asleep, or rather, he returns to her, from some place where he is always present, just below the surface, within her inner cells. Now it is his childish, still perfect face she sees, as their mother shooed them out of the house, pushed them out against Kolya's pleading eyes. A whitewashed farmhouse in Provence. It must have been Provence, that was where Lena brought them, to stay with a group of Argentinians, ebulliently cheerful even in their exile. That was in Lena's peripatetic stage, when she ferried her children to and fro, between a baffling succession of other people's houses. And everywhere, she turned away from her small son with a casual, careless cruelty . . . Isabel can still feel Kolya's tiny, listless hand in hers, holding on as they walked along a narrow whitish path, between fields of enormous sunflowers. The glaring sun. The flowers' big yellow heads turning toward it on their long thick stalks. They walk slowly, in the stretchy, toffee time of childhood. They're not all that pretty, she remembers thinking about the sunflowers, and she didn't like the absence of clouds, the acuteness of light which made her sense a shadow somewhere at the back of her, coming from the house, from Lena's sensuous, deprived body and her aggrieved, indifferent face. The shadow of the object falls upon the ego: Freud. But of course then there was no ego. Not yet. There was only silky childish skin and a defenseless porousness of soul. She was permeable, everything entered in, Kolya's sad little face and helpless blue eyes, the transparency of the light, and the sunflowers' heated menace. She might as well have been drinking in Kolya's hurt, his sense that Lena threw him out even though he tried so hard to be good, to make her smile. He walks along silently, his eyes fixed on the ground. The gratuitous suffering of children, Isabel now thinks, the memory of his hurt piercing her again . . . Kolya had not been flogged, or thrown into an orphanage, or even spanked; but his eyes in her memory have the look of a suffering small animal, a creature that can't make out the rights and wrongs of the situation, but only knows it has been wounded. Is that the shadow? She stoops and embraces little Kolya on the white path, and strokes his head and back. Nothing is said, but when they start walking again, he's almost cheerful. "Oh look!" he cries, pointing to a sunflower which for some reason seems more beautiful to him than the others. "Look at this!" Now she almost gasps from the recollection of the sudden shift in his childish face, how easy it was to make him happy, and how easily the childish happiness was shattered.

In her bed, Isabel tosses and turns restlessly, as if to escape the memory, which now comes with the knowledge of its consequences, the knowledge that what was shattered could never be fixed again. Now it is a young man's pale face she sees, in some unearthly distance. It has the haunting presence of a revenant; someone who is no longer of the reachable world, and yet not completely vanished. He looks at her with a sort of reproach, but also in consolation, as if trying to convey a complex message. I have been so abandoned, his expression seems to say; but I am no longer suffering. As she falls asleep, she feels a line of purest longing stretching from her to Kolya, to his spectral presence. If only she could console him, tell him he had been loved . . . A swell of still living anger at her mother comes at the heels of her grief, at the injustice of what she did to her small son, so unthinkingly, unseeingly. At the gratuitous withholding, the dearth of love. The Incident comes back to her, with its larger consequences. By comparison, this is such a . . . private matter. She married Peter shortly after Kolya's death. Was that also part of the story, some hidden, half-known narrative unfolding in that other lawless realm, the realm of the heart?

*

July 21, 1982

The cellist again. She burst in with her bouncing body,
seemingly without inhibition, giving me her white-
toothed smile. "I'm going to surprise you today!" she
announced, and proceeded to play Bach's Second Suite,
with her breasts bouncing beneath her T-shirt. The
incongruity was so great that it struck me as shameless
. . . But undoubtedly, this Jane would not recognize the
concept of shame. She would think it a quaint
inconvenience interfering with her right to pleasure.
I wonder what would happen if the human kind lost its
sense of shame. What would emerge from bodies
allowed to speak themselves, without brakes or scruples?
But no, I cannot imagine such a condition, do not want
to imagine it. It is impossible to imagine Bach without a
sense of sin. Without recognition of our wrongness,
which drives us to imagine something more perfect than
ourselves. Without knowledge of our mortality, which
impels us to produce timeless symmetries. No matter
how hurtful to discipline our spirit, to make it rise out
of the flesh and our earthbound selves.

This is what this Jane doesn't understand. She has
virtuosity, it must be admitted. But she has no faculties
with which to grasp the profound, the necessary
conflicts impelling Bach or Beethoven.

July 22, 1982

Isabel Merton. I wait for her lessons . . . impatiently. This
has to be admitted. I am not yet so lost to myself as not

to notice. She played Schubert's B flat, beautifully. The autumnal beginning, the melodic lines not so much haunted as finding their way to epiphany . . . I thought of that Warsaw room, the utter stillness, our hands moving over each other's bodies . . . I put my hand on Isabel's shoulder when she finished playing, to indicate my approval. Her eyes widened with feeling, and she lowered her head to conceal how much she was moved.

In her enclosed capsule, her resistless meta-space, Isabel is moved again; by all that Wolfe discerned; by the braided conversation, with all its accumulating meanings; accumulating weight.

Amsterdam

In Amsterdam, she waits for Anzor to collect her at the hotel. Oddly, she's feeling more skittish, more shy, than before. They're meeting by prearrangement this time; she cannot pretend to an irresistible or errant impulse. She's doing this with her eyes open, and is proceeding despite what she felt the night before.

She sees him before he sees her as he comes into the lobby of the hotel, with a quick long step, looking for her impatiently. Then he does notice her, and his eyebrows gather into a funny V, as though he's been taken by surprise at a tender sight. He embraces her as if they'd been parted too long.

They walk out into the autumn day with no particular plans, but with some unspoken agreement to avoid excessive eagerness about falling into each other's bodies. The narrow streets are packed tight with tourists, consulting their guides and going about their task with the determined, dyspeptic looks of tourists everywhere. Youths of both sexes, laden with enormous backpacks, move with the resigned patience of slow beasts of burden. Middle-aged couples click their cameras in front of Anne Frank's house. The great nomadic republic. But in the historic city, the light falls with an almost fleshly warmth on the dark brick of the tall narrow houses, a light filtered through the miraculous paintings she's seen of just such brick and such tall narrow houses. Pleasure doubled by the doubling of perception.

Anzor, who seems to know the city well, ushers her among the crowds, talking informatively and inconsequentially. He points out a house whose interior was once apparently painted by Vermeer, and she's pleased by the thought of pleasure she'd glimpsed in his magical rooms just behind the brick, the quiet women at their lutes or their washing, the ordinariness from which people had always extracted so much loveliness. She's in the loop between the virtual and real, in the seamless cosmopolis; but this time, she feels the thrill of it, rather than irritation.

Allegretto; leggiero. A lightness of spirit comes upon her. There's nothing she wishes for outside the sparkling light of this moment. They're making their way across a cobblestone square, when Anzor places his hand on her shoulder, to detain her. His grip tenses; and following the direction of his gaze, she sees a small demonstration of some kind, a cluster of people holding posters, someone taking up a megaphone and shouting. She focuses on the posters, makes out the word "Kosovo." There's an instant, tight constriction of her chest. Anzor's hand continues to hold her shoulder, in a command to stay still. His attention is fixed on the small group, and whatever is being shouted into the megaphone.

"What is it?" she asks. "What's going on?"

He speaks casually, in a tone which doesn't quite match his alert stance. "You know, the usual. A demonstration. Something about independence for Kosovo."

"Does this have anything to do with . . . what happened in Rotterdam?" she asks. She hasn't mentioned the Incident to him; there seemed no need, no call for it.

The glance he directs at her is sharp in its inquisitiveness. "I didn't realize you follow the news so closely," he says. "Was it in the *Herald Tribune*?"

"I happened to be there," she says, and feels the return of the previous day's sensations. The strange excitement, strange desuetude.

"I didn't know . . ." Anzor says, turning her gently away from the demonstration. Then he says firmly, as if to make sure she understands: "They're actually protesting what happened in Rotterdam. They are on the right side."

The right side . . . She cannot make out where that might place them, on whose behalf the demonstrators, who seemed to be shouting both in Dutch and in Yugoslav, are raising their voices, or against whom. But Anzor seems to be completely sure. Another statement in C major. She resists its four-square simplicity, then yields to it. She looks at him, and knows that the focus of Anzor's gaze, the very directness of his presence, are fueled by the same energy as the words. By comparison with him, she is vague, uncertain, dispersed. By comparison, everyone she knows is dispersed. He takes her hand reassuringly, and she feels herself coming into focus, as if the scattered filings of her inchoate thoughts were being gathered by a strong magnetic force. The constriction in her chest gradually dissolves. She lets him lead her through the thickening crowds back to the hotel.

Later, there is the great effort of the concert, the lift-off and then the comedown. When they finally fall into each other's bodies, it is as if after an enormous postponement, with a ravenousness fed by everything that happened that day, and whose own certainty cannot be gainsaid.

*

The next day she tries to practice, but finds it hard to concentrate. Images of Anzor interfere. They've agitated her in the very places from which the music springs, and instead of finding her way to the Debussy pieces she'll be playing next week, she finds her way to him, his tenor and rhythms . . . "Poissons d'Or" is nothing more than a dry dutiful exercise . . . She is in her own watery medium, of longing and yearning and flowing into something, someone else . . . She wonders, as she has before, if Rothman is ever so unraveled, so undone. She wishes for greater grit, and then unwishes the wish. She cannot undo this fluidity any more than she can undo her being. She is permeable, that is her flaw and her advantage . . . It is how she experiences the world, how she lets music enter. She remembers Wolfe: "You must know, Miss Merton, that if you want to be an artist, you must have a will of iron. You must be uncompromising in your pursuit." He meant, you must unwoman yourself. She turns to the opening section of Chopin's Fourth Ballade, and forgets all else. The theme, with its rueful half-tones, compressed and repetitive like the circling of obsessive thought, the line curling and uncurling from itself, till it eventually expands into openness of major tones and wide arpeggios, pulls her into its vortex till there is nothing outside it. The delicate modulations and intermixings, pensive thought wistful melancholy the breathing of beauty, big and spacious. She grunts, from the effort of adjusting to the shifts with her breath and inner body. She goes over the beginning bars again and again, making sure that no note, no left-hand chord stands out too jaggedly from the fluctuating diminuendos and crescendos. Ah yes: the leap in the left hand is a semi-quaver too sudden. She repeats it several times, till the jump is perfectly incorporated into the flow. By the time she looks up, she realizes that two hours have passed. For two hours, she has been inside time. Then she shakes the Ballade off, remembers the interview she has later that afternoon, and beyond that Anzor, who will meet her in the next city; and the anxiety of the passing minutes, the beating of restlessness against the skin, is upon her again.

In Between

July 23, 1982

The cellist again. She's always a few minutes late for her lesson, and bursts in saying, "Hiya," as if I were her best friend, and there were no question of my being annoyed. A big, indulged child. I wonder why on earth she has decided to become a musician. Her body seems designed for making babies. Still, there is undeniable fluency in her playing, undeniable energy. This must be admitted. But there is no restraint or postponement; no darkness, no struggle with Time. I tried to talk to her about understatement, about working toward a dramatic resolution so that it seems earned. "You mean you have to earn the satisfaction?" she asked. She looked at me with a saucy expression, as if she understood that this was provoking. I told her it is not a question of satisfaction, it is a question of musical logic. Of conclusions that have to be arrived at after a struggle. "Struggle?" she asked again. The notion seems foreign to her. I told her music wasn't hockey, it was complex thought. The most complex we know, perhaps. "But shouldn't it be fun?" she asked with complete disingenuousness. "Shouldn't we enjoy it? Otherwise, what is the point?" Her soul is so alien to me that she might as well be from another planet. I wonder what will happen to our

great tradition in hands like hers. She exerts a fascination, this must be admitted. But I do not like being fas-
cinated by her. It disturbs me. Perhaps it is no more
than the dubious fascination of the new, of the future.

In her airplane seat, Isabel remembers a demonstration class at
the Retreat. Jane, playing a Beethoven Sonata, and Wolfe
looking on sternly, as if he wasn't going to give away anything,
certainly not his almost unintentional excitement. Isabel can see
his sensitive face responding only with a sort of grinding of his
jaw, an extra sharp gaze. His raised finger, interrupting: "You're
not riding a horse, you're reflecting thought," he said, addressing
all of them. "Music is thought in sound. You have to follow it,
like an argument. Reveal the structure. Pare away the excess!"
Jane, clearly displeased with the interruption, pouted and made
an exasperated gesture with her bow. "What should I pare
away?" she asked. "The notes?" You could hear the collective
intake of breath among the small group. Nobody else would
have dared say such a thing to Wolfe. Jane looked at him with
a saucy defiance, then, before he could answer, swung up her
bow and played the passage again, with more restraint, more
tension. Wolfe allowed himself a barely discernible nod of
approval. "That's better," he conceded. "You must remember:
All art is in the resistance." He turned to all of them. "I'm
quoting Franz Liszt, who may seem to you an unlikely source
for such a remark. But every artist worth his salt knows this
from his own hard experience and in the bones. You must con-
sent to the struggle, or you will not create anything worth-
while."

All art is in the resistance. Isabel knows that now, knows the
obscure struggles she has to wage with heaven knows what
obstacles in order to make music yield its truth. Like hewing
away at stubborn stone, even though she is molding the most

109

impalpable element. But Jane's pout said she did not really believe that, refused to believe it. To Isabel's half-envious eyes, Jane seemed to glide through the world as if it offered no barriers to her wishes, and as if there were no price for getting what she wanted. You can always get what you want . . . That was surely the provocation to Wolfe, and the secret of her charisma. For there was no doubt that Jane had her own, feckless kind of charisma. "The Great Refuser vs. the American Id," someone summed up the contest between her and Wolfe. The two stars of their little constellation. There was, also, the subordinate contest between Jane and Isabel, for the Great Refuser's attention. For Jane was not immune to his kind of power, to the need for some insemination of interstellar dust from his older, almost extinct galaxy; for some kind of musical benison.

As it happens, Jane will be playing in Copenhagen when she arrives. They're in the habit of catching each other's concerts whenever possible; she'll go and hear her, of course.

Copenhagen

There she is: Jane. The air in the small concert hall sizzles in response to her appearance. She is wearing a carmine-red dress, flaring spectacularly at the hem; but she walks out on to the stage like a rock star, like a motorcycle driver. Forceful applause, scattered gasps of appreciation. Jane's unruly black hair descends down to her shoulders, and she takes big steps, with an easy swing and swagger, gripping her cello nonchalantly in front of her, milky shoulders carelessly hunched. A corpulent, rather abashed-looking pianist in a tuxedo waddles after her with diffident air. Isabel remembers a much younger Jane, wearing her frilly skirts and heavy, laced-up boots, half-waif, half-punk. Now, as she sits straddling her cello, the piano makes a great backdrop for the carmine red. Jane was never shy about going for the obvious, for the main chance.

The pianist plays the opening bars of the first Mendelssohn Sonata. Jane doesn't exactly straighten out, but it is as if something in her has stood to attention. She readies her bow mid-air, and makes the first attack: the sound is so unerring, so honey-full and resonant, that you can feel the audience startling in turn. And then it pours out, lush, golden sound, unhesitant momentum. Jane's body sways above the cello, and her bow swings wide; her mouth opens and almost twists with the abandon of the playing. The same expression as all those years ago. Isabel feels a surge of competitiveness, speckled with respectful admiration.

The third movement: Jane's right leg works up and down with the music, her motions unmistakably inflected by blues and hard rock, by all that euphoric dancing years ago to Aretha Franklin and the Rolling Stones. She gallops through the bravura passages, fully unstopped, black hair falling into her face, milky shoulders working muscularly into the cello, the music flowing with lubricious ease. The ease that Wolfe objected to, not entirely without reason. Jane's Mendelssohn is sexy in the idiom of her very own time; and yet the jerky jabs and thrusts of her bow and body bring out something true to the music: its original, radical energy.

In the second half, she plays a new piece especially composed for her, with bluesy jazz melodies, and thumping rhythms of square dancing, and scratchy country fiddle bits, eliding into something newer and stranger still.

Isabel goes to the Green Room afterward, and Jane greets her with sparkling eyes, and without missing a beat. "Hey, girl, this is a surprise!" she exclaims. She's in frisky spirits, though the pianist is sitting on the sofa rather limply. "Well, so how was I tonight? Tell me! You know you can always be honest with me." This, Isabel knows, is true; Jane has always taken criticism like a fighter; without ducking or caving in. But this is not a moment for caviling. Isabel says the Mendelssohn was terrific, and means it.

"Well, what do you know," Jane says, not hiding her pleasure at the compliment. "And you haven't been doing so badly yourself, have you, girl? Wolfe knew talent when he saw it, I'll give him that, the old sourpuss. And he was sure betting on you."

"Well, not all the way."

"So you've got the *Journal* too. I guess all his disciples rushed out to get it . . . Did you read the parts about me yet?" Jane asks, bending her head coquettishly. "The good parts? Pages 73 to 81."

"You're incorrigible," the pianist utters appreciatively from the sofa.

"Ah, Tim, my darling." Jane turns to him, with a mock purr. "I almost forgot about you. You ready to make tracks?"

"Sure," he says, not moving from the sofa.

Jane turns to Isabel with a coy expression. "We'd invite you along, but we've got plans . . . You know how it is, right?"

"I couldn't come anyway," Isabel says. As she leaves, she sees Jane flopping down on the couch beside Tim, and raising her creamy face toward his, as Tim's arms come up to the nape of her neck. Well, Liszt would have understood, who in his erotic life seemed to encounter practically no resistance at all. You can always take what you want, if you're an Artist of a certain kind. Jane is drawing on the great tradition after all . . .

The air outside is agreeably warm, and Isabel ambles back to the hotel unhurriedly, scenes of that Wolfian summer floating through her mind. There was the afternoon walk she and Jane took through a wooded thicket near the Retreat. The sun was dappling the path through the thick foliage and a deer stood absolutely still at the wood's edge, before fleeing. They were discussing some compositional problem Wolfe had set them; and Isabel said she'd stayed up the whole night trying to resolve it. Jane pawed the path with her sneaker like some impatient pony. "You stop it, girl, you hear?" she said. "Or I swear you'll turn into Wolfe yourself. You shouldn't *punish* yourself like that. The thing about art is that it should be *easy*, don't you know that? I mean, otherwise, what's the point?"

Isabel still remembers the shock of that sentence. The Retreat was dedicated to the cult of the difficult, to art as heroic effort, the most exalted of quests. If art wasn't that, then what was it?

Standing on the dappled path, she finally asked, "No pain, no gain?"

"Oh c'mon, don't let them sell you that," Jane snorted. "No gain is worth the pain, that's the real truth of it."

A smooching couple seated on a bench briefly pauses in their transactions as Isabel walks by through a little square. The world is becoming lighter by the minute . . . Sometimes, she can almost catch the drift of Jane's way, the insouciant logic of her proposition. Why should being-in-the-world be difficult, when there's no choice but to be in it? Why should anything be difficult at all? Just go for it, girl, she hears Jane's voice say. Go for it! And yet . . . some intricate complexity is working its way through her, and she probes it, listens; she wants to know what is in it. What sort of creature is she, what is she driven by and toward . . . She wants to grasp it all, as music grasps it, in its wholeness; its essence. Her meaning bug, undoubtedly. A flicker of apprehension seems to illumine the transience of the moment, a brush as of a wing against her mind. She tries to catch it, but cannot. A line of longing shoots up through her body and consciousness, out into the Copenhagen street and beyond, seeking something beyond its own horizon, and then turning, with a sort of inevitability, toward Anzor.

*

113

They are meeting in Warsaw, the next step on her itinerary. Anzor has assured her that he has reason enough to go there, lots of things to do. The Poles are more sympathetic to the Chechens than the rest of Europe, they've had their own history with the Russians. There are people to see, groups to talk to. There are the refugees, who are living in pretty terrible conditions, idle and disoriented. He should visit them. "So you see," he said, tracing the outline of her cheekbone with his fingers, "I have good reasons to meet you there." She narrowed her eyes at him mischievously, bemused by his anti-sentimental reassurance. He knew she would have been nervous if he followed her yet again for her own sake. Now she's sitting at an outdoor café, in the city's old square, rebuilt from its wartime rubble. The city of Wolfe's Passion; but now it has the pastel-colored charm of any old quarter of a bustling, mid-sized European city. The scars covered up, even here.

She looks up as if in response to an unheard signal and sees Anzor across the square, walking toward her with his long, rangy stride. His jacket, loose over his shirt, swings open lightly in the breeze. It is the way he moves that rivets her, paying no attention to himself, or even to the surroundings. A presence, vivid and palpable, against the meandering topology of the crowd.

And now, she is already half out of herself, halfway between herself and him, somewhere in the pure visual field, pure seeing. She has leapt out of herself, and he has to take her up, or else she will be nowhere. At least so it is in this moment. She directs her gaze straight toward him. He's still at some distance, but he catches her signal as if it were carried by some invisible transmission line. She's picked him out, or he's picked her out; and they hone in on each other through some inaudible ultrasound. She feels a sort of delight, tension mingling with deep concentration, as at the beginning of a concert, before the full plunge. In this moment, that's all there is.

He takes her hand in his and inspects it tenderly. He asks her details of the last few days; they are now in the phase of details. She tells him about Jane's concert and their rivalry at the Retreat. They've also entered a phase in which she's beginning to disclose personal information to him, as much as the other way around. Some balance between them is quickly changing. She's telling him about Wolfe's *Journal*, when a compact, broad-faced man in a leather jacket approaches their table, and, without acknowledging her presence, speaks to Anzor in a foreign tongue. Anzor turns away from her without letting her finish a sentence; and the two men talk as if picking up a conversation they had interrupted shortly before. Isabel looks up, startled by the suddenness of the intrusion, and then by something else. Anzor's voice is quite different in his own language, deeper and more guttural. His gestures have altered too, to something more abrupt and rougher. It gives her an instant glimpse of the modifications he has made in himself for her; for his life here. She thought she's seen him exposed . . . But this is in some way more serious than their intimacy. The men are speaking to each other in sharp, businesslike tones. There's no pleasantry in their expressions, no camouflage of polite restraint.

The stranger leaves as unceremoniously as he'd come, and Anzor, running his hand through his hair distractedly, tells her he must go to see some of his people who are living in Warsaw. Does she want to come along? He needs to talk to them about new information which has emerged regarding the situation in Chechnya. It's very urgent, he must go immediately. She hesitates, then says yes. She's suddenly in the midst of an unfamiliar world, and she feels briefly nervous. Maybe she should go back to her nice hotel and rest. But of course she cannot draw back, she wants to know what is behind Anzor's forehead, wants to enter his mind more deeply . . . Besides, she's not ready yet to leave his physical presence, the honeyed mutual draw of their bodies.

Anzor gets up abruptly and flags a taxi, which takes them to another part of the city, where the buildings are ugly and drab. He holds her elbow reassuringly as they walk through the grim hallway and ascend in the metallic, urine-permeated elevator. How do people living here bear it, she wonders, how do millions upon millions bear their lives . . . The door he knocks on is opened by an old woman in a kerchief, bent into diminutiveness by osteoporosis, with a heavily wrinkled face which lights up with deferential pleasure when she sees Anzor. From her bent frame, she directs a questioning look at Isabel, and Anzor says a few words to her in Chechen.

The room they enter is small and dismal, with frayed brown sofas and an ancient TV placed on a pile of carton boxes. A sickly odor of stale cigarette smoke thickens the air. Not a madeleine shabbiness, this, Isabel thinks, trying to get her bearings. This is something more deeply impoverished, or damaged. Three men sit at a Formica-topped table, drinking and smoking. One of them seems older and more authoritative. It is he who gets up to greet Anzor and who embraces him vigorously, shaking his hand at the same time. He gives Isabel a brief, unsmiling glance and indicates she should sit on one of the frayed sofas. She hesitates; she's not feeling entirely comfortable, not comfortable enough to settle in. She leans against the kitchen counter instead; another man, who has been making coffee, joins her, introducing himself in English as a Polish journalist. He pours her a cup of strong, thick coffee and she stands beside him, sipping. He follows the conversation intently, and from time to time, translates for her benefit. The men at the table are talking about the refugees, there are more of them coming in and it's hard to know what to do with them.

The ones in the camps are beginning to fight among themselves, from inactivity and frustration. There are fears of infiltration, by spies. "Spies from where?" Isabel asks in an undertone, but the journalist says, "Wait, this is important," and listens closely, as the conversation gets more heated and escalates into an outbreak of shouting—until the older man raises a warning finger, and says something in a voice of such steely authority, that Isabel instinctively stops sipping her coffee. She's now staring at the group around the table together with the journalist. Anzor begins speaking agitatedly, jabbing the air with his forefinger. She is, again, startled by the rough authority of his hand. Nothing urbane or tender about it. This is another Anzor, drawing on some more primal, more direct repertory of gestures. Now the older man places both his palms on the table with a thud, as if to say "enough," and Anzor instantly stops. The older man speaks, the others follow, nodding. Anzor's olive skin, in the yellow light, looks nearly transparent. There is something in the undivided attentiveness he directs to the older man that makes Isabel feel an incongruous pang of jealousy. She wants to pull him away from the rectangular table, wants to turn the attention, the focus of his eyes, toward herself.

"What is this about?" she asks the journalist, in an undertone.

He hesitates. "There're all these factions," he says, as if trying to explain in shorthand. "In Chechnya. There's a question of methods. Which are the most effective to use."

"Which faction is . . . this?" she asks, indicating the table; but he again raises a hushing finger. The conversation proceeds in softer tones; then Anzor puts his face between his hands, as if some piece of terrible news has been delivered to him. Another gesture from the deep. "Anzor . . ." she begins, but her voice comes out as a wispy trace of itself. She doesn't register here. Anzor's lower lip, as his face emerges from between his hands, hangs low in some distress. For a long time, a few minutes it seems, the men at the table sit silently, stolidly, as if they were experiencing something together with Anzor, or thinking in tandem, without having to speak. What is she witnessing here? The scene has an esoteric familiarity. Has she dreamt something like it, seen it in the movies, read it?

"Which faction are they?" she again asks the journalist. He is slim and intelligent-looking, he induces trust. He looks at her with quick sympathy. "They're OK," he says. "I believe so."

One of the men nods his head slightly, as if, in their silence, they've reached a conclusion. They begin to talk in a different register, low and steady. She can almost feel their gathered, concentrated heat. They're a quartet, acting in concert . . . She understands this, the currents of energy traveling back and forth through the small group, as they travel through a group of players, till they are all encompassed in the thing itself, a piece of music or a common task.

The leader writes something on a piece of paper he has torn out of a notebook, and hands it to Anzor, placing a large hand on his shoulder. The men clasp hands in some sort of compact, or promise. Then the conversation is abruptly over, and, to her surprise, the older man comes toward her, and clasps her hand in turn, looking closely into her eyes. The hand clasp seems to declare her a comrade, a friend; but his eyes examine her with chilly antipathy, and for a moment, she thinks she sees in them a sort of disgust. He turns away from her without smiling, and gestures to the Polish journalist to translate something for her. "He says you shouldn't talk about what you've seen here," he says. "It would be unwise."

"I haven't seen anything . . ." she begins, but Anzor signals her to leave. The old woman reappears from another room, and bows from her already bent frame as she lets them out, with a pleading, trusting expression directed at Anzor. Then they're out in the bleak corridor. Anzor looks straight ahead, and says nothing.

"What is going on?" she asks, as they descend in the foul elevator. "What was that about?"

"There'll be another war," Anzor says, in a choked voice. "That's all. Another war. They want to grind us into dust. The bastards." His face seems distorted by something in the elevator's yellow light, though she cannot tell whether it's by distress, or anger, or something like inadmissible fear. Now she is frightened, too. The word "war" seems too big for this dirty metallic box. She puts her hand on Anzor's for some kind of reassurance, but he winces, as if she's hurt him.

"Is your family in danger?" she asks as they emerge from the oppressive building. It's drizzling grayly, and the area seems stripped of life.

"It isn't only about my family," he retorts sharply. "It isn't so . . . personal." He sounds as if she's insulted him, and she walks alongside him in baffled silence.

"Isabel," he says after a while, grasping her by the elbow, "let us not talk about this. I don't want to draw you into this . . . matter. Into my country's affairs. They're not your affairs."

"I wish you'd tell me what's going on," she says.

"Nothing yet," he says, in a voice that is less bruised, more like his own. "So let us stop talking about it. I want to be with you. For as long as I can."

But later, in the hygienic hotel room, between the white sheets, he says, "I didn't tell you the truth earlier. My uncle . . . he died. He wasn't killed, but he had a heart attack after the Russians came through his village."

"I'm so sorry," she says, and is afraid to say more, afraid that Anzor will wince again, at whatever words she might choose.

"He was old," Anzor says. "But my father will be right if he doesn't forgive me. I should be there, with them."

"Tell me about your father," she says. "If you want." She realizes she knows nothing of Anzor's family, his actual history. The narrative. She knows only the way he moves and seeks her behind her eyes; the way his voice travels to certainty or fills with feeling. Perhaps the narrative matters too.

"He's an engineer," Anzor answers, with some reluctance. "Soviet-trained. Everybody had to be, if they wanted to be professionals. He had good training."

"But what is he like?" she asks, and this time he doesn't answer for a while. "Do you know Gorky's book about his childhood?" he finally says. "Those scenes in the peasant hut with everyone beating each other, all the time. Men beating women, women beating children. The stronger beating the weaker, and the weaker taking it as their due. Everyone sleeping in the same bed and beating each other." His voice has gone grainy with the effort of saying all this; but he doesn't break contact with her. "Well, my father—that's where he came from, that kind of place. He was just one generation removed from such scenes. They're in his bones . . . He is a Soviet engineer, but he is also . . . a peasant . . . peasant patriarch."

Anzor's voice has traveled into some bitter past; and she remembers a shack she once happened upon on the pampas, with a drunken man in it and a large-eyed child crouching in the corner. The history of cruelty, she thinks, everywhere, so close and so ordinary. The intimate history of violence. "But he didn't beat . . ." she begins, and Anzor quickly interrupts. "No," he says, and stops again, as if trying to find the right words. "He was just educated enough to stop himself from beating us. But he didn't need to. He just . . . stared. That was sufficient. He is not a large man, but he had a sort of . . . force. They do, in my country. But his power was . . . unusual. He had very strong arms. A bull's neck. And the eyes . . . that was where the power came from. Sometimes he raged, and shouted. But it was when he got very still that he was . . . really dangerous."

Anzor's breathing is coming harder, and she places a soothing hand on his chest. "Once . . ." he begins, and pauses, as if deciding whether to continue. "There was this Soviet recruiter who came from a university in Moscow to talk to me. I was fifteen. I really wanted to go. We all did. I mean, we were young and we were dying to get out, to be part of the world. So I suppose . . . I was nice to the recruiter. He was not much older than me, and I drank with him and maybe laughed too much."

"What happened?" she asks, although she's half afraid of what he'll say.

"Nothing really *happened*," Anzor says. "After the recruiter left, my father simply looked at me. He sat still and stared straight at me. His eyes were filled with this . . . contempt. Cold contempt. I tried to stare back, to say something icy and disdainful. But I couldn't. I was . . . paralyzed. Finally, I looked away." He pauses, before bringing out the next sentence. "I had been defeated."

"And he didn't say anything . . ." Isabel says wonderingly.

"He did. After he knew he'd . . . squashed me. He said, 'We in this country have very little. But we have our pride. Our honor. Today you have dishonored yourself.'"

"But—" Isabel begins.

"No," Anzor cuts in, curtailing her protest. "The old man was right. That day I lost some part of my honor."

She has been following each turn of his account as if she had been part of the scene he has summoned; but she is suddenly impatient at the solemnity of his tone.

"Oh, come on," she says. "Isn't that a bit . . . exaggerated?" She hears him breathing harder, and backtracks. "I mean, aren't you being hard on yourself?"

His voice is knife-sharp in its disdain. "Hard on yourself," he repeats, scornfully. "Those wonderful . . . phrases you have here. Hard on yourself. You can say that only if your life has been . . . very easy. If you don't understand what people must do to retain their honor. Their dignity."

"I'm sorry," she says. "I only meant—" He turns to her sharply. "I meant that you were so young," she says, trying to sound casual, to dispel the tension. "You couldn't be expected to behave like some . . . ancient Roman falling on his sword all the time."

She thinks he might see the humor of it, but he doesn't. "No, not Roman," he says instead. "A Chechen. We have our sense of honor too."

"Oh, I am sure . . ." she begins, and then realizes she is about to fall into some kind of deflating irony again; and that she mustn't. For a moment, she wishes she could lighten up, crack a joke; wishes for Marcel's blithe cynicism. But Anzor is speaking out of something entirely serious in himself; the core place untouchable by irony. The center, around which his urbanity is spun like a removable, flimsy fabric.

"You see," he resumes, speaking again to her, seeking her understanding, "my father was a tyrant. Sometimes I wanted to hit out at him . . . punch him." His voice is taut with old anger, then changes. "But I can't stand what's happening to him now. I can't stand to think of him being treated . . . without respect." She nods wordlessly. "I keep seeing him . . . You see . . . before I left, there was a bunch of these Russian . . . soldiers who burst into the house. These young thugs. They're just thugs, you know, just stupid, illiterate . . . hooligans. Drunk out of their gourds, reeling and laughing. My father shouted at them to get out. In his most authoritative voice. But these bastards . . . just laughed. What is it, old uncle, you don't like having us around? No? Ah, that's not nice, we're such good boys . . . Then one of them . . . he . . . shook my father, with a sort of . . . insolence. It was sort of . . . casual."

"Don't tell me if you don't want to," she says quickly. She isn't sure she wants to hear more.

But Anzor goes on, as he apparently must. "Then this thug . . . he took my father . . . by the ear . . . his earlobe between his fingers. And then he twisted, hard."

Anzor stops, as if this were the truly unbearable thing, the detail on which torment hangs. Under her hand, she can feel his chest inflating and falling. She is afraid he is telling her too much, that he will later regret it. But he seems to be speaking to himself, as if the scene in his mind has to unfold till the end.

"You know," he continues, "my father is in his way a simple man. Simple and proud. His pride is who he is. Or who he was . . . He tried to give them his stare. The stare which used to frighten me into submission. But they hardly . . . noticed. One of them laughed, with a kind of . . . merriment. As if they were just having fun. And then my father . . . he lowered his head." Anzor falls silent.

When he speaks again, his voice is flat, as if he has reached a desolate plateau, his private bottom line of shame. "I stood there the whole time," he says slowly. "And I . . . didn't do anything. Nothing."

"What could you possibly do?" she says.

"I wasn't ready to take the risk."

"But how could you . . . ? There were several of them. You could have been . . ."

"It was . . . a failure." He states this as if the right, the only conclusion has been reached. "You don't know this . . . here, in your . . . nice countries. Your nice peaceful countries. But sometimes you have to be willing to risk . . . everything. You have to be willing to die. If that is what it takes to do the right thing. If you do not want to be ashamed. If you do not want your life to become worthless. What is the point of living a life of shame?"

He breathes deeply, as if he has said what needs to be said.

She takes his words with a kind of wonder; a sensation that is beyond, or beneath, fear or finicky doubt. She is close to some fundamental calculation, the axis around which choices about the human condition revolve; and she understands that in the calculation, it is possible to choose death.

Then the sensation passes, and she feels the dizziness of having traveled too far away from herself, lost in the antiseptic hotel room, in the alien city. Where has she wandered to, through the milky fog of her own freedom . . . She peers into Anzor's eyes, which have become more deeply veiled through all his revelations.

"Your eyes," he says. "Your wide green eyes."

"Am I staring?" she asks, but feels a sort of shift, looking now at him directly from within, as he looks at her.

"I want to know you," he says, intimately.

"What do you want to know?"

"You. You."

Then their dance begins, urgent and lyrical, and she presses on, as if the lovemaking were also an inquiry, as if she could penetrate through Anzor's body to some truth at the heart of his darkness. There's that, she thinks—the music, the stillness of the stage before, and the different stillness after—and there's this. That's all I know. Or rather, she corrects herself, this is the only way I know how to know.

Budapest

In Budapest, she walks along the grand avenues and the ordinary streets, feeling the pull of their long narrow vistas, the somnolent gravity of the darkened stone. The city draws her into itself as into a deep funnel, with the promise of age and richness, a languorous heaviness. Madeleines of the imaginary. For she has never been here, and yet the city corresponds to something she recognizes. She meanders into a spacious arched courtyard in which doves are cooing. She catches the soft, sublunar sounds of Hungarian. But throughout it all, she is waiting. Underneath the rhythms of the city, she's suspended in waiting time, a time in which every second grows large and in which, beyond each second, there's no extension. In which every second is distended with expectation and compressed with absence. Only the presence of Anzor will disburden her of this pressure, will restore time to its imperceptible flow. Is this kitsch, is she caught in a banality? She has no words for this, or at least none of which she's not ashamed. She will not let them come, not even in her own mind. And yet, how is she to think about what she feels, unless she stifles it into silence, sours it in her skepticism? She thinks of Brahms and Schumann, and their simple, oh-so-simple melodies; the motifs which, through variation and alteration develop into sonatas and symphonies, epics and edifices. Begin with the cliché, she thinks, because that is where the heart begins. Then elaborate. She stops fending off Anzor from her mind, and thinks, better the clichés of love than no love at all.

On the way back to her hotel, the taxi stops suddenly, jolting her forward. She breaks her movement with her hand, winces at the twinge of the back-stretched wrist. The taxi driver rolls down the window and shouts at someone outside; then apparently realizes it's hopeless and shakes his head in disgust. Now she hears and sees: the sound of shoes, or boots, stamping on metal, glass breaking, brutally loud, deliberately harsh young voices. A bunch of kids—that's surely what they are, though the words don't seem to fit—are jumping up and down on the hood of a car, while others are throwing stones at its windows. Another car is being tackled in the same way. The kids are very young, some of them not grown to their full height. Their figures, illuminated by the yellow street lamps, look wild, baffling, unhinged. Their faces are distorted with a sort of orgiastic fury. She stops up her ears against the awful sounds, but keeps looking. She wonders if these are rites in some local gang war, but these youths—that's better, youths—seem too aimless and bacchanalian for warfare, as if they were striving for some anarchic climax rather than a specific aim, some violent epiphany which will come God knows how.

"*Scheisse,*" the driver swears, apparently looking for a common language with his passenger, and hurtles on with a string of phrases in German.

"*Ist* . . . punk," he says, changing his tactics when she doesn't respond. "*Ist* . . . hooligan." He blares his horn very loudly, and the car jumpers turn toward the taxi and hurl some mocking, threatening syllables at them. One girl makes an obscene gesture with her navel, touching herself on the crotch. The driver swivels his head and waves to the car behind them, signaling they should back off. They do so, a string of cars going into reverse and making their way carefully out of the street, as the sound of police sirens approaches from the opposite direction.

"Sorry," the driver says when they're finally in the clear, and he makes an abrupt, angry turn into another street. "*Ist* . . . *Scheisse.*"

She doesn't respond, but she thinks, they must be unloved children, unloved and abandoned. Surely. No child which has been loved would turn that feral, that ugly. It's the chain of uncaring, small and large. The history of cruelty, or of small uncaring, with its large, its enormous consequences. Kolya, she can no longer fend off Kolya, and with a twist at her heart, sees again his small hurt face as clearly as if he were very near, and raising his eyes toward her, with their burden of meaning.

The taxi driver repeats "*Ist Scheisse* . . . hooligan," as if to make sure she understands; then as she fails to respond again, shrugs his shoulders and they make the rest of the trip in silence.

At the hotel, she goes through her ablutions, tries to shake off the figures of the stomping youths. Instead, as she applies soothing night cream to her face, she sees Kolya's face within her own in the mirror, staring back at her with its revenant presence, with eyes so much like her own, looking at her as they did that night. Yes, she knows it was that night, in the thudding disco in lower Manhattan, where the scene was in those days. She no longer remembers why she went along with Kolya and his buddies, the older sister, but not so much older as to constitute a restraint. She may have just wanted to see how he lived, her genius brother, who had moved into a world of incomprehensibly abstract mathematics, and whom she didn't see very often anymore. She can still bring back the heated excitement of the cavernous room, the figures of the dancers leaping and twisting with the thudding, pounding rhythms of the music, faces emerging and disappearing under the rhythmic strobe flashes, distorted with angled light or their own ecstasy, half exalted, half infernal. The Dionysiacs of lower Manhattan, the Dionysiacs of Budapest . . . Kolya took her into some dimly lit back room, which was apparently the drug room. A young woman, thankfully only vaguely visible in a corner, was injecting something into her arm, and Isabel turned away so as not to see the needle working its way under the skin. Kolya was talking to a young man dressed in an incongruous blue blazer, who was handing him a plastic sandwich bag. A marijuana purchase, clearly routine. "My sister," Kolya introduced her. "Bel, meet Rex." "Didn't know the genius had a sister," Rex said. So Kolya was known to be exceptional, even here. "You should look after him," the boy said. "Somebody should." He was only a boy. She remembers a pang of resentful guilt. Why should she have to look after Kolya? "You're right," she said. "I will."

"You want some grass?" Kolya asked. "It's good stuff. Isn't it, Rex?" "Only the best," Rex said, with the cheerful politeness of a good salesman. "You have no worries, I promise." And so she smoked the thin cigarette, and when they went out on the dance floor, the ecstatic faces seemed even more luridly beautiful, more luridly grotesque. And at one point, Kolya brought his face toward hers—they were dancing together—and held her very tight. It was like looking into a powerfully angelic version of herself, with Kolya's wide-spaced green eyes indistinguishable from her own. He kissed her, unequivocally, on the lips; and she returned the kiss, yes, she definitely returned it, bending her neck backward under his touch, accepting his tongue in her mouth. The sensation was so deep that it went beyond the erotic, to some perfect androgynous completion. A Wagnerian swoon, she thinks in her Budapest room . . .

They never alluded to that moment, which happened under the merciful cover of marijuana and the hypnotic lights. Transgression, her peers would have called it. Incest is nicest . . . Not that she ever told anybody. Still, she winces as she remembers Kolya's face coming close to hers. Her reckless, abandoned brother, moving toward her in abandonment, wanting, perhaps, to avenge himself on Lena, who had abandoned him.

But after that evening, she started dropping in on him in his minuscule walk-up apartment in the East Village, to check that he was still there, that he was all right. Kolya seemed to keep up with his studies, and had written a paper for a professional journal that was thought to be precocious. He fed himself intermittently from the Chinese takeout below, and took marijuana, which, he said, helped him grasp the strange shapes of matter on which his equations were based. "I just don't know how Einstein and those guys did without," he said, humorously. There's nothing more reassuring of a person's sanity than the ability to crack a joke. Except, Isabel now thinks, when it's a sign of a deeper crack.

Often, she found stray friends of Kolya's when she came over, crashing, as they put it, on a mattress placed next to the grimy kitchenette. The places they lived in then . . . Isabel particularly remembers a girl named Sabine, who seemed to stay there forever. She was on the plump side, and wore slovenly T-shirts, under which her big breasts moved about amorphously. When Isabel asked her about her studies, Sabine revealed that she'd dropped out of school, and all that nonsense, and that she was working at a strip club. "Isn't that dangerous?" Isabel asked, trying not to betray that she was appalled. "Nah, I just dance," the girl said. "I'm good at it, too. I like it . . . Actually, I'm a kind of artist," she concluded proudly. "That's what I'm called." The word which constituted the imprimatur for just about everything. "Besides," Sabine added, in further explanation, "it's kind of . . . romantic." "Romantic?" Isabel asked incredulously. "Yeah," Sabine confirmed, drawing the word out dreamily. "The men there . . . they can look but not touch. You should see how they look at me." Isabel remembers Sabine's young mouth twisting downward, in an odd expression that combined a barely camouflaged eroticism with something like shame, a wounded shame.

After another two weeks, when the girl's clothing had taken over such floor space as there was in the pathetic room, Isabel asked about her parents. "Aren't they worried about you?" she asked. "Do they know what you're doing?"

"C'mon, give her a break," Kolya intervened from his bed. "What are you, some kind of parental substitute figure?"

"That's OK," Sabine said quickly, and rather politely. She clearly didn't want to get thrown out of Kolya's miserable quarters. "They know . . . I mean, they don't really care . . . I mean, you know, they want me to go to university. They're, like, so standard . . . But they're away a lot. They're in the Bahamas right now."

Where are the parents, Isabel thought then, where are the real parents. But Sabine's mother and father did show up eventually, and took her back to their apparently chic SoHo loft. Kolya said they practically screwed up their noses in disgust when they came to collect Sabine. "Like some package," he added. "Like she was some big lump." Isabel privately thought this was not an inaccurate description of the girl.

Their own parents had been long absent; Carlos dead of a heart attack, and Lena back in Buenos Aires, from where she communicated with them irregularly. Occasionally, Kolya asked Isabel to talk about their father, whom he didn't remember at all; and, sitting at the foot of his large bed, which took up most of the apartment, she had tried to bring up scraps of memory. The atmosphere of their house on the pampas, where they spent part of the year, with the long grasses outside; the cowboys she sometimes glimpsed on their horses. The tangos Lena and Carlos often played on their old record player, and whose fierce syncopations whipped Isabel's small body with near violence. The figures of her parents dancing to the scratchy melodies, moving across the wooden floor glidingly, gracefully . . .

Then there was the mega-fight, as she described it to Kolya, in an attempt to make light of it. Though it was the great caesura, there was no doubt of it even then. She doesn't remember how it started, but she can see her parents standing up and shouting at each other loudly, without restraint, as if she weren't there. Then her mother beginning to cry, copiously and unwillingly, as if the tears were a further humiliation. Her mouth contorting horribly, she picked up the nearest thing to her—a Dresden porcelain figurine standing on the table—and hurled it, almost at Carlos, but not quite, all her uncertainty, her impotence, contained in this curtailed trajectory.

"Please, Lena, you've known about her for a while now," her father said in a pleading tone. Isabel remembers this exactly. The primal scene.

"Of course I know, you made sure I'd know," her mother shouted. Then she sat down at the table and put her head between her arms, still trying to hide her tears.

"And I mean, what were you doing when this was going on?" Kolya had asked, but Isabel found her sensations at that moment difficult to describe. She can still envision herself, though, as if she were looking at someone else: a child seated on a tattered couch, wide-eyed and perfectly still, a mere conduit for what was passing between the man and the woman; absolutely attentive, absolutely absorbent. She was so quiet that the two of them forgot about her, and she seemed to disappear even to herself, so powerfully was she suctioned into the hurricane of emotions in their little living room, into the two large creatures, struggling with each other. She was equally dispersed into all points of the room, the light and the blowing curtains, her mother and father, and the passions hurling between them. She was in all of them at once, at every point of the configuration, an absorbent reed for the passage of light in the room, and the passage of grief and rage.

Then her mother started crying, terribly and openly. Isabel remembers the return of something like her own being, her will. She slipped off the sofa, wanting to go over and console Lena. But it was Carlos who bent down over her, and stroked her hair, and then held the nape of her neck as if to steady her. Her mother quieted; Isabel can still sense the full ambivalence of that moment, and the sensuality of her mother's response to her father's large fingers. A strange lethargy, almost like sleepiness, suddenly invaded her own small body, and she got up on the sofa again and lay down. That, in turn, brought her mother's attention to her, and she looked at Isabel with awful, red-rimmed eyes. "Oh my poppet, I'm so sorry," she whispered. "Please go, Carlos," she said, no longer storming. "Really, you'd better go."

She still feels the stab of that sentence, declaring the end of her childhood, of simplicity. But as she moves through the memory, she thinks, if Schubert moves within me, it may be partly because of this.

What Kolya remembered best was being taken by Lena to Sunday services in the Orthodox church in New York, where they all settled for a while, after their wanderings. He loved the heavy scent of white lilies and incense, and the gorgeous basso profundo chants. Isabel remembers the chants as well, vibrating even more deeply than the tango, with their dense, almost unmoving power, as if the sounds were concentrated matter, rather than voices in motion. Lena's turn to religion was brief, but intense; it was her way, Isabel understands now, of mourning her marriage. Their mother still understood something of religion's claim on the soul, and Isabel dimly sensed it through her: the basso profundo acceptance of suffering, the promise that we experience ourselves most wholly in giving ourselves up. For Lena, it was only what happened to her that counted, rather than anything she made happen herself. It was only when she was plunged into love or disaster that she felt she had a deep, human fate. So, after the catastrophe of her husband's departure, it must have consoled her to be in a place where she could imagine that she had been subjected to a fate, rather than anything smaller or nastier; and where she could try to acquiesce to it, rather than thrash against it in fruitless protest.

Lena lowering her body to kneel, Lena bowing her beautiful head till it touched the cold church floor . . . Isabel remembers the gestures of surrender with a sort of queasiness. But maybe her mother took her growing children to church because she wanted to pass something on to them after all, out of the scattering of her own life. To pass on something especially to her little son, from whom she had so carelessly turned away, in rejection or just indifference. Indifference, Isabel says to Lena's imago, which is worse than rejection, because it renders you nil. That was the heart-twisting thing about Kolya's pale childish face that day in Provence. He looked somehow erased, as though he knew he had been rendered null and void, expelled from the circle of love. So perhaps Lena was trying to give him something instead. Poor substitute, Isabel thinks bitterly . . . And of course Kolya didn't take up her compensatory offering. No religious option for him, except maybe for some leftover seeking, which Isabel felt in him like a pulsation; seeking for . . . what? Something to pour himself into, with all his keenness and hurt, something outside the boundaries of his own self, although it had no shape or name. A trace, old and seemingly as useless as the appendix. Certainly, Kolya had no words for what he wanted, except for some vague notion of Experience he'd caught from the general air, and which kept eluding him with a vicious irony, the harder he pursued it. He only knew that he wanted to be transported; to abandon himself. An ecstatic without a cause, like so many. For a while, Isabel worried that he would follow a friend who had joined the Moonies. But Kolya was simply too lucid to fall for something so, as he put it, "un-dialectical." He needed his meaning-systems accompanied by logic. So he spent his days in the bleak flat, and at night ventured out into his clubs, where the drugs got stronger and more expensive. He was trying to pry the doors of perception wide open, he told Isabel. Surely, she wasn't such a nerd as not to understand that? Not to appreciate a whole twentieth-century tradition of experiment, of trying to find the truth behind the paltry appearances of reality? Was she, like, from another century? Isabel, in her Budapest hotel room, winces at the memory of one awful afternoon, when he told her, his eyes wide open and hypnotic, about a dream in which the governing spirit of the universe had telephoned him; and the phone number from which It was calling was a perfect circle. Kolya kept trying to dial the number repeatedly, in her presence; then curled on the bed in a posture of fetal despair, and said, much more terribly, "Nothing ever works in my life. Nothing that really matters. I am an unloved person, how can anything ever work out?"

Such a small injury, Isabel thinks, his mother shooing him out of the house, turning away from his small face, as though it didn't please her. Surely not enough to account for what happened . . . But the worm of desolation had bored into him, and kept burrowing deeper and further, until there was nothing but desolation, and then the sight of his young body on that awful bed, in his open-necked shirt and mauve scarf. Sitting up in her hotel bed, Isabel emits a small gasp. The mauve scarf was Kolya's signature, his small sign. Pain adheres to such details. The two terrible friends, drugged and panicked. One of them, with matted filthy hair, kept pacing the room with a sort of impotent defiance, as she held Kolya's wrist, willing the pulse to continue until the ambulance arrived. "It's not our fault!" he suddenly shouted, and hit the wall with his fist. "Fuck it, it's not our fault!" "Yeah, man," the other one muttered from his position on the floor. "He shouldda known." The one seated was swaying to and fro in a sickening, automatic gesture, and with a look of abject, absent fear on his face. Isabel ran into the bathroom and threw up. When she came back . . . the Adam's apple under the mauve scarf was moving even more faintly. Isabel still hears a remote scream, coming from herself, not a controlled, coloratura scream from a Verdi death aria, but a dissonant, graceless eruption of raw pain.

And that was all. And that was all. Just one of his generation's scarifying statistics. The best minds of my generation have been undone . . . Part of his generation's story; that was what Isabel's

friends kept offering as solace, as if making Kolya into a sociological fact would somehow make it easier to accept his death.
When did that begin, she wonders, the conversion of ourselves
into sociological facts. It won't do; won't do for Kolya, whose
young man's face is still appealing to her in all its bruised
puzzlement. It won't do for his spectral presence, which she
wears like a gauzy shroud on her soul, and which impels her
search, as though she could offer him something still, some kind
of counterpoint, a consolation.

In the morning, a recording session. The studio is in a low stone
building, picturesquely overgrown with green vegetation. From
the white-walled room where she will play, she can see the
control console, the gleam of high technology. The piano, in the
middle of the white space, looks like some geological beast, left
over, in its great bulk, from another epoch.

She warms up with some arpeggios, waits for her cue. "Ready
to roll?" the technician asks through his microphone, and smiles
at her encouragingly. She gives him some test sounds, pianissimo,
fortissimo, treble, bass. She's recording a sequence of Beethoven
Sonatas, and she starts with Op. 109. The technician tells her he
won't interrupt till the end of the movement; they can go over
the corrections later. When she finishes, she looks up at him to
see how she's done. She respects the views of technicians highly.
This is where real criticism happens, in praxis. He gives her a
thumbs up, and summons her to come into the cubicle and
listen with him. She sits in front of the console, with its array
of buttons and levers. The sound, through the earphones, is
startlingly clear, pellucid. No surround of moisture or breath is
perceptible, just crystalline notes. It always takes her a moment
to accept this sonic perfection, this distillation from her breathing, roiling effort. The technician is following with the score
open, and when they come to a transitional passage between

theme A and B, he presses the stop button. "Did you hear that?" he asks. "Yes," she says, and though she hardly knows this man's name, this is a moment of precise communion. They've heard exactly the same thing: the bass figuration in the left hand is a decibel too loud, and several notes have fallen out of alignment.

"Do you want to redo it?" he asks, and she nods, and goes back to the piano. There's no need to discuss what she needs to do, they've heard the same thing. She waits till her concentration returns, and begins a few bars earlier, so as to elide into the passage in question, then segues into a bar on the other end. She gets a high thumbs up, and joins the technician in the cubicle again. "Perfect," he says. "It will go right in." There's another passage to redo toward the end of the movement; and then they go over the whole thing bar by bar for fine-tuning. A ritardando, she thinks, is too exaggerated, and he speeds it up by a smidgeon on the computer. The graph on his screen pulses just perceptibly faster. He takes a few bars apart, and makes a few bass notes more pronounced. Now the line fits, seamlessly.

"Shall we have a listen, then?" he asks. He stretches his arms and crosses them behind his neck; the concentration of their task has been intense. They follow the completed version in silence. When they come to a singing bel canto passage, he gives her a small, approving nod. The startling, pure sounds. Is it still Beethoven, she wonders. Is it still she who is playing? But it is. It is. She sighs, in a release of tension, and lets the music enter her more impartially. From the distance created by the recording and the high-tech console, she is stirred as if it were anybody playing. She's just an instrument. She thinks, but this is beautiful. Or maybe she is moved by this strange process, the decomposition of meaning into subparticles of mere sound, and then its unaccountable, its utterly convincing return. The gluing together of what has been taken apart, so that the aural molecules fill up with sap and flow, so that they add up to this Sonata, this verisimilitude of the human soul. Which is the illusion, which truth . . . ? But that's how it is with meaning, she thinks. Or that's how it is these days. She thinks of Anzor, and her disallowable, archaic emotions, her atavistic yearnings. Too late for that, too late. And yet, they return, the same desires, as if they had not been decoded into hundreds of particles and stories. She takes in Beethoven's sudden shifts of feeling, and she thinks yes, it returns, as if encoded in something, maybe in some microscopic DNA sequences, activated by switch genes, like the console with its on/off buttons. Now you see it, now you don't . . . It's the ultimate trick, and she's moved by it, the unraveling of meaning into sonic neutrons and electrons, and then their conversion back into music. Music, which itself is nothing, and which is everything, in which we recognize ourselves as if reading some deep-encrypted information from an old manual of longings, for love, truth, beauty.

The cubicle is blank with silence when the movement is finished. "Ready for the next one?" the technician asks, and she girds herself for the second movement.

Anzor arrives in Budapest just in time to join her for dinner with her friends. Sheila and Larry are spending a year at an international institute of scholarship in Budapest, released briefly from their own university in Minnesota, whereto they feel themselves to have been unjustly expelled from their native Manhattan. Isabel has asked if she can bring Anzor, and as she changes from her concert dress to slacks and a loose shirt, she feels oddly jittery about the outing, and then embarrassed about her nervousness. It's not as if this is a performance, she admonishes herself; not as if Anzor is going to be on show. And yet, she cannot deny a certain sense of risk at this breakout from their privacy. Who exactly is Anzor, outside their erotic cocoon? How will he be seen when he is exposed to the normalizing judgment of her friends, the appraisal which comes with being seen from any distance, outside of interlocked eyes and entangled flesh? She will know what the judgment is, even if it is not spoken.

So it is with some stiffness that she tells Anzor about her friends on the way to their apartment; about their long-standing habit of having Sunday brunch as a threesome (she suppresses the thought that it was a foursome, not too long ago), and afterward, a leisurely walk through Central Park. Sheila and Larry practically wept from nostalgia when they returned to New York the first time, after being exiled to bleak and unnatural Minnesota. Anzor looks at her quite sharply at the word "exiled," and she's instantly aware of its falseness. Then why did they go? he asks, reasonably enough. With a dutiful loyalty to her friends, she tries to explain that academic jobs are hard to come by, especially for a couple in disparate fields. Larry is in cultural history; Sheila in psychology. It's a second marriage for them both, so they didn't want to be apart too much. "I see," Anzor says tersely, and without much interest; and Isabel says no more, conscious that she is describing the rarefied difficulties of the privileged.

"It's so great to see you!" Sheila exclaims in her effusive, wide-open voice, as she lets them in. She embraces Isabel heartily and examines Anzor with frank curiosity. "Welcome," she says enthusiastically. "Anzor, from Chechnya, right? I'm very happy you could come."

Isabel feels Anzor tense up behind her, though whether it's at Sheila's greeting, or the penetrating cheeriness of her voice, or the grand apartment they are now entering, she doesn't know. Larry greets them heartily in turn, and shows them around their Budapest quarters. He's wearing a striped shirt with several top buttons open, and his compact body exudes a sort of adrenaline-enhanced confidence. "Can you believe this?" he asks, pointing to a Rembrandt drawing. "An original. Made it through the war and everything after." He is clearly in his element in this dark-wooded apartment, with its authentic art and heavy furniture, and its suggestions of a complex history. Isabel notes that Anzor is observing him closely, from under hooded eyes; she senses some determination on his part not to be charmed, or to charm his hosts too willingly; too easily.

"Drinks, anyone?" Larry asks, and he tells them about the institute and how great it is to have books brought to you from practically any library in the world, by well-dressed assistants.

"He really approves of the local fashion sense," Sheila says, deadpanning cheerfully. "You should hear him carry on about those assistants."

"The fashion sense is impeccable," Larry agrees, "but the impressive thing is the quality of service. Such politeness, and they find anything I ask for, no matter how obscure. Music scores too. I do a lot of listening these days," he informs Isabel. "I'm doing the German Romantics, you know, and their influence on modernism, and there are all these lieder. Nonsense, most of them, of course. But informative nonsense."

"Nonsense?" Isabel repeats. "Do you mean the music?"

"Oh no no," he assures her affably. "I mean those slushy sentimental lyrics. Swooning maidens and dying swains. Trust the Germans. Always overwrought."

"But there is the music," Isabel says. As it happens, she agrees about the poetry. She tries to ignore it whenever she listens to the songs, to the modulated subtleties of Schubert and Schumann.

"Yeah, but as a matter of fact, the lyrics give you clues to the music," Larry says energetically. "I mean, to the tropes from which these things are constructed. With which the Romantics worked. Lots of swooning in the music, too."

"Tropes?" Anzor asks sharply. She suspects he knows what the word means.

"Conventions," Larry genially explains. "Units of phrasing, which have certain associations and trigger certain emotions."

"You make it sound like some behaviorist experiment, testing reactions in mice," Isabel protests.

"Well, what do you think, that we are moved by the Holy Spirit when we listen to Schubert?" Larry asks briskly.

"We are moved by something . . ." Isabel begins, and as usual, when she tries to speak on such topics, doesn't know how to end. "Aren't we?"

"Ah, you've always had these mystical tendencies," Larry says dismissively. "Or should I say, mystifying."

"Surely, you don't need to be mystical in order to believe that a Schubert piece is driven by something . . . more than the sum of its parts," Isabel retorts. "That there is some . . . unifying principle which makes us feel a sense of its wholeness." She has meant it to come out lightly, but a note of defensiveness has stolen into her voice. It's odd how much this matters to her, how much is at stake.

"Ah, those are very bad words!" Sheila throws in. "Don't let him get started on unifying, or wholeness, or principle. He thinks the idea of unifying principles has been responsible for our decline. I mean, the decline of Western civilization."

"Well, I certainly wouldn't want to be responsible for *that*," Isabel responds, this time with a more successful insouciance.

"Honestly, you play these things," Larry persists, impatiently. "You know that these pieces are made. Constructed. Composed. That the impression of unity is an illusion. The whole notion of a work of art is an illusion."

"Then analyze the illusion!" she bursts out. "I mean, why we're entranced by it, why we feel it captures something . . . essential. How does Schubert achieve it. Or Beethoven."

"Ah, there you go, with your idea of the Artist. I thought we've done away with it a long time ago . . . The Great Artist. The Genius. The grand unified agent. I mean, Schubert was a bloody syphilitic drunk and Chopin was a bloodied consumptive. Beethoven was barking mad, as far as I can tell."

"But, somehow, they created beauty."

"Oh come on."

"Then what would you call it, exactly?"

"You just don't get it, do you," Larry says curtly.

"Leave her alone," Sheila orders her husband. "She's a performer, not a theoretician. It would probably screw up her playing if she thought like you."

"OK, Bel, you can retain your innocence if you want. Your theoretical virginity." He has used her younger nickname to soften his sarcasm, summoning her back to their long friendship.

"Given the rites of initiation, maybe I will," Isabel says, and wonders if he is right; if she wants to retain a certain innocence, or even ignorance. Then she thinks of her recording session, the coagulation of meaning from its separate units, like the exfoliation of a plant; the rising of bread. She doesn't think Larry's skepticism would survive the test of such a session; of what the computer graphs can and cannot tell you.

But Larry now turns the full blast of his keen-eyed, thick-browed attention on Anzor. "This must be boring for you," he says unapologetically. "You must have more urgent things on your mind."

"You mean politics," Anzor says, carelessly. "The savage politics of my country." His manner has become positively languid, and he's contemplating his whisky glass pensively.

"Well, we can't help but wonder . . ." Larry says, uncharacteristically failing to finish his sentence. "I mean, we know terrible things are going on in your country, but we don't know much."

"That's all you need to know," Anzor says politely. "Terrible things are going on." Isabel tenses, and wishes she could say something apologetic, or conciliatory; or move the conversation away from this mined area altogether.

"Was it very hard before?" Sheila cuts into the brief silence, in her eager voice. "I mean, growing up over there. I mean, your country has always been . . . sort of repressed, right?"

To Isabel's relief, Anzor looks up from his whisky glass with something like a friendly expression. "Believe it or not, one could have a happy childhood in Chechnya," he says, this time making Sheila a partner to his irony. "Of course, I was lucky to be born after the return."

"The return?" Sheila asks, and Anzor explains, about the great deportation, and how the entire Chechen population— "All of them?" Larry asks with some skepticism, as she did the first time she heard the story—were herded into refugee camps. And how, after eleven years, there was a change of policy in the Politburo, and the Chechens, all one and a half million of them, were reunited with Chechnya. He has his tropes too, Isabel thinks; but Anzor would never put it that way. These refrains throb with too much meaning for him, too much reality.

"Extraordinary," Larry says, and again falls uncharacteristically silent. His authority, in the face of such disclosures, recedes. Persecutions, totalitarianisms, the Gulag: History, the real thing.

"But you said your childhood was . . ." Sheila interjects, almost pleadingly.

"I had the sheer good luck to grow up after," Anzor says. "A kind of golden time, as long as you didn't realize what kind of world you were living in. It only got unpleasant later."

"What do you mean?" Sheila's voice has turned less bright.

"I mean it's not pleasant when your friend is beaten up by official thugs or taken off to a labor camp from which he may never return." Anzor's tone is very even and without a trace of pleasantry. "Or when he has stopped talking to you because he is afraid you'll inform on him."

"I guess they were really awful, the Soviets," Larry says, in a tone which suggests that he's making a concession.

With a sudden roughness, Anzor gets up and goes over to a

side cabinet, where he unceremoniously pours a large amount of whisky into his glass. Larry and Sheila follow this not entirely proper initiative in riveted silence. Anzor's presence in the room is suddenly very large.

"As a matter of fact," Anzor says, as he sits back down, "the gulag was a very good school for learning about the unified agent." He stops, as if not deigning to explain further.

"What do you mean?" Larry asks, after considering this briefly. He doesn't like to be in the interrogative position.

"I mean," Anzor says, with a sudden passion, "that when you're being beaten or tortured, you don't doubt there's someone doing it to you. An actual person. Or bastard. A real unified agent. You don't have to worry if what's happening to you is a whole experience. No need for analysis. None." His voice has stiffened, this time unmistakably with anger. Larry raises his eyebrows, in a sign that he is not entirely convinced; but says nothing.

"Did you have personal . . . experience of . . . any of this?" Sheila asks.

"No," Anzor answers, with an abruptness just short of rude. A brief silence falls upon them again.

"Why don't you tell them about your friend?" Isabel intervenes. She wants to defuse the growing tension; to bring him back on board.

Anzor considers her as if he'd forgotten that she was there. "I don't think anyone is interested," he says finally, making a sort of concession in turn. He's only trying to be properly sociable.

"Oh but we are!" Sheila protests and Anzor tells them about his friend, who grew up in a religious Muslim family in a village near his grandparents, and ended up in the Gulag for attending secret prayers. Anzor had visited him in his village over several summers; then one summer the friend was no longer there. The people in the village, once they got over their secretiveness, told Anzor that he had been badly beaten because he wouldn't give away names of his co-conspirators. His fellow Chechens in the camp tried to take care of him; Chechen solidarity held strong in the camps. But the beatings got worse and worse. "That was probably how he died." Anzor's voice catches and he stops.

"What is happening to such people now?" Larry asks.

"They want full revenge," Anzor returns, with a sort of satisfaction. He knows this is not the sort of sentiment his hosts will like. Then he shrugs, and adds, "Some of them have turned fanatical. Or are about to. What do you expect?"

"We do it every time," Larry says, regaining his air of authority. He leans forward, and the gathering of his brow is assertive. "We repress them and then we're surprised when they turn violent. Our politicians should read Foucault, he could have told them all about it."

"We?" Anzor queries. "Actually, I don't see what this has to do with your politicians."

"Oh, believe me, I'm ashamed of the way we muscle our way around the world," Sheila throws in eagerly. She's back on certain ground, the moral high ground of proper guilt. "Ashamed. I mean, look at what's happening in Kosovo. There we go again, sending in some big planes as if dropping big bombs from the air were going to solve anything. I mean, how crude can you get?"

Anzor looks at her with open incredulity. "Would you rather watch innocent people being slaughtered daily?" he asks, no longer bothering to sound polite. "Massacred? Put behind barbed wire? Maybe it doesn't matter because many of them are Muslims?"

Sheila's face crumples a little, as if she were a child being rebuked. "Oh no no," she protests in confusion. "Of course not. It's just that . . . intervention . . . I mean, bullying, pushing everyone around . . ." Anzor looks at her acidly.

"I appreciate what you're saying." Larry leans forward toward

Anzor, like a boxer rallying. "I can see your point of view. But what you must understand . . ." Anzor, at this phrase, turns toward Larry with an excessively calm expression and the slightest rise of his eyebrows; and Larry, in brief confusion, pauses and swerves to another tone. "You see, what I have come to understand is that American power is always dangerous. We have lots of it, and we like to flex our muscles. You know, we are still cowboys at heart."

"Oh yeah, I'm aware of it even here," Sheila picks up. "The way we have . . . infiltrated everything. The ads. The movies. We're like some . . . Godzilla, walking over everything."

"We don't get a lot of American movies where I come from," Anzor puts in, speaking in an informative tone. "But we do get a lot of dead bodies."

Isabel looks at him, startled. He has never been so explicit, has never mentioned bodies.

Another silence falls upon the room, in which she sees Larry recede from his pugilistic forward lean, and back into the sofa and a more thoughtful posture. "I appreciate that your country's situation is very . . . difficult," he says, "but surely American intervention wouldn't help."

"No," Anzor agrees. "I just mean that America doesn't control the entire world. Whatever you may think." His expression has become veiled in a way Isabel is beginning to recognize as camouflage for terrible anger.

"I always thought . . ." Sheila begins, and then looks a bit desperate. "I mean, if we could just have been smarter about it . . . If we could just have been . . . well, nicer to them."

"Nicer to whom?" Anzor sounds as though he is merely asking for clarification.

"Oh, you know. Them. The Soviets. If our government didn't go around saying those stupid things about the Evil Empire. I mean, how provocative can you get? And childish."

"You wanted to be nicer to the Soviets?" Anzor asks, with a more candid incredulity. "You think that would have helped?"

"Well, you know, I study psychological dynamics," Sheila explains eagerly, "and studies definitively show—I mean, really definitively—that if you treat people as if you expected the best from them—as if you trusted them—they'll respond more trustingly. I don't see why that shouldn't apply to politicians too."

"Politicians is not the word I'd use for those Soviet . . . gentlemen," Anzor begins, and then—only Isabel sees this—makes a private, dismissive shrug, as if to say, I give up.

Sheila looks confused, and Larry puts his hand on hers to silence her. "You know, I think it's time to have something to eat," he says, resuming the jovial tone of a good host; and they transfer to the dining room, with its splendid long oak table. Everyone takes the opportunity to turn away from the subject. The elusive elephant in the room is successfully ignored; or perhaps has left altogether, as Sheila and Larry offer food and Hungarian anecdotes with equal generosity. To Isabel's great relief, Anzor joins in, turning into a perfectly charming, jovial dinner companion.

On the way down in the elevator, however, he doesn't say a word. Insofar as is possible in his light jacket, he hunkers down into the collar, as if it were a fur coat or a large woolen scarf. He opens the door for Isabel politely; and then, as they come out into the half-lit courtyard, he says, loudly enough so that she's worried Sheila and Larry might still hear, "What utter . . . crap. What world are they living in, anyway?"

"Please," she says, pointing her finger up toward a window. She thinks she sees their silhouettes through the semi-transparent curtains.

"And these are the rulers of the world. The master class."

"Oh come on," Isabel says. "They teach a few students about

abstruse theory. Or some self-betterment techniques for people who are . . . unhappy. I don't think that qualifies them as the masters of the universe." Her own annoyance is finally matching his.

"You don't understand how the world works," he says flatly. He's walking at a deliberate distance from her, as if touching her might ignite him to open violence.

"You're right, I probably don't," Isabel says. "But I understand that they mean well. That they're my friends and . . . yes, good people. They actually wish the world were a better place. They hate the idea of power, didn't you see that? They don't want to *rule* over anyone. As you so quaintly put it."

"They don't have to *want* to," Anzor says. "They just do. That's why they can talk like that. As if the whole world were like them. As if they controlled everything. As if everyone were just reacting to their bloody . . . niceness. Or the lack of it. This bloody . . . moral imperialism." He pauses for a moment; his breathing is agitated. "They have all the power in the world, that's why they can pretend to hate power. Such nice people." His sarcasm is acid. "It's bloody faking, that's what it is. Didn't you see how . . . he . . . talked to me?"

"They seemed to be interested in what you had to say—"

"Seemed. Seemed. As long as I told them noble savage stories. 'What you have to understand . . .'" He mimics Larry's tone, accurately and furiously. "All we are allowed to have is great stories. People behaving like noble savages. Of suffering like savages. Great . . . *material*. Thinking, that's for them. It's they who understand the world."

"Oh, Anzor . . ." she begins, and then stops. She looks at his hunched silhouette, his glowering eyes; she sees that he feels he's been slighted, patronized, though she can't grasp why. In all his vulnerability, he seems to her more powerful than her friends. Much more powerful. He's fired with the injustices his people have suffered and the justice of his cause; he can hold them moral hostage with surprising ease. But she doesn't say any of this to him.

"Perhaps you took this remark too seriously," she says instead.

His voice is cut through with acid. "So it means nothing, what they say? They don't mean anything, they're just talking? Is that what you mean?" He turns toward her angrily. "Because that's exactly the problem!"

"I guess I have lower expectations of dinner-party conversations than you," Isabel says.

"You don't even expect people to be responsible for what they say," he goes on, ignoring her attempt at conciliation. "Not even your intellectuals. They can say anything they want. Like children. Self-indulgent children. The best and the brightest, isn't that what you call them?"

"Stop saying 'you'," she says in exasperation. "I'm not a representative of the country."

"Well then, what do you want me to say?" Anzor asks. "At least you can stand up for . . . something. For your position."

"I have no position," she says quietly, feeling a kind of resignation. She thinks, I don't. I was not meant for this. This is not the way I understand the world . . . She feels an obscure sense of bad faith. Is this willful ignorance, willful innocence . . . Perhaps Larry is right about her; perhaps everyone is right.

Anzor grips her by the shoulders roughly, and turns her round, so that she faces him. "Don't," he says through tightened lips, his eyes hooded—"At least don't patronize me."

"What do you mean—" she begins.

"You don't even have the respect to get angry at me," he brings out. His grip remains tight. "To take me seriously."

"I'm getting angry now," she says and pulls away.

"That's the problem with . . . all of you," he says grimly. For the first time, she sees something hard in his face, some twist of his mouth that has cruelty in it. "You have all this power, and you don't care. You think if you say a few nice things over dinner . . . that reprieves you from everything. You're without passions. How can you understand people who have them?!"

"You think I have no passions," she says quietly.

He releases his grip, and hunches more deeply into his collar; then looks up. "No, not you," he says, and his face clarifies, as if he were coming back to himself, out of some inner storm. "You know I don't mean you."

He takes her hand and lays it in his, to examine it wonderingly. She can feel his anger receding, being replaced by something else. He says, "You can summon . . . everything with this hand."

She thinks that maybe now she is being patronized, and that perhaps she deserves it. No ideas but in music, that has been her credo. Insufficient, perhaps, to the world in which she finds herself. In which she never expected to find herself. But as he brings her hand up to his lips, as if it were a small living creature, as she feels the heat of contact and of his wanting her, she senses, again, his fleshly vulnerability and his breathing presence; and she responds with her own heat, her own need.

Prague

Prague, the burnished city, the throbbing site of still fresh History, the latest playing field of the international young. The human traffic on the Charles Bridge is in gridlock. She weaves her way laboriously among the squatting street musicians, the couples nuzzling each other's mouths, the young nomads with their humped backpacks; she's part of the crowd. In Wenceslas Square, a camera is thrust in her hand by a young couple wanting to be photographed. "Against that building, there!" the

149

young man requests excitedly. "Where Havel spoke!" She smiles at them and wonders if they feel they're unique individuals standing on the stage of history, the most exciting play of all. If everyone in the endless stream crossing the bridge feels that. Further on, boutiques with Bohemian glass; an inconspicuous house which for some reason reminds her of a Sienese painting she saw recently, somewhere. She looks up at a flurry of robins swooping down on some treasure of breadcrumbs; looks up at the wispy white cloud, passing; and is suddenly pierced by incompleteness. There are only these fragments, grazing the retina, only her one self, moving in and out of the great historical museum, as provisional and wispy as all the others. She sidles into a crowded café, opens Wolfe's *Journal*.

August 7, 1982

The cellist today. She had the sheer nerve to tell me I should live more in the moment. Aside from the arrogance of such a statement, I was struck by its naivety. Living in the moment! Does she not understand the supreme difficulty of such a feat? What it takes to free a moment to be itself? Of course she doesn't. She thinks living in the moment is equivalent to "having fun." I have observed these youths of both sexes trying to "have fun" at their drunken parties, throwing each other into the pond at night, or hooting at each other on forest paths. I have heard their false and grim sounds, straining to laugh the hardest, to shout loudest, until, presumably, they reach the acme point of fun . . .

One of the young nomads, a hefty, pasty-faced girl, has approached her table, and is asking if she can sit down. Isabel gives a cursory nod, and the girl—she reminds her of someone, who is it?—carefully swivels herself out of her large backpack, which promptly trips up a fast-moving waiter. "Oooff," she emits, self-explanatorily, as she plops into a chair. "*Sprechen Sie Deutsch?*" Isabel shakes her head no, hoping that'll be the end of it; but the girl obligingly switches to English.

"Many people, yes?" she interrogatively declares. Isabel nods, minimally; but the girl doesn't need encouragement.

"I travel through seven countries already," she states, with satisfaction. Isabel is about to pick up her book, but the girl continues confidingly. "I enjoy the travels very much. I keep a notebook, every day. I feel it is important to do this. So it will not get lost, you know, my experience. My adventures. I've had very interesting adventures."

"Oh yes?" Isabel asks. She now knows who the girl reminds her of. It's Sabine, Kolya's long-ago tenant.

The girl looks at Isabel slyly. "In Bucharest, someone tried to make me a slave."

Isabel is mildly interested in what story the girl might concoct. "A slave?" she repeats.

"Yes," the girl says eagerly. "I was traveling with some girls from the Ukraine . . . and they tried to trap us in this house. So they could sell us later."

"But why are you telling this to a stranger?" Isabel asks, hoping this will indicate her disbelief.

"Oh, my name is Monika," the girl says, as if that would take care of the problem. "And I don't mind telling about it. It was kind of . . . exciting."

"Ah," Isabel says, and Monika proceeds to tell her story pell-mell, and with enough unlikely detail so that Isabel begins to believe it.

"They just trapped you?" she nevertheless asks. "On the street?" Even though Monika doesn't seem to be lying, the tale she unfolds is improbably medieval, with its girl-snatching and pirates on the global highway.

"No, it wasn't like that, they invited us into their house, and we went along, and then, you know, we were locked up."

"I hope nothing . . . awful happened," Isabel says. Monika seems very young, and is biting her lip childishly.

"No, because I called my mum on my mobile phone, and she called our embassy and they did something about it. But it was interesting, you know? A real adventure. It's all in my diary."

"And the others . . ." Isabel begins, but Monika's attention has been diverted by something outside the window. "Jan!" she calls out, waving energetically toward a tall, long-haired young man passing on the street. He waves back lazily, and makes his way desultorily into the café.

"He is a friend," Monika announces to Isabel in an undertone, but with some excitement. "He's nice. We met in Barcelona. That was also an adventure."

The boy puts down his backpack, and lowers himself into a chair in the spirit of defeated impassivity. His left leg begins jiggling very fast, his knee lifting quite high.

"Jan is going to Africa," Monika informs Isabel proudly. "He is going to do some work in the refugee camps. In Egypt. They've lots of people from Liberia there. I might go too, after I do some college. I'd like to do something good, you know? To help. Things are really terrible there, like the worst. You tell her, Jan."

The boy proceeds to tell her, at first lazily, then with increasing seriousness, about the wars in Liberia, the maimings, the killings, the child soldiers and the refugees who have fled from there, and with whom he wants to work. His leg stops jiggling, and his sentences begin to emerge in unwilled grammatical entirety. Isabel asks why he has chosen refugees in Egypt out of all the possible horror-riddled places. That seems to be the wrong question, though, because his face falls back into its bored affectlessness, and the knee begins its autistic movement. "Because I googled it first," he says.

Isabel begins to get up, but Monika, in an effort to detain her, wants to know what she's doing in Prague. Isabel hesitates, then tells her she's giving a concert.

"Wow," Monika responds wholeheartedly. "What kind of concert?"

"A piano recital," Isabel says, wondering whether they have reached the limit of common vocabulary.

"You mean, like classical?" Monika asks, incredulously.

Isabel nods.

"Wow, that's like so . . . romantic."

Isabel laughs at the incongruity of the word; the word which will not die. On an impulse, she asks her entirely accidental acquaintances if they'd like to come and hear her. She could leave tickets for them. She isn't quite sure why she's proposing this; perhaps it's some youth-improving impulse, her form of the missionary urge.

"Oh, that would be so cool," Monika says enthusiastically. "Don't you think it would be cool, Jan?"

Jan stops jiggling his knee and looks at Isabel with a perfectly sensible, polite expression which seems to emerge from another personality, another kind of life. "That's very nice of you," he says, in his compacted, gutturally accented English. He's told her he is Danish. "I've been listening to a lot of Schnabel lately. We would very much like to come."

. . . the acme point of fun. They think by doing this, they will at last experience the moment to the full. Poor young brutes. Do they not know that such a feat takes nothing less than Belief? That in order to experience any one moment, you need to understand the meaning of Time itself? Try to hear a note, or a chord, outside the edifice of structure. Try to compose a succession of notes, without having some idea about the ends to which they are used.

That is our difficulty, at the present time. We need to know our ends, before we can invent the means. Otherwise, we will only produce groping, meaningless sounds, as these youths produce their strained, jarring noises.

No liberty but in structure—even if the aim of structure is the abolition of structure. But we have tried that too. We have come to the end even of abolitions. Where, then, can we go next? Through what forms can we begin to liberate sounds that will express new meanings? That, in essence, is our great problem. Or perhaps my problem. My thorny dilemma, my sting of nettles, my bloody battle on the blank death-riddled ground. And she'd have me live "more in the moment."

In the Green Room, she hums to herself. She's feeling quite relaxed. Maybe it's because she won't be able to read the reviews, which will come out in Czech. Or maybe because, in this musical city, making music seems like a natural activity. As Jane would wish it. She's just going to sow some musical beauty among the audience; she trusts them to recognize it and absorb it without strain.

. . . hah, listen, it's kind of neat, thinks Monika, Row P, Seat 13, and I know her, I know the artist! / what is she playing, *Davidsbündlertänze*, crazy title, but it's kind of sexy / mmhmm, close your eyes, it's soft like being caressed / like when Mother took care of me / before all her stupid boyfriends / tender, tender / Isabel, great name, so glamorous, she must have lovers / close your eyes, yes, candlelight, he holds her hand, so handsome

/ Jan, so handsome / I would like to / but he doesn't / maybe he's shy / me too, I'm actually sort of shy // . . . ah, that's lovely, thinks Jan, not like Schnabel, more tender, intimate, she's a woman / ah, but she's good / how does she get to be that good, must be lots of practice like carpentry / my music lessons / I wish I'd done more / must take CDs to Africa, in case / in case / don't want to be maimed tortured—no! / don't mind dying, but no pain / Dad said I'm too valuable / too valuable for what? / why am I valuable? / ah, listen, that music curling, uncurling / like singing, softest voice / jerk wanker like wanking off fuck fuck fuck who're you kidding, who're you kidding, I'm so afraid / but that piece, her up there onstage, so calm / I'll remember this // . . . ah, listen, the tenderness, poetry, the distillation, thinks Sunil Patel / pure lyricism, no dross / how to do that in my novel, writing so *prosaic* that's the problem / no lift-off, oh God why can't it lift off like music, into pure motion / listen, new section, ah, *interesting*, short sections maybe that's the answer / why spell everything out stupid words, stupid story business, this happened then that happened, plod plod plod / Aahh!! What, what was that, why did it grab me seize me, was it the sudden drop? / wow / contrast, yes, must remember, more contrast, light and dark chiaroscuro / bravura, brava, bravery / courage you need courage / and look, she's beautiful, the lips just slightly opened St. Teresa head thrown back / St. Teresa . . . orgasmic, yes, ecstasy, yes, except she's doing something, controlling the piano / ah, listen, that melody meandering weaving not making a point, just suggesting / the way we meander inside our lives our thought not knowing / ah, the leaping chords God it must be difficult / to say everything at once, yes, more courage more nakedness say what you mean / dare to say it / naked truth, raw truth / how express it // . . . and she is mine, thinks Anzor, I've held her fucked her had her / ah, but listen, look, that glow up there, she has it, Isabel / I know how she loves, I've loved her / they wouldn't believe,

none of them would, would throw me out of here, the savage /
ah, listen, the line, sinuous, like her body when she turns toward
me, the curve of her hip the thigh lifting / yes I know where
the music comes from, know exactly, all the places / her hands
so strong, so sensitive / ah, the quiet, tender quiet, how does she
do it / she has truth in her, a kind of truth except / she doesn't
understand none of them understand, they're stupid, they do not
understand the hatred our hatred the passions which burn / they
think they are safe superior good / ah, it makes me sick, their
goodness their niceness, my people are smarter faster, they know
more, they've lived more, they deserve their country we will
kill for it whoever it takes, it is kill or be killed / these cow-like
soft slow unsuspicious people / so good / honestly, I could stran-
gle their goodness, their time is over, they do not deserve what
they have / ah, but listen that line, she grabs me again, twists
my heart, Schumann knew passion, he must have known, you
can hear it / her hands I know them, touched them, they have
touched me, tonight her body it will bend as she is bending
now . . .

Stockholm

This time, Anzor is coming to meet her in her hotel room, late
at night. It's a new intimacy, this nocturnal arrival. She imagines
an aerial map of the routes they've traveled, the traceless trajectories along which he has followed her. He's probably getting off
the plane right now, moving swiftly through the always moving
crowd. She thinks about Monika and Jan, who might be anywhere at all. Peculiar nomads, with no tribe to accompany them,
no song lines to follow. But now she waits, in this northern city,
jeweled lights warming up the windows across the street.

Anzor is agitated when he comes in, and paces around the room, picking up objects aimlessly, and putting them down again unseeingly. He removes a small bottle of Scotch from the minibar, and drinks it in a large, rude gulp. He tells her the conflict in his country is escalating. One of his friends has been killed. One—and this is much worse, he says, pouring himself another slug of whisky from another miniature bottle—has been caught by the Russians. The thugs. He will be tortured; he will be humiliated.

"How awful," she says.

"It is going to get worse," he says grimly. "I am a worse traitor every day I stay away."

"Anzor," she begins, carefully, "what is this conflict really about. I mean, is there no peace possible, must it go on like that?"

He bends his head backward and pours whisky into his throat like a peasant, like the Russian boys she saw on the train a long time ago. Then he looks at her from narrowed eyes, with a sort of brazenness, a nearly open hostility.

"You don't know what you're talking about," he says, just controlling contempt. "If we compromised now, all that we have done would be meaningless. The death of my uncle. My father's only brother. The deaths of my friends."

"But the violence . . ." she says.

"We will do anything it takes," he says. "They've done . . . everything to us." His eyes are filmed now with some excess of emotion that gives him a half-blind, an entranced look.

"I hate them so much," he says. "My hate is complete."

"You frighten me," she says, and hears her own voice deepen into a more complete seriousness.

"I hate," he repeats, evenly. "But in my hate is my love. That is what you must understand. I hate because of everything I love. Because of how . . . strongly I love."

He looks at her directly, a straight gaze; and she can feel her own eyes going still as she looks back at him.

"Please," she says nevertheless, trying to rein in the quickening dark currents of excitement between them, the escalation of her pulse, "I don't recognize you when you talk like that."

"I tell you the truth," he says quietly. "It is . . . who I am. I do not want to lose my rage. It is the fuel I burn with. And as long as my country is burning—"

"You're frightening me," she repeats.

"There's no love without hate," he says, as if stating a QED. His QED. "And no dignity. You must know when your enemies wish you ill. And you must answer them." He looks at her almost threateningly. "Do you understand?"

"Yes," she says, in a kind of submission.

He reaches out his arm and pulls her toward himself, speaking to her more directly.

"I love my country," he says. "I want to defend it with whatever I've got. It is what I stand for."

"But what is that, what is it you stand for?" she half whispers, out of her own, hypnotized state. "Aside from your anger . . ."

"Can you not understand," he says, as if she were a student slow to learn her lesson, "that there is justice involved? Something more than myself? That our cause is just?"

An announcement of a theme, a clarion call. His credo. From her proximity, she sees raw emotion working its way into Anzor's eyes, the muscles of his mouth. She is riveted by the naked simplicity of it, the dense disturbing force of his conviction. She gets up, and walks across the room, trying to regain her composure, to reclaim herself. She begins to formulate a question about what it is he does, exactly; but some civilized impulse stops her from doing so. She's not used to not believing people. Or perhaps she doesn't want, exactly, to know.

Later, she stares up at the ceiling in the dark, thinking, what does it mean to stand for something, what is it she should understand . . . Standing for something: is that what gives Anzor his upright spine, his straight direct gaze? She imagines the mountainous vistas that for him have the spaciousness of beauty, and wonders what it is that matters to him in that distant landscape, as only the nearest things matter to her, only what enters and lives inside her till it is transmogrified into inner music, her cells, her skin.

Next day, in a morning mood, Anzor suggests they go to an exhibition of new Euro artists he has read about in an English-language paper. "I still have some resident . . . no, residual interest in this kind of thing," he says, sounding again like his urbane daytime self. "And anyway, I want to forget . . . other things for a while."

The gallery is in a low, industrial-looking building, and the spaces inside are airy and white. In one, a Dutch artist, a tall man with close-cropped blond hair, is beginning a talk about his work. "This is my sculpture from a few years ago," he says, pointing to an object in the corner of the room. As far as Isabel can tell, the artefact is a chunk of dry wood, with some indefinable feathery material and bits of shiny metal affixed to it in a seemingly random way. "That incrustation," the artist says, "is a trace of a once-living creature, a bird that died against the tree. But there are also chemicals on the wood which have pervaded the forest." He pauses to give his audience time to absorb this. "I wanted to make a reflection on this. On natural and unnatural decay. On the way we are killing nature so it is disappearing. Nature dies anyway, but we are contributing to its dying." He turns on his PowerPoint and an image comes up, which causes some sounds of discreetly suppressed dismay to emanate from the small audience. The image shows a man—he looks like the artist, though his face is obscured by some impasto effects—undergoing multiple torments, or humiliations. His arms are tied in front and marked with reddish cuts. From the back, a knife held by an anonymous hand approaches his sternum; from the front, something like a baseball bat is lifted against his groin. "This is the work I am doing now," the artist says. "Because I believe today we also need to reflect on the death of man. Of the human." His voice is soft and tinged with compassion, as if to suggest that it gives him pain to inflict this pain on the audience; but it must be done.

A hand goes up in the small audience, and a woman speaks. "Do you think this degree of . . . violence is necessary for art?" she asks.

"Art must take us closer to the edge," the artist answers, in an explanatory tone. "The edge of where we are. Because the edge is *where* we are. That is what I as an artist believe." He looks wan suddenly, less certain. "That is my credo, you see," he declares again, as if he wanted to persuade his interlocutor, or perhaps himself. "We must dare to go beyond where we are. Otherwise, we have nowhere to go."

The woman nods, without looking convinced. The artist clicks his PowerPoint to more images. A muscular arm, incised with Xs and Os, as in a child's game; a woman's face, with a flap of skin peeled open, perhaps in plastic surgery. A painting of a man's upright body, surrounded by large penises.

"The death of the human," the artist repeats, pointing to the images with a sort of resignation. "That is the precipice for us. The new abyss."

Anzor turns to Isabel, and points his thumb toward the door. She nods in agreement, and they get up, with the artist pausing briefly as they exit.

"I'm sorry, there's only so much I can take," Anzor brings out, once the door is shut behind them. He's walking fast through the gallery, without looking at her.

"Yes," she says, in a mollifying tone. "That wasn't . . . great, I agree."

"I suppose he thinks this is *transgression*," Anzor picks up, as they walk out on the street, his voice rigid with scorn. "This . . . triviality. This . . . pretend danger. He should come to my country, if he wants to experience danger. This stuff . . . it's safe, ugly and safe!" He has gripped Isabel's wrist, and she edges it out of his grasp, careful not to do it irritably.

"It's probably *subsidized*," Anzor continues, infusing the phrase with all his contempt. "I know the Dutch, they subsidize this kind of thing with lots of money. The more . . . vile the better. They can't stand how safe their lives are, so they have this . . . subsidized transgression. So they can thumb their noses at . . . anything that matters and not pay for it. They get paid for it instead. He probably got some nice vacations in Dubrovnik out of that . . . rubbish. They love coming to Dubrovnik, the Dutch."

"Yes," Isabel repeats, in a conciliatory tone. "It's quite appalling, I agree."

But Anzor won't be interrupted. "You have this puny idea of freedom," he continues, in full furious flow. "You think that if you mock things that matter, then you're *free*. You think . . . urinating all over a few religious symbols is freedom. Or having more . . . bloody options. You think you can give human beings what they need by giving them *options*. Or letting them play these games. These 'I can do whatever I bloody want to' games. And you expect the rest of the world won't find this . . . ridiculous. You expect people not to choke!"

"I agree," she says, baffled yet again by the escalation of Anzor's anger. "Please notice that I agree."

The expression he turns on her makes her recoil. "You agree, but it doesn't matter to you," he says, coldly. "You don't see . . . the implications."

"What are the implications?" she asks. "This was just . . . an art exhibition. What possible consequences can it have? I mean, what on earth would you like to do about it?"

"I would like to blow it up," Anzor says. His voice is strangled. "The exhibition and the whole rotten show. Then start over again." Well, she has had similar thoughts, in strange streets, in the becalmed cities. Smash it all up and start from the beginning, from the ground up, from the smithy of the soul.

"And what would you do then," she asks, and this time she wants to know the answer. "What would you put in its place?"

"Some natural human dignity," he answers instantly, and hurls on, his passion hardly spent. "Some respect for . . . what matters. Because you can't have anything . . . beautiful, or good, without respect. No matter what these . . . types think. They're not serious. They have no . . . honor. If anyone *remembers*"—his voice is acrid with bitterness—"what that is."

"Please," she says. "At whom are you so furious?" They're walking down a narrow street, lined with enchanting houses, their windows sparkling in the clear northern sun.

He makes an effort to calm himself. "Not you," he says. "Not at you."

"Shall we go into a café?" she suggests, and they do. They sit silently for a while, and then he takes her hands in his. She sees that he is looking for a way to backtrack from his fury.

"It's probably what's happening in my country," he finally brings out, although it clearly costs him an effort to say this. "That's why I can't stand . . . these stupid games."

He was talking on his mobile phone when she woke up; and she now asks, carefully, whether there was something in the conversation to upset him. He hesitates, then says tonelessly that a friend, who was badly wounded a few days ago, is dead. Aslan, he adds, as if not naming him were indecent. They had known each other since elementary school.

A shadow has entered the Stockholm café, and she senses it,

like a brush of darkness, an ominous dark wing. She thinks, this is more reality than I've bargained for. The violence of the world has penetrated the quiet interior, with its marble-topped tables and gleaming mirrors, and she wants to fend it off, protest that it has nothing to do with her. She feels small; vulnerable. Too small even to try to understand. She's here to give a concert, that is her mission.

"How terrible," she says. "I'm so sorry."

"He will not go unavenged," Anzor states, and the word, too, jars, like a small explosion. "This is what the Russians don't understand. Because they're fighting without faith. Just for oil. For power. We're fighting for our survival. Our freedom. Yes," he says, as if to counter her objections. "Freedom. As that . . . *artist* would never understand it. As none of . . . them"—he makes an inclusive gesture toward the street and passersby—"would understand. Because you can only understand what it means to be free if you have been . . . a slave."

His voice is choked with fury, and she imagines it expand till it covers the café they are in and the city; till it covers everything. It seems that limitless. She wants to flee to her practice room; to her music, in which violence and rage are already transmuted into beauty.

"It must be awful to lose a friend . . . this way," she finally says, in a muted voice.

"Yes," he cuts in, icily. "It is. But it is not only about one friend. It is about much more."

"I mean, I understand how this . . . must affect you." She sees a flicker of annoyance on his face, and rephrases again: "I mean, how much is at stake. I think . . . I understand."

He says, "Good." The word is menacing, like a well-aimed bullet.

"It's just your rage . . ." she starts again, and then stops. She's floundering.

"So being angry is not nice, is that the idea?" Anzor is looking at her evenly, and his voice is compacted to solid ice. "I know this idea. About how you should be nice to everybody. No matter what they've done to you." She feels hurt, as she knows she's meant to, but he doesn't let up. He fixes his eyes on her, to make sure she's following. "I know this idea and I find it . . . contemptible. I know your nice men. They don't care. They don't give a damn. That's why they can pretend to be *fair* to everybody, even if somebody wants to kill them. Because actually nobody has done anything to them. That's why they can be so *nice*." Anzor stops briefly, and then continues, as if carried on the wind of his argument. "People whom I . . . love have been hurt. They have been killed. It would be . . . ignoble of me not to avenge them. Not to hate those who have killed them. If you lose your rage, you lose . . . your self-respect. And then you begin to live . . . like this." He indicates the street again, with a comprehensive gesture. "Dishonorably. For nothing at all."

But that evening, they fall into hungry closeness again, with a ferocity that is almost impersonal. What do Anzor's words matter, the overlay of stiff clumsy assertions . . . In the abandon of the lovemaking, it doesn't matter what he stands for, or who she is. She is body, mind, a conduit for experience, part of the human chain on the Charles Bridge. As she is a conduit for the music in the concert hall, music they all exchange like a substance which binds them together . . . Her consciousness, wide-open and impersonal, enters Anzor's, and senses his shame at being here, in this safe place, senses the call of his comrades, the high emotion of battle, fear and trembling transmogrifying among the warm bodies and burning eyes till they rise to a self-forgetful exaltation . . . till death does not matter. Yes, she can sense it with all its dread, its awe. Anzor is talking, from some great dreamy distance, he is telling her about Kazakhstan where he went as a child, the empty majestic desert and a tent where he stayed with the muzhiks. The horses, Anzor is saying, the horses were so wild and beautiful, that was what I wanted to tell you about, and the muzhiks had such grace as they rode without saddles, and Isabel isn't sure whether she has seen the horses herself, galloping across a reddish plane, they seem to arise out of her mind, dreamlike and wild, with a rider raising his long whip and squeezing the animal's haunches in a shared fierce dance. Perhaps she knows this from Glinka and Mussorgsky, this wild ballet, the steppe, wild and spacious. Then he'd stride into the tent and get dead drunk, Anzor is saying about the muzhik, it was so stifling and smelly in that tent, and the whip was always with him, and sometimes he'd pick it up and turn it on his wife and children. "How horrible," she says, beginning to come out of her trance, but Anzor is saying, and yet the horsemen were beautiful, I rode with them once and I thought I was made of that earth and the wind . . . Bellum, bello, bel canto.

Then Anzor says, "Isabel!" emphatically, and she feels instantly brought back, summoned by his call, the pressure of his demand on her.

He rolls over on his back, and says, "Ah, I need those spaces; the mountains, the stones, the stone towers. I cannot breathe free when my country does not breathe free."

She says, coming into ordinary consciousness now, "But isn't that a sort of . . . fantasy?" and he rears up above her as if he could hit her. She quivers slightly, and says defensively, "I mean, you could live here too. You would be fine here."

"What would you have me do," he asks, sarcastically. "Take some academic job, like your friends? Anyway, what job could I get, except some low-paid junk? You think I am a candidate for anything but . . . crumbs?" He half turns away from her, and she puts a soothing hand on his chest.

"I would rather have a real purpose," he says, in a deeper

voice. "That is more than your friends have, with their great Midwestern jobs and their great *theories*. At least, I can have my fate."

"Those are very big words," she says, partly out of loyalty to Sheila and Larry.

"They are not just words," Anzor says stubbornly. "They are how I live."

She sighs and thinks, if this were only in the music. She thinks of Chopin, frail and ill in Paris, conjuring up out of his instrument the grandeur of his country's revolution as if it held the essence of human beauty. His tears for the revolution's failure. His music, in which everything is contained at once: fierceness and tenderness, violence and love, triumph and the most wistful sadness. She thinks, if this were in the past, I would be waving good-bye to my freedom-fighter sweetheart, I would raise flags to the passing soldiers, would sew mourning shrouds. Too late for that, surely. Too late. But there is the living man beside her, his chest rising and falling, filled with his Cause, his fate. Is there something she does not recognize when it's near; which she understands only when it's shaped into music, or into the past?

After a while, the lovely duet which ends in blending takes them over again. But some tension has entered into their dealings with each other, making her body more taut, attuning her to the darker undertones in his intensities. She tries to remember, memorize them, so she can decode them later. For now, she wants to yield to this, to be lost to herself so she can be wholly herself, as though she were infused by some vital essence, molding her body into unerring motions, lines of longing, lines of beauty. Wholly herself, if only for those moments.

*

She straps herself in for the short flight with a sense of relief. In no-place, there is nothing she must conclude or decide. She can weave in and out of her thoughts; her conversation with Wolfe.

August 10, 1982

Lesson with I.M. She was playing parts of the *Kreisleriana*. For some reason, she was having a hard time with that piece. Suddenly, she stopped, without even coming to the end of the section. Her head was lowered so that at first I did not understand what was going on. Then I saw. She was crying. She was wincing from her effort to stop, but she couldn't. There was a steady trickle of tears. What is wrong? I asked. Has anything happened? I was worried that something I said had bruised her. For all the strength of her playing, she is a delicate creature. But that was not the case. When she calmed down, she told me that the *Kreisleriana* brought back her brother. She had to gasp and wince before being able to say the next thing. He was a younger brother who died in tragic circumstances. The *Kreisleriana* had been one of his favorite pieces. They'd listened to it together shortly before he died.

I looked at her more closely than ever before. I did not want so much to calm her down, as to assure her that what she was feeling could be borne. That it even had a kind of beauty. I said, "Death has always been the great source." She turned her face up with her sudden, transparent curiosity. "A source of what?" she asked. "Of music," I said. "Of art." She looked at me more calmly. "I'd rather have my brother back," she said. "You cannot," I said. "But you have your grief. It is a very human feeling." She seemed to be absorbing what I said with her wide eyes. Then she sighed as if she had been relieved of something and, with a great simplicity, said, "Thank you." I asked her if she wanted to continue the lesson, and she said yes. She insisted on going back to the *Kreisleriana*, and this time, played it with such limpid simplicity that there was no need for me to make any comment.

I felt such sympathy for her; almost a camaraderie. And yet, although I am ashamed to record this, I envied her too. I envied her the ability to feel so tenderly for one particular person; to have one particular person to mourn.

Vienna

The beginning of Beethoven's 111th calls for an almost martial resolve, the foreshortened, abrupt rhythms a summons to a kind of action, some necessary battle. The sounds she hears herself making as she practices express a different foreshortening, a lack of breath. She misses Anzor, her body misses Anzor. She cuts herself off in mid-phrase, in annoyance. Rothman would never allow himself to be undone like this, would never give up his force, his musical potency. But then, Rothman loves his power, and uses music to express it. She's heard how he once competed with a fellow pianist for the loudest fortissimos. She laughed when she heard this, but perhaps she shouldn't have. She knows that music calls for power, as being-in-the-world calls for power. And yet, if she loses her ability to be undone, she'll lose her strength, she's sure of it . . . That's her source, that's where her kind of power begins, in her willingness to register the tremors inside herself and give them voice. She goes over the short difficult trill in the opening passage, begins to feel a gathering of momentum, of forward force. It is still not finished, she thinks, the woman question. Perhaps it's never finished, as the question of desire is never finished, the question of giving yourself up to something you love. Perhaps Rothman after all knows this too . . . As Beethoven surely knew it and Schubert. Without that, what are you, she thinks, except a mind arrested in a body; without being permeable how can you expand beyond your borders, without submitting how can you burst through your confinement. She puts her fingers on the opening notes of the Sonata's second movement, the simple chorale progressions. "This is how it is, this is how it is," the theme seems to be saying, with the most gentle acceptance. Her breathing deepens at last and alters to comport with that mild and lovely statement, and then quickens with the music's labor out of the quiet accord into a storm of syncopated rhythms, working and winding through a dense, strange complexity to a crystalline register beyond turbulence and desire. Yes, she thinks; yes. This is where truth lies, without statements or conclusions; this is where it can be attained.

Dinner. It's post-concert, and she'd rather not go. But she must, she's promised Jonathan, whom she has known since their student days at Juilliard, and who is now an important executive for a recording company. She must go, must meet people, must converse. Bourgeois heroism, rather different from what Anzor has in mind. A sotto voce pang of guilt follows: bourgeois heroism is Peter's phrase.

"Well, I'll be damned!" Jonathan exclaims genially on opening the door, and gives her a robust bear hug. "This is great! Our star has come." He still has the powerful physique of a lumberjack, as he did when he so incongruously chose the flute as his heart's instrument. He is wearing a black shirt and a fashionably loose jacket; his hair, like an allusion to an earlier persona, is tied into a short ponytail.

The apartment is a hypermodern space carved out of a nineteenth-century interior, with high ceilings and white walls, and impressively sleek pieces of furniture scattered on the polished parquet floor. A slim Japanese woman in a flat graphite-gray dress, looking as streamlined as everything else in the apartment, comes out soundlessly into the foyer. "Noriko," Jonathan introduces her, with a sidelong glance of proprietorial pride. "She lives here too. She does futures. I mean, the markets," he clarifies, on seeing Isabel's confusion. "She's a whizz at it."

At the table, she is seated next to a loose-limbed Englishman, who turns out to be the literary editor of a London paper, here on a brief visit. "A sort of reconnaissance expedition," he explains, "to look at the literary scene here, and how it reflects the political scene. Or doesn't."

"You know, I have a gripe with you," a woman across the table, dressed in a multicolored silk kaftan announces, addressing the editor rather sharply. "Or rather with that place you work for."

"I am interested in all complaints leveled at my humble paper," the editor responds with excessively polite alacrity. "We like to know our readers' views."

"Not so humble," the woman retorts, refusing to be jollied along. "You exercise lots of influence, and you know it. I understand, for example, that the prime minister was very pleased by your review of his biography. Or should I say hagiography."

"But surely you're not suggesting that we ran a good review *in order* to please the PM," the editor politely distinguishes. Ah yes, Isabel remembers this technique from her London days. Spell out the implicit insult, so the opponent has no insinuation behind which to hide. Do the English learn it in their debating clubs?

"Well, you did assign it to a total . . . shall we say acolyte?" the woman persists. "Though how anyone can still be an acolyte of that toothsome hypocrite is beyond my understanding."

"If he were at least an effective hypocrite," a dark-eyed bearded man speaking with a German accent throws in. "But from what we can observe here, his government is incompetent to govern. I do not want to suggest the British are inefficient, I do not believe in such stereotypes. And yet we cannot help but observe the mess they are making of everything, from taxes to transport."

"Taxes notwithstanding, the economy seems to be on a definite upswing," the editor throws in casually, skewering a piece of boeuf bourguignon with his fork. He knows he's making a provocation.

"Don't tell me you give him credit for that," the woman in the silk kaftan rears up. "He's been lucky to have overseen super-growth in the global markets, that's all."

"Well, I suppose we would give him full credit if the economy declined," the editor observes, speaking even more languidly than before.

"What do you think, Noriko?" someone asks. Noriko has been silent till now. "Is it luck or good policy?"

"It is all faith," Noriko responds in a startlingly loud, clipped voice. "Faith in the future."

"Ah yes, faith, that's very important," someone mutters, and the man who asked the question nods slowly, as if unsure whether Noriko has uttered a platitude, or given him a Zen koan to contemplate.

A small silence falls upon the table.

"What I don't understand is why there's no protest any-where," a Canadian woman bursts out passionately. "I mean, where's the dissent? The ideology? The idealism?"

"What would you protest, the improving economy?" the editor annoyingly asks.

"The betrayal of . . . all ideals," the woman proclaims, an edge of high-minded righteousness in her voice. "Certainly, in our neighboring country—"

"Oh, c'mon, you guys." This from a long-haired local rock musician. "Can't we lighten up? Put on Oasis, or something?"

"My country is like a terrible awkward giant—" Jonathan interjects, ignoring the rocker's appeal; but the Canadian woman leaps in to finish the thought. "Awkward giant is exactly right. You just *walk* all over my country, without even knowing where you're stepping. I mean, what do Americans know about Canada . . ."

"It's good to have someone to hate," the editor states neutrally, bending over a cube of meat which he places on his fork with painstaking precision.

A small silence again, after which a clean-cut American in a black suit and tie speaks carefully. "I regret having to say this, but in my line of work, you can see why we are not liked by the rest of the world. I'm afraid I've been forced to see this clearly." He apparently studies models of transition. "I mean, have you read the figures on the gap between the rich and the poor in the last years? Not to speak of the rich and poor nations? Now the reasons for it . . . you know, in my line of work you get to understand that things are very complicated."

"Well, that is certainly true," the editor says, this time with apparent sincerity.

"What do you think?" someone asks Isabel. "You see so much. So many countries."

"I see concert halls, mostly," she demurs, and isn't sure what she should say, or even what she thinks. Or why her errant observations should count. Anzor has been hovering in her mind, in the vicinity of the conversation, providing a tacit commentary. "And from there, you could get the impression that we're living in comfortable times. I mean, on the whole . . ." She feels oddly embarrassed. "But you know, I live this cocooned life . . . I mean, I stay in nice hotels."

"But maybe we all live cocooned lives," the editor cuts in, speaking with some earnestness again. "That's the problem for all of us grizzled revolutionaries. We have won. We don't want to admit it, but that's our problem. The terrible stuff, that's else-where. We got ourselves our welfare state and our equal rights and spa vacations if we're a little stressed, and let's face it, that doesn't leave us in a position from which to hurl grenades, does it? Or even get up on the barricades, supposing we could get up on them after our very nice dinners. Very dispiriting, really. Very discouraging." His tone has slid all the way back from serious-ness to multi-edged irony.

"Oh, honestly, you guys . . ." the rock musician protests again, but nobody takes him up on his mini-revolt, and the conversation moves on, along its familiar grooves. The Discourse; is there anything outside it? She stops following, listens instead to Anzor's hovering commentary. It's just as well he didn't come, he'd hate it all, hate the self-hate, the rightness and the righteousness, the cleverness, the *talk*. Anzor hates his enemies, not himself. But then, Anzor has enemies. The country he professes to love has enemies. But we, Isabel thinks, we've had our bloody bouts and our battles, our civil wars and our revolutions. Now what we have is this. The virtual loop of discourse, circling the globe in some meta-space, carrying its reit-erated messages from Prague to San Francisco, and for all she knows, to Tokyo as well.

"And then, here we are, in Vienna . . ." This, vaguely, from a tall Swedish woman.

"The true land of amnesia," Jonathan states, perhaps a bit too cheerfully. "As is well known."

As everything is well known, Isabel thinks irritably. She's fatigued; she's coming to the end of post-concert adrenaline.

Then the talk moves on to a book about memory and forgetting, and a candid gay novel which is the sensation of the season, and which someone bravely tries to connect to the previous conversation by saying it's actually all about amnesia and repression, and the sublimation of perversity into the Austrian cult of *Kultur*.

"It's actually about high snobbery and low buggery," the editor pronounces unhurriedly, and finally, everyone laughs.

The rock musician stands up suddenly, and announces that he's leaving. "I'm hoping for a little perversity myself before the night is over," he says. "Preferably polymorphous, if I can find it at this hour."

Jonathan beckons her to stay after the others have left, and they move over to a comfortable sofa, while Noriko places herself uprightly in a wooden chair. "You know, you really should record something for us," Jonathan says to Isabel. "You wouldn't believe the weird stuff one finds here. From the fifties. Kind of retro, but you know, in a really hip way."

"Yeah, it's really weird," Noriko throws in in her clipped accent. "He makes me listen to it sometimes."

"We've played some pretty strange things in our time, haven't we?" Jonathan says, directing a comradely look at Isabel. "Remember that piece for sound and silence we did? Half sounds, half silence. I think those were all the directions we had."

"Do I ever," she says, and remembers a younger Jonathan, his long hair half covering his face, as he bent over to blow into the small, elegant instrument. It was never clear why Jonathan, who came from money, and who was large and bursting with energy, wanted to pursue the strait and thankless path of a classical musician. Except that he wanted to be Good; he wanted to find some way to restrain and chastize his power, and music, art, was the last good thing in a world cruddy with greed and big power and money. So they all believed, ardently, and up to a point. It wasn't clear, either, what it was that he lacked as a musician, what kept him from being merely competent. Perhaps it was just musicality. Whatever that is, she now thinks, the intangible element. There is Jonathan, with his large, somewhat stiff frame; and she reflects that for all his wish to give up his power, he could not yield himself to the inward motions of the music, the dancing flux between the notes, or within them.

"You want to do some coke?" Jonathan now inquires. "I have some really good shit, it would perk you right up."

"No!" she says, somewhat too sharply, taken aback by the offer. "No thanks."

"Why, you think only pop musicians get to do drugs?" he asks, more challengingly. "You should see some of your fellow stars. You should see Rothman."

"Oh yeah?" she asks. For some reason, her curiosity has been piqued by Rothman, and the way he seems to sail through his famous life with such seemingly triumphant ease.

"Yeah," Jonathan confirms. "He's really into it. Brings it to the recording studio."

"Well, I don't do that," she says.

"Hey, come on. Why limit yourself?" he asks with a hint of provocation. "You can do anything you want. It's not a limited world."

"I guess because I've got to get up early tomorrow morning," she answers, deflecting the challenge. Noriko in the meantime has got up and now returns with a mirror on which she places, with careful precision, some white powder.

"I'd better be going," Isabel says. "It's late." Jonathan gives her a perfunctory hug in the foyer, and she sees that his eyes have gone vacuous. Some sort of sadness has slid into her own fatigue as well. What is it, she thinks as she walks out onto the yellow-lit street, why the melancholy. She remembers Jonathan and herself, in their overheated, aspiring, competitive student days. He tried hard then to stretch beyond his limits, even as he hunched over his slim instrument. And now what? Jonathan seems sad in his big bulky frame, with the sadness of having gotten most of what he wanted. He's hit his spirit level. It's not a limited world, he said; and she adds, and none of us know how to live in it . . . It's a mood, she thinks, the post-concert specter, with its acrid thoughts. Tomorrow, she will remember the party with pleasure. It's just as well, though, that Anzor wasn't there; she won't even tell him about it. She knows the icy judgment he would pass on Jonathan and his friends. He would think they're the masters of the universe, arrogant with privilege, and she feels a sort of protectiveness on their behalf. They're only trying to live out their lives, she tells him. Trying and floundering. What would *they* make of him, of Anzor, with the embers of anger lighting and darkening his eyes? They might think him quaint. But she could tell them that the cool ironies of the Discourse are no match for his certainties, or for the four-square simplicity of his phrases. She suddenly misses him, wants to get back to his three-dimensional presence, to the strange subterranean thicket of their exchanges and their contrapuntal music.

London

Anders has carved out a few days for her in London, and now she is doubly glad because of Anzor. This is where he has his main base. She has asked him if she can pick him up in his flat, and in the end, he said yes, although she could hear his reluctance. "It's just a temporary place," he told her. "It's not mine. It's not how I really live. Or how I choose to live." She insisted, lightly. She has some need to ground him to an earthly spot, to reassure herself that he actually lives somewhere, is surrounded by furniture or books, some paraphernalia of ordinariness. A need at odds with the urge to leave him as ungrounded as she found him, to leave intact the sensation that he glides through the world unimpeded, following some unknown, not quite gravitational laws. So she feels uneasy as she ascends the poorly carpeted staircase of a terraced house in Camden, to the third floor.

It's a while before Anzor responds to the doorbell. When he does, he's running his hand through his hair, frowning, as though he didn't quite recognize her or expect her. She looks back with bafflement, hurt by his lack of welcome.

"Did I . . ." she begins. "Is this the wrong time?"

"Sorry," he says distractedly. "Some friends are here. We need to discuss something."

For a moment, he examines her as if deciding whether to invite her in at all; then ushers her in with bare politeness, informing her curtly that his guests will leave soon. Maybe she can wait. The room he brings her to is small and cluttered with furniture, but not awful, as she feared. There are three other men there, and they get up stiffly when she comes in.

"Let me introduce Isabel Merton," Anzor says, speaking as if in a formal tongue. "She is a friend." One of the men—he's dressed in a black turtleneck and jacket—nods at her, inspecting her warily. There is also the older man from Warsaw, the one she thought of as the leader. He is now wearing a kaffiyeh, but it is definitely him. She tries to extend her hand to him, but he has already turned away. He has not made a rude gesture, quite; but he has made it clear he does not want to greet her. She's sure, though, from a flicker of his eye as he moved his head to ignore her, that he has recognized her.

"Please excuse us," Anzor addresses her, without a hint of intimacy. "Please make yourself comfortable."

She sits in a chair slightly distanced from the men, and has no choice but to observe them, as they proceed with their business, speaking in their language, in this low-ceilinged, very English room, made stuffy by wall-to-wall blue carpeting. Not Anzor's room, clearly. Nor theirs. The four of them, bent over a table with their severe expressions and big frames, look incongruous in this domestic space, their gestures too broad and abrupt. Only the man in the kaffiyeh has the stillness of posture which seems undisturbed by any surroundings. The sheikh, Isabel thinks, because he fits some stereotypical movie part so perfectly. But then she brushes away the feather of irony, for there is something about him that does not permit it, something in his expression, or stance, that suggests a perfectly focused concentration. Isabel understands concentration, and respects it; even if she doesn't know what its object may be; what the man is gathering his attention toward.

The others try to talk quietly for a while, aware of her presence, but their voices rise to their natural level, guttural and brusque. They bend over a xeroxed piece of paper, covered over with Arabic lettering and point to parts of it, speaking in short, impetuous utterances. Then the man in the kaffiyeh clearly clinches whatever argument they're having. He points at the printed page with an extended finger; then looks at the others to confirm, or demand, agreement. They nod, making noises of assent. She tries to overcome the intimation of fear, suddenly clutching at her chest. Fear of the men, their voices, the suppressed violence she senses in the discussion. Of Anzor's sudden distance. Calm down, she tells herself sternly; these men are undoubtedly planning some propaganda campaign. In their circumstances, it is normal. Part of their work, their task.

The sheikh now holds Anzor at arm's length, and looks at him with utterly sober appraisal. He then turns toward her, and says something to Anzor in an undertone. Anzor shakes his head in denial, and she's chilled by the gesture, by the men's complicity. But the sheikh now clasps Anzor in an embrace which suggests that something has been agreed on; that a compact has been reached. The men shake Anzor's hand with silent nods, without looking at her at all, and abruptly leave.

For a strange moment, Anzor stands unmoving in the middle of the room. Then he runs his hand through his hair again, as if to remind himself of something, to locate himself in the room, the actual space.

"Sorry," he says absently; into the air. "This couldn't be avoided."

"Of course," she says, uncertainly; and then, because she's feeling unsure of how to speak, she indicates the room with her hand and says, "This is not too bad."

He shakes his head as if to swat something away. "It's not mine," he says, as he did before. "It's not how I choose to live." Then, more bitingly, "None of it is of my choosing."

She decides to be more direct. "What was this about?" she simply asks. "It looked so . . . conspiratorial."

He looks at her sharply, somberly. "Of course we have to plan our actions," he says. "We have to be at least as smart as the others. Or smarter." His eyes have gone hooded, and he looks at her appraisingly, as the sheikh looked at him. "If I were you," he says, "I wouldn't mention this to anyone. Not, for example, to McElvoy."

"McElvoy?" she asks, utterly confused. "But why . . . what does this have to do with him?"

"Nothing," Anzor says impatiently. "He's just the one person we know in common. That is why I mentioned his name."

"I hardly know him . . ." she says, her disorientation now infused with the chill of rejection. "Anyway, I don't know what you were talking about."

They stand there, facing each other; his face unyielding. She feels a sort of panic, tries another tack. She needs to bridge this distance, to get him to acknowledge her presence.

"Have there been new developments?" she asks, softening her tone, assuring him of her sympathy.

"There are always developments." His voice is just short of hostile. "Horrible things are being done to my country. Even if the world is not paying any attention."

"What is happening there?" she asks again.

"People are getting killed," he says. "That's all."

"Anyone close . . . this time?" she asks.

"When you fight together, you are all close," he says acidly. "You are all brothers."

She nods, forlornly. She knows that anything she might say will be wrong.

Anzor finally looks at her with actual recognition. "Oh, Isabel," he says, his voice altering as he approaches her and puts his arms around her. "I'm sorry. Let's have our day in London. That's why you are here. We must have our day." She stays close to him, listens to his heartbeat, feels his warmth. She thinks, I do not want to lose him, not yet.

And so they drift through Camden Town, bits of rubbish drifting up in the breeze, among the familiar flotsam and jetsam of the young and the disaffected; the outrageously dressed and the bland-eyed, the drugged-up girls with bright pink hair and exposed navels, the genderless boys with metal studs affixed across belts and ears, a woman's tongue extended toward ice cream showing a large rhinestone pierced through it. Isabel winces at the sight; Anzor grips her elbow more firmly. Smells of overused oil waft across the breeze from a grubby eatery. "It's all going to the dogs," Anzor says, grimly. "You've let it go to the dogs."

"What do you mean, you?" she asks, though she is slightly repelled too by the spectacle, the greasy smells and the aggressive ugliness. A youth, thin and sharp, with a spiky tomahawk hairdo, strutting braggingly but unsteadily on his high platform shoes, weaves in her direction, hitting hard with fleshless elbow against her upper arm. She brings her other hand up instinctively. The arm has to be protected, everything depends on it. In the same instant, Anzor grips the youth by the thin shoulder, and pushes him away with sudden and surprising force. He doesn't let go instantly, but retains his grip on the shoulder, as if considering what to do next. He's regarding the scraggly figure with utter hatred.

"Hey, man, I didn't mean anything," the youth protests.

"You . . . punk," Anzor says. His tone is low and menacing.

"Let him go," Isabel says, feeling jittery.

"Hooligan," Anzor says, packing a punch of almost comical contempt into the word.

"Lemme go," the youth says. He doesn't look strong. Anzor beholds him as if he were a piece of rubbish among the other debris, and pushes him away disdainfully.

"Please," she says. "Let's go. It doesn't matter."

"Doesn't matter?" Anzor repeats. His anger is turning toward her. Authentic anger, flaring suddenly, in ways she's beginning to recognize. "Look at this . . . this . . . rubbish. In the center of London. The once great Empire."

"It hasn't been an empire for a long time," she hazards.

"Do you think these . . . hooligans could behave with such impunity, if they didn't think they were at the center of the world? Do you think they could be so . . . arrogant?"

She shakes her head wonderingly. "This is supposed to be the West," he continues, with over-heavy irony. "The wonderful West."

"Please," she says again. "It's only Camden Town. A kind of . . . spectacle. A scene."

"Only. It's always only. But it's not only. It's for real." He fuels the colloquialism with fury. "These . . . wretches could kill you from not caring. Or themselves. Just for the hell of it. Because it's

181

a . . . *scene*. Maybe we can have some ritual murder. Maybe we can call it *art*." The force of sarcasm brought to the last word is considerable. "Because they don't care. That's what makes them so . . . ugly. Not caring. They make everything ugly with their callousness. Their stupid . . . cynicism. That's for real, even if you think it's all part of a *scene*. Even if you think it's cool."

"I don't," she says. "For the sake of accuracy. I don't think it's cool. I just don't think it's that . . . important."

But he's in no mood for fine distinctions. "They're perverted, don't you see that? Twisted . . . They twist themselves into something . . . graceless. They're not even clean." His contempt is eliding into disgust, and he is breathing almost painfully. "They have no dignity because they have no . . . legitimate purposes."

"Legitimate?" she repeats. It seems an improbable word, to apply to these scruffs and strays.

"Yes, legitimate," he repeats. "Because you can have legitimate purposes, even if you're not . . . very important. You can choose to live with dignity. You should see the people in my country. Simple peasants. But they have more dignity, more grace . . . than these punks will experience in a lifetime."

He's gripping her elbow too tight again, and she eases it out decisively. The flow of energy through the arm has to remain unimpeded. Anzor winces, as if he'd been hurt himself, and removes his hand. They've reached the tube station, and they enter its inhospitable interior. On the escalator going down, he stands behind her and places his hand on her shoulder lightly; a kind of apology.

They walk up the grassy incline of Primrose Hill, sloping at a mild but long angle that Isabel associates with the morphology of the English landscape. The day has uncovered itself as gloriously autumnal, sunlit and through-woven with quick white clouds and feather-light breezes. The sky, adjusting to the hill's contours, is a diagonally bent blue overhang. They pause at the hill's top, contemplating the low London skyline. A group of Indian women, in swaths of color, proceed across the hill's ridge, a row of human figures moving with easy grace. London, which can accommodate so much, and yet remain itself.

Some dogs are playing friskily with their owners, and Anzor bends to pick up a stray ball, and unbends to throw it with that strong, effortless arc. Yes, the gesture that started it all; that ignited it all. She thinks, I'm in for it, for even through the anxiety of this morning, she feels connected to him, literally connected, as if by a web of tendrils, except this is more intermingled and more dangerous. It is as if part of her has been poured into him, and part of him is now within her; so that a tearing away would inflict a wound. No matter what she knows about him, or doesn't. She shudders a little, and gives him her hand. He must feel something like this too, because he picks up on their last nighttime conversation, as if it had not been interrupted, as if they were still in their undercover, underwater darkness.

"You know, the other thing I didn't tell is that he killed my dog." Who, she asks, who killed it? "My father," he says, and she watches his face fill with gloom.

"Why?" she asks. "Why did he have to kill the dog?"

"It was to hurt me," Anzor says curtly. "To show me. The dog snatched some chickens from a neighbor's yard. It was my dog, I was supposed to train it. And I had trained him, he was a good dog . . . But the neighbor was furious. The dog came to my father with its tail wagging. And my father . . ."

"How?" she asks, recoiling from what is coming. "With a stone," Anzor says, and his voice lowers and dims. She pulls slightly away, out of his reach. She tries to imagine the awful gesture of bringing down a stone on the animal's head, the animal not understanding . . . Kolya, not understanding, his hurt child's face. She is suddenly suffused with pain.

"I loved that dog," Anzor says simply. She realizes she has never heard him use the word "loved" for a particular creature. Only for his country.

"Why was your father so . . . violent?" she asks.

"I told you, he was practically a peasant," Anzor says, his voice shifting to defensiveness. "He was doing what he thought was right."

They stand silently for a while. "The only person who understood him was Aslan," Anzor resumes. "My friend. Remember, I told you about him."

"The one who died," she says.

"Yes. I went to him after the dog . . . expired. It took a while." He pauses, and she feels, again, that she has walked through a thin membrane into another landscape, far from this benign and sunlit hill.

"I wanted to kill my father," Anzor resumes. "Or to run away. Aslan . . . he calmed me down."

"How?" she asks again.

"He understood how I felt," Anzor answers, speaking as if to himself, into some inner distance. "But also how my father felt. He had a great sense of justice. That's why I could trust him."

"What did he say?"

"He thought my father did what he had to do. By his own rules. His own code of honor." Anzor's eyes are now intense to the point of being clouded; he's certainly not seeing her, he's looking at something else.

"It seems cruel," she says, not bothering to conceal her dismay. "What sort of code of honor can you apply to animals?"

Anzor turns toward her, as if he has been singed. "You mustn't judge him by your standards." His tone is sharp, cutting. "The code of honor applied to me, not to the dog. My father was acting as he thought he should. He was trying to teach me a lesson."

"Isn't that a . . . horrible lesson?" Isabel brings out. "An inhumane lesson." She feels suddenly that she must have the right to say what she means.

To her surprise, Anzor responds calmly. "No, I suppose it wasn't humane in your sense," he says thoughtfully. "My father didn't care about that kind of . . . niceness. He didn't think you should forgive someone who did something wrong. He would have thought that was even more wrong. Do you understand?" he inquires, and Isabel shakes her head stubbornly to indicate she doesn't.

"He thought I *deserved* punishment," Anzor rephrases. A beautiful, shiny-furred spaniel has run up to them, panting; and Anzor bends down and throws a stick for the dog to run after. This is undoubtedly why he's remembering the awful story . . . Even dogs are not everywhere the same; even dogs meet different fates.

"Truth to tell," Anzor says, after straightening out, "I hated him after the dog died." His voice is matt with old anger, and he pauses briefly. "And yet . . . I loved him too. I could see who he was. Just himself. Straight and solid, all the way through. He had no . . . side. He didn't pretend. He believed what he believed. That was his . . . integrity. He couldn't be anything except what he was. That was the real lesson, the one I will never forget."

His voice has grown impassioned, and she looks at him inquiringly. He is speaking out of some old fire, from close to the core; and she wonders how he spans the distances within himself between here and there, and which man it is she knows.

"I suppose you can't really hate your own father," she finally says.

"No," he says. "Not unless you're some spoiled . . . stupid brat." She knows he's substituted "stupid" for "Western" this time; it is a concession of sorts.

She nods, and they remain silent for a while, contemplating the mild expanse of the hill, with its gentle activity. She feels him returning to her, in their wordlessness. Silently, he takes her hand, and they walk back down, into the low houses and the pastel-colored quiet of a prosperous London street.

The parenthesis is coming to an end, but she doesn't know it yet. In the morning, she practices intensely, putting Anzor aside in her mind, knowing that she will see him later. She dives into the Rachmaninov Prelude she'll play that evening with an abandon, surfaces as if through a thick buoyant element an hour later. Wigmore Hall is her favorite place to play, containing in its size and shape. On the way out, she says a few words to the technician who will work on the piano before the concert; some of the middle keys are too tightly tuned; they are in danger of sticking. She must visit Mrs. Brownley, she has promised. Anyway, she has fond memories of Mrs. Brownley, who was her landlady one summer when she studied at the Royal Academy. She takes the tube to Willesden, walks down a small side street, lined with identical, decent small houses. Mrs. Brownley's house still has pots of red begonias arranged on the exterior stairs, as they were all those years ago.

The little parlor is unchanged too, though time has marked Mrs. Brownley, whose broad, once pink face has become paler and pastier; the skin around the jowls looser. She moves more carefully in her chunky frame, as she brings her tray into the room she calls her parlor. The same sturdy tray, Isabel notices, as she brought then, when she used to call Isabel down each afternoon for scones and tea and a half-hour of gentle conversation. Isabel feels a sort of amazement in the familiarity, as if she'd stumbled into a lost corner of the known world. Traveling along her virtual loop, she sometimes forgets that lives like Mrs. Brownley's go on in millions of uneventful side streets, as they have for decades and more, in some quiet zone always bypassed by more turbulent currents. She briefly wonders how Mrs. Brownley bears it, the sameness, the size of her life circumscribed by borders as visible as the lines on the palm of her hand. But then, she remembers from the past, Mrs. Brownley doesn't compare herself to anyone else; she's innocent of the thought that her life is taking place on some larger stage, or that she is observed by an external eye. Blessed relief . . . Mrs. Brownley lives within the frame of her own life, and what happens there seems to her sufficient. Isabel butters her scone, and feels she could sink into the ordinariness of this parlor as into a comforting warm quilt. "You've been traveling such a lot, haven't you?" Mrs. Brownley notes. "My son has told me. He found out on that thing called Google, he looked you up." Yes, Isabel says, she moves around a lot, although sometimes it seems as if she is forever going to the same place. "Still, it must be very exciting for you," Mrs. Brownley says soothingly, maternally. Isabel promises to leave her a ticket at the box office for the evening's concert, and Mrs. Brownley says she will be sure to come, if only her old bones permit it.

. . . ah, look at her, thinks Mrs. Brownley, all different up there, might as well be a different person / so elegant / what is this tune, too bad I know nothing about it / hmm, look at her how she moves, head thrown back almost not proper / but it is art / the little ones, maybe they should have lessons they could afford it, not like when I grew up in the village we never saw heard anything like it / listen all those notes all pearly coming out from under her fingers, like little jewels / I just wish Keith were still with me / I miss him, never a rough word / sitting together in the parlor in the evenings, nice and quiet / tears in my eyes, haven't cried in ages I'm not that sort / must be the music, so sweet and goosey // . . . ah, the tenderness, thinks Norman

Lawrence, I have never had it, listen, this murmur, not even with Jenny when she comes, maybe such tenderness doesn't exist in the world, but how can that be, has it disappeared, no more tenderness, or is it just me who doesn't know it? / how awful if somewhere it exists for the reaching and I have never known it / my whole life, without it, can I bear it, can I bear it? / ah, what happened there, that alteration major to minor, maybe only music only music // . . . ah, here it comes, thinks Anzor, the build-up, the chords, ranged, arranged, like a cathedral, mountains, elements / larger than us, in excess of what we are / that is what she said, and I said yes I understand I understand / in excess, I feel it, my hate my love building up / my country, larger than me / must do whatever it takes, more machine guns, yes, more power, the power of it, the passion, Lenin loved the "'Appassionata" // . . . ah, Schumann, thinks Marjorie Lempinsky, lovely, tender, Clara and Schumann, great love, so romantic, then he went mad / why did he? / listen, you should listen, follow / get that skirt fixed, the flower pattern feminine, will he notice? / would you like to have dinner tonight? / don't get carried away, only that nod in the elevator that time / get a new skirt, one of those skimpy ones, cunty skirt yeah a bit of tease / ah, that passage, so sad listen / don't be pathetic no new skirt but I want . . . I want // . . . Lenin loved the "Appassionata," monster, bastard, even so, he knew / must have will, total will, no hesitation / but Isabel / but I must, whatever it takes, no hesitations none / can't make an omelette without . . . without breaking / must break // . . . listen, thinks Lydia Marvis, the susurrus, the murmur pianissimo, like Proust, like that stream in the forest / pure movement seamless, she's good so delicate, head thrown back / tomorrow, they're all coming, how shall I seat them, complicated, who will talk to whom / but oh, I am suffused, the music enters, it is in me, so beautiful as if I were playing / a sort of gift // . . . breaking eggs, breaking bones, full justice nothing less / my rage, it will lift me will tear me, those Soviet punks, mocking father / here, different but I can see it in their eyes, the contempt, they're good at hiding, their eyes go blank, pale neutral words, but I know / supercilious, pursed lips / those friends of hers, slow-minded, they don't care, don't need to care don't need to feel, sluggish with money power, oh I could pour the acid of contempt on them, their time is up / their time is up // . . . absolutely beautiful, thinks Frances Manning, a kind of nobility / the chords, forte fortissimo, the march . . . why does it speak like that, to me? / directly to the heart / Richard . . . oh my darling, when you look at me like that / and you spoke so well tonight / I was proud of him / ah, listen, the finale, a kind of pride too, pride and tenderness all intertwined // . . . the logic of history, thinks Anzor, no doubt, no regret / no way back, it is my fate I am meeting my fate / ah, but the sadness / am I frightened? / I am frightened / could have been a scholar, quiet study, beauty of thought, logic / Isabel, bending her head like that / for me / it's the music it is undoing me / No! / gather my forces, act, the absolute act! / must be prepared braced for anything mustn't flinch no FEAR / listen, that line of music, line of beauty / pure, so pure / the comrades brothers long nights in the mountains, the stone towers, severe, beautiful / violence tenderness all intertwined / I wanted to embrace the world, shout, love the flame within, leaping / look at her hands, her face she is an instrument, receiving the music, so malleable her body, her wide eyes her strange eyes, when they fill up / No. No music. Ruthlessness. My task. / no doubt, no fear / my rage will lift me up make me fly / I can feel it the exaltation I am filled with it, violence love contempt overbrimming, it must spill must explode, must be expelled, the excess the rage / let it explode, let it burn whoever is in sight it doesn't matter they do not matter, I am an instrument / must sacrifice myself let it be / let it end, let it all end, let something else begin . . .

*

Anzor collects her after the concert, and as they walk into her hotel, she sees a man in a long black robe and a kaffiyeh across the lobby. She peers at him out of her post-concert fog, the still coursing adrenaline, as if he were not clearly visible; but as he moves toward them, there is no doubt, this is the man she has seen before, the man from Anzor's room, the man whom in her mind she has dubbed the sheikh. She is startled. How does he know where to meet them, or that Anzor is with her? His figure, in his black robe, is more expansive in this larger space; he moves toward them with a sort of flowing gravity, but when he comes closer he does not even glance at her. He is being deliberately rude, and she wants to make a gesture to show him up; but as he and Anzor exchange silent signals, she understands that she would not have Anzor on her side. A signal from her own innards tells her she should be frightened. The sheikh lowers his head minutely in her direction, indicating he wants her to leave. "How does he know—" she brings out, but Anzor grips her forearm and presses it, decisively, to get her out of the way. She steps aside, but stays; she's going to stand her ground. The two men talk with low-voiced absorption. Now that they're standing close to each other, she sees that the sheikh, for all his compacted energy, is shorter than Anzor; and when he raises his finger toward Anzor's chest, as if to make an important point, the gesture grazes her mind with its familiarity. A déjà vu, perhaps, or a fragment of somebody else's gesture she's seen in a crowd . . . Then it comes back to her: the bar in Berlin, a man in a leather jacket talking in the dim interior to a man who may or may not have been Anzor. A man who may or may not have been the one standing here, in a kaffiyeh and a flowing robe. Who seems to know where she's been staying. Who knows what else? She must find out, she must pin Anzor down. She has been much too willing not to know, not to imagine the concreteness of his actions. She's been too willing to leave the world inexact. She is beginning to feel awkward in her pointless pose, and takes a step toward them. The sheikh makes a dismissive turn of his head in her direction, as if to remind Anzor of something. His expression is chilling; it says she is entirely dispensable.

Anzor looks at her with an absent gaze, then comes up to her and spreads his hands, as if to say he cannot help what he is about to do.

"Anzor," she says urgently, and the syllable of his name is suddenly like a small explosion, "were you in Berlin recently, did I see you with that man?"

He looks at her in puzzlement, then shakes his head impatiently, as if to say this is an irrelevance with which he really cannot be bothered now. "I do not know what you're asking of me," he says, his locutions, as always under stress, becoming more formal. "But I must tell you . . . I must inform you . . . that I cannot be present for a while."

"That's a bizarre way to put it," she says, finding her anger at last. "When did you suddenly become a complete stranger?" His forehead furrows, as if he were trying to make out what she wants of him.

"I'm sorry," he says. "I will have to go away for a while."

"You're going . . . there, aren't you? You're going to fight in that . . . awful war. To . . . kill people." She's surprised by the calm with which the sentence comes out. She has been crossing over to Anzor's zone, Anzor's element, for a while now. His eyes are suddenly very hard, and his face falls into the odd angles it assumes when it's filled with acute emotion.

"Do not insult me," he says, and his words are an implicit challenge. A glove has been thrown, and he is no longer on her side. "I will do whatever I need to help my country. Whatever is required of me. Even if it doesn't please you. Even if you don't understand . . . very much."

"How can I understand when you've told me so little?" she begins, and then stops in a horrible confusion, a fog of inarticulate feeling. She has come to know this man in his every gesture and reflex, and now he is going to disappear into alien landscapes, the violent scenes she's glimpsed, the maiming . . . She thinks of the plastic-wrapped limb in Rotterdam. He will kill people, or he will be killed. Both are impossible thoughts. She was not meant to have such thoughts. She was not meant for this, not meant to know the world in this way, or to know such a world.

"Why must you go?" she asks, her voice muffled with hurt and accusation; although she knows it is a superfluous question.

"I must," he says. "I have been summoned. I am needed in my country. It is my turn."

"For how long?" she asks, her voice fragmenting a little with the chaos of her feeling.

"For a while," he says, impatiently. "I do not know."

The sheikh comes up close to Anzor and looks at him as if to say, it is time. He may have something to say to Isabel as well, because he's turning toward her, when a man in a Burberry coat walks past them hurriedly, brushing against the sheikh so that a small briefcase falls out of the folds of his robe, and to the floor. Anzor, in a coiled movement, seizes the man's shoulder, stopping him in his tracks.

"Anzor . . ." she begins, but the sheikh directs a look of such disgust at her that she stops.

"Apologize," Anzor brings out, detaining the man with his grip, his voice strangled to the point of incoherence. "Apologize."

The man looks taken aback, then coldly angry. He tries to take Anzor's hand off his shoulder, but Anzor holds on, and the man stands still, in a display of perfect self-composure. "Apologize to whom?" he asks in a deliberately unexcited voice. "For what?"

"To him!" Anzor shouts, jabbing his forefinger in the sheikh's direction. "You think just because he is—"

"I think nothing," the man says coldly. "I was in a hurry. I am in a hurry. Please excuse me."

"Anzor . . ." Isabel begins again, but again, the sheikh throws her a look of unmistakable warning. She must not speak. She must know her place. His finger, extended out of his robe, reinforces the message.

"You owe him an apology," Anzor repeats, with a low, explosive emphasis.

The clerk behind the counter has been observing them closely, and is clearly trying to decide whether to intervene. The sheikh, who has picked up his briefcase, now shakes his head in Anzor's direction, and makes a subduing movement with his hands, palms down. The man in the Burberry coat gives Anzor a look that is now frankly contemptuous, and walks out through the revolving door.

For a moment, Anzor looks as though he might run after him. Then, with an effort, he restrains himself. He stands as if not knowing where to turn. His face is flushed. He's not looking at her, or at the sheikh.

She's been following Anzor's every gesture with her eyes. "For God's sake, why do you get so angry?" she asks in genuine bafflement, some impulse to make contact with him overtaking her, as if it still mattered; as if they weren't about to part.

Anzor snaps his head to face her in fury. "Didn't you see his arrogance? His . . . condescension? They think they can be rude just because—"

"I think you're imagining—" Isabel begins, and then stops. She realizes, in a flash of clarity, that to finish the sentence would be to undo what has happened between them; that if she thinks Anzor only imagines the offense, imagines all the slights against which she has seen him ignite, then she can no longer assent to her feelings for him freely. Some measure of respect will have been lost. And the loss of respect, she instantly recognizes, is the beginning of the loss of love. Not that it matters any longer, she recognizes in the same flash; and yet it does.

"It is you who doesn't see what's going on," Anzor hurls in an undertone, and his mouth twists with an expression that has cruelty in it, and a kind of weakness. "You don't see what's in front of you."

Then he too stops, and they stand facing each other, his gaze filled with such ambiguous embers that it might as well be emitting its own infrared spectrum. She returns his look; she is, as yet, incapable of not doing so.

The sheikh summons Anzor to come closer with his expressive finger. They speak in an undertone, with the sheikh throwing glances in her direction as if she were an inanimate object of reference. They're deciding what to do with her. Or about her. Then the sheikh, in the first English phrase she's heard him utter, says, very clearly: "Stupid bitch."

Anzor winces and half closes his eyes, as if in pain. She knows her own eyes are very wide open. She stares at the men, at the sheikh. A long moment passes.

Anzor comes back toward her, and spreads his hands, in a gesture of resignation. He looks tired now and very distant. "I'm sorry," he says. "I mean, I'm sorry we have no more time. I must go now."

"I wish you didn't," she says, before knowing that's what she will say; but as she looks at his lean body and his face, which has gone pale and drained from the expense of emotion, she knows that this too is true.

The sheikh nods at Anzor sternly, and she allows herself to respond with a look of contempt. The sheikh moves toward the door, in his stately way. Anzor takes her hand in his, and brings it close to his eyes, as if to give it one last inspection. She's still surprised by the delicacy of his long-fingered hand. Her own, muscled through years of practice, is probably stronger than his.

The sheikh holds the door open, as if to say, it's time. Anzor's eyes, as he lets go of her hand, gather to a new focus; and, without a word, in an odd repetition of the gesture she remembers from their first meeting, he turns away from her abruptly, and follows the sheikh through the door. Outside, a silver Mercedes-Benz seems to be waiting for them, and a compact man in a dark turtleneck sweater emerges from it and holds the door open for them to get in.

The parenthesis has come to an end. Just put brackets around the whole interlude, she commands herself, pacing around her room, or a fermata, to suggest a long pause. Then move on. If I could, she answers herself from some other part of herself, if it were not for what I actually . . . feel. This, it seems, cannot be bracketed, it sloshes and swirls and threatens to spill. Unmediated, immediate, hurtful. The swirl includes her moment of clarity about Anzor, the clarity of doubt. She wants to rewind, to ask him questions. To shake him, shout at him, make him tell her what was really going on. Although, in a general way, it has been obvious enough. It is the specifics she has avoided, the awkward literal specifics of his ideas; his beliefs; his four-square declarations. Ideas, which have seemed to her to be mere surface, foamy froth of the mind. What did Anzor's errant convictions matter, compared to the glow of Conviction itself, the dark light in his eyes? That was what convinced her, spoke to her with its own eloquence. That was what she wanted to be close to, essence to essence, flame to flame. Without rules or contracts, or limits on what to take and, especially, what to give. Without mediations.

The very thought of this is beginning to fill her with queasy embarrassment, as she winces to herself, goes down to the fateful lobby for coffee to distract herself. Larry once compared her, meanly, to Madame Bovary. He was always big on tropes and archetypes. But was he right, was she misled by the promise of music, as poor Emma was once misled by her cheap romances . . . Was she misled by the intimations of beauty, truth, love? She read *Madame Bovary* in one of her literature courses, where Emma's yearnings were taken apart sentence by sentence and shown to be cheap illusions, sentimental and paper-thin. Surely, she should know better. She comes after. She has read *Madame Bovary*, surely she cannot be Madame Bovary.

After a few days, she tries to call him, but his London phone has been cut off. His mobile number is no longer valid. Cut. Cut off. The unkindest cut of all. The loss, now that she really admits it, stabs as if a shark fin emerged from the deep, to puncture her through her diaphragm, her lungs. Perhaps her heart. The heart is a pump, she thinks, a mechanical instrument. We know that now, it's the easiest part of the body to fix. We can take it apart and patch it together. She could get a new one if necessary, if this one continues to behave in this unacceptably retrograde way. She could get a more up-to-date organ. And yet she cannot stop the erratic movements of something inside her, the ebb and flow of blood, which informs her she's suffering, as no one has suffered before. As everyone has suffered before.

She wonders where Anzor is, what he is doing. But she doesn't know enough to imagine the setting in which he is operating, never mind the dramatis personae. She remembers the Kazakh horsemen whom he once described. Is it possible he is on a horse? Surely not, surely no one travels on horses anymore, and certainly no one goes to battle on them. The man on the horse is as outmoded as the heart, although men go on stabbing and killing. Is he, then, on one of those trucks, rattling and comfortless, surrounded by men casually holding their Uzis or Kalashnikovs, or whatever they carry, how is she supposed to know about such things? She doesn't want to know, surely she is allowed that much delicacy. But Anzor too is delicate, his hand, his mouth, how is he faring on a thuggish truck among men willing to maim and mutilate. Has he done so already, are his hands capable of it . . . But of course it is not his body which has taken him there, it is his mind and his rage, that is what has transported him all the way to the heart of violence. The shark fin surfaces and stabs. She's pierced by fearfulness, for him, but also, for something else. What has she lost, what was she seeking . . . Anzor seemed to promise . . . what? Relief from the banality of the flat, concrete world, she tells herself sternly. She thought she could find in one person the completeness whose intimations she hears in the music. She wanted to be taken beyond her own borders, up into wholeness, and down into the innermost center, the molten source from which music proceeds. Was she, instead, falling for a tawdry metaphor, threadbare from overuse? Was Larry right about that too? Center, beyond, wholeness. How he would satirize those words. Her disappointment begins, gnawingly, to turn on herself. She has been her own biggest blind spot, and she peers into the void left by Anzor, trying to discern what it is she has failed to see, or so badly misunderstood.

Barcelona

The explosion comes—she'll be sure of it later—simultaneously with the last chord of the Chopin Scherzo. It has been obviously well timed. Or perhaps whoever it was that set off the deafening inchoate noise had the natural impulse to wait till the Scherzo came to its inexorable, its bravura culmination.

She comes down on the last chords with her full force, gripping the keys with capturing fingers, like a large bird landing.

Something locks into place. It is complete. Simultaneously, an inarticulate roar shatters the air and reverberates through her like a horrible, distorted augmentation of the chord she is still gripping. In that distended moment, she is astonished, but not really surprised. Her hands come off the keyboard with their accustomed gracefulness as the thud reaches its climax. It is too late to modify the gesture, though she becomes aware, even as her hands fall softly into her lap, that it is somehow wrong. Inappropriate. Then, from the haze of her extreme focus, a realization comes forth. She has heard a bomb going off, she knows that instantly, though she's never heard one before. The splintering, deafening ugliness: a bomb. The anti-music: a bomb. She stands up abruptly and doesn't know where to turn. In the dark auditorium, there are angry shouts, fearful shrieks. In a second, the lights go up. Coming forward to the rim of the stage, she sees people scrambling toward the aisles, standing in awkward poses, trying to crouch in the narrow spaces between the seats, pushing others out of the way. A few remain calm, and they are oddly moving in their stoical dignity; but in a minute, the audience will turn into a herd, dangerous in its fear. A solitary shout of "Help!" rings out, small and trivial. A word from another era. Her gaze, from her stage promontory, alights on a figure at the back, standing still and looking at her very directly. It's the sheikh, she's sure of it, although he is now wearing a smooth suit and looks like any other member of the audience. Except for his demeanor, which seems entirely unaffected by the melee around him. Even from this distance, she can tell he is looking at her with a sort of brazenness. He has sent her a warning signal. Stay away. Do not dare to interfere in what is beyond you; in what is not your business. Well, she's been warned. In the moment's preternatural lucidity, she stares at the sheikh across the auditorium, and feels the force of his loathing. Then he turns away with deliberation, pushing a dark-haired woman in front of him, steering her toward the exit. Amid the mass of clumsy, frightened bodies, neither of them looks disoriented or frightened.

Somebody is approaching her from the stage entrance, and putting his hands round her shoulders. She is led out quickly, while the man mutters reassuringly that it's all right, it's going to be all right. She nods, even as she's beginning to shake. In the Green Room, someone sits her down and hands her a glass of water. She notices that her teeth are chattering. Then her Barcelona minder is there, taking her by the hand. What's his name? Soldano maybe, that's good enough. "Are you all right?" he asks, his voice concerned but very controlled. After all, he is the man in charge. Illogically, she wants to scream at him that so much control at such a moment is indecent, that it is immoral. They should all be screaming, in rage and protest. But he's right, someone must stay steady, and she answers, through her chattering teeth, "Yes, I'm all right. Of course I'll be all right, I'm fine, I'll be fine."

"The bastards," he now spits out, having ascertained she's not injured, and injecting the furious force of his Spanish pronunciation into the word. "*Salauds*." She is in Barcelona, how long has she been in Barcelona? The wrecking noise back there has warped time. She's been here . . . she doesn't know how long. Something has been going on for a very long time.

"What happened?" she asks. "Is anyone hurt?"

"They . . . they put it in the lobby," he says. He's stuttering in agitation, and his fists are clenched. His self-control apparently goes only so far. "We don't know who. One of our groups maybe. Or one of the others. *Canaille*." Is French the international language of curse and condemnation?

"It's probably the others," she says, speaking with difficulty. She regrets the phrase as soon as it is uttered.

"At a concert too," he bursts out, shaking his head, as if he couldn't help making this obvious observation. "I mean . . . why do they attack this? Music. They have no . . . respect. No respect for anything."

"No," she says, with a grim certainty. "At least not for . . . this." She means not for us; but she cannot bring herself to say it.

"Who are they," he asks, rhetorically. "What do they want. From us. From you. What do these . . . people want."

"Has anyone been . . . hurt?" she repeats, her teeth beginning to chatter again.

"I do not think so," he says. "I need please to excuse myself to find out what is happening. Will you be all right?"

"Yes," she says. "I'm fine. Will you please let me know . . . what has happened?"

"I will, I will do this," he says, and then she's alone, and lets herself shiver violently, thinking, maybe this is a time for prayer. For I want somebody to make sure that no one has been hurt, even though it is too late, even though it has already happened, whatever it is.

Soldano comes back a few minutes later and closes the door behind him softly. She looks up at him anxiously, and he shakes his head no. "No one has been hurt. Very fortunately," he says.

She feels immeasurably grateful to him, as if he were personally responsible for this news. Kiss the messenger. "Oh, thank God," she says. "Thank heaven."

"One person is in trauma," he informs her. "But maybe it is not so bad. She is just shocked. She is taken to a hospital." Isabel nods. That much can be accepted.

"The lobby is destroyed," he adds drily. "It will take us a long time to repair it. We will have to cancel the rest of the season."

He looks bleak and pauses before asking the next question. "The police want to . . . want to talk to you," he says. "Can I ask them to come in?" He's looking at her with a concern, but also a more neutral curiosity.

"Oh," she says. "Yes. I mean, I see why they need to talk to me. But can I . . . can this wait till tomorrow?" She would give anything to postpone this conversation. She is feeling, she now notices, shattered with a deep fatigue. The stuffing has been knocked out of her with the thud back there; with that one comprehensive sound.

"I do not think so," Soldano says, in a voice that is suddenly very firm. "I think they will probably insist on speaking with you now. They are right here. Can I please ask them to come in?"

"Yes," she says, a lurch of anxiety twisting her stomach. "Of course. Please ask them to come in."

One of them is black-haired and black-eyed, the other short with a reddish moustache. They are very young, and she feels a wave of sympathy for them. They've been out there, looking for bodies, although, thank God, no bodies have been found.

"We are sorry to disturb you," the tall one says. "We are also sorry for our English."

"No, please," she says. "I wish I could speak Spanish. I knew some as a child, but haven't spoken it for many years." If she could only extend the chit-chat. She is wondering what on earth she will say to them when the questions come, and feels a sudden, sickening sense of wrongness. She is in the wrong, even though she has not done anything wrong, as in dreams in which she is guilty of murder, even though no murder has been committed. Dreams in which Kolya hovers abstractly in the background, and from which she has woken up sweaty with unspecified dread.

The short one takes over. "We need to ask you a few things. To help us in what we are doing. To see if you have any, how do you say, clues. We'll try not to take too long."

They ask her the predictable questions, about whether she knows anyone who might have a grudge against her, perhaps someone wanting revenge for something, a jealous pianist who is less successful—anything is possible. She keeps saying no, thinking she will stick to the facts, even though the facts are not exactly the truth. Surely she has that right, after all those years with Peter she is perfectly aware of defendants' rights. The thought of Peter, the very possibility of his calm rationality, induces a rise of longing, and also of shame. She has failed on grounds of rationality, has wandered into a morass where nothing clear can be made out. She's responsible for something vague and awful, even though she never intended to hurt anybody. Do her intentions count, can she be reprieved on grounds of good intentions?

"Or do you personally know anyone who might be involved in something like this, some kind of group?" the tall one asks, looking at her very attentively. He is young, but his face has the lines of habitual skepticism, the expression of someone who knows he should expect the worst of everyone. "Sometimes you may not realize what your friends are involved in, but please think hard. You meet so many people. Was there anyone suspicious? Anyone who asked you strange questions? You never know. Someone might have wanted to use you. People like that have very, how shall I say, very strange purposes. Perverse purposes, one might say. Or is it perverted?" His English is really excellent.

She turns away for a moment, to make her decision. "Yes," she says, facing them again. She has decided to tell them whatever she knows. And in a flash, she has understood that she knows more than she has wanted to acknowledge.

They listen, carefully, and take notes, even though the tape recorder is on. Just another kind of interview, she thinks, with low irony. Though this one has rather more real implications than her usual interrogations. The real, once again baring its sharp teeth. The policeman asks her about Anzor's London base, and a wave of sickliness makes her stop mid-sentence. Is she committing some awful act again, some literally murderous

202

betrayal; or is she doing the right thing? Once again, she tells them what she knows.

They thank her. They say she has been very helpful. They write down some things, lingering at the table, consulting with each other about what else they need to do.

"What will happen now?" she asks. She has gone beyond fatigue, she is feeling dusty and gray, made of ashes.

"We don't know," the red-haired one says. "These people are very hard to track down. But we'll try. Believe me, we'll try."

She feels nauseous with ambivalence, or perhaps with the effects of the questioning. They may not find Anzor. She may not be responsible for his incarceration, or torture, or whatever awaits him if they tracked him down. She doesn't want to think of his flesh being tortured . . . But if they don't find him. The flesh of others. She has seen, in Rotterdam, what a bomb can do. She reminds herself that it is he who has been traitorous. He and his comrades. Their contempt apparently extends to her, and everything she stands for. Her and all the others, the people who came to hear her.

The red-haired policeman looks at her carefully. "Please do not feel bad about this," he says, with real kindness. "You are a musician. You did not do anything bad. You do not have anything to blame yourself for." She looks at him with gratitude, as if the thread of redemption were hanging on his words.

"I agree with my colleague," the tall one adds warmly. "I agree with him very much. I know how you feel. We have some experience of this. Often the victims feel the worst. It's very disturbing, very unjust. You shouldn't . . . feel guilty. You didn't set off this bomb, right?" She nods, trying to absorb what he's saying, its impeccable logic. "I hope you have some friends in Barcelona," the policeman concludes. "To have dinner with them. Perhaps a good, how do you say, stiff drink."

Another question occurs to her. "Do you think they might try again . . . ?"

"I do not think so," he says. "We cannot guarantee anything, of course, but this looks like a one-off, for these people. Very strange, actually. They do not usually do this kind of thing. If we are thinking of the right people. Of course, your friend is probably back in Chechnya, where we cannot reach him. Outside of our sphere of influence, you could say."

She is queasy again at the word "friend." On some level, she knows, she cannot be absolved as easily as the policeman suggests; but she is glad of any absolution she can get, any reasoning which extracts her from the obscure murk of guilt and shame. Under her eyelids, she feels the burning of incipient tears.

"Thank you," she says. "Thank you very much."

Then the cops leave, and Soldano takes her out through the stage door to his car. As they round the corner, she sees police cars in front of the concert hall, and bright lights illuminating a pile of broken stone and glass, a hard mess, wreckage. She begins to feel the onset of a different anger, turning on Anzor, with a bitter sense of betrayal. She must expel his body from her body, where it has taken residence; must reject his words from her mind. She begins to shiver again, this time with the agitation of her wrath. She is against him, utterly against him. She must take sides, it is indecent not to. She must hate as it is right to hate.

Marseilles

It is upon her again, the death of meaning. She walks around her white-carpeted apartment without sound or thought. She feels right in this geometric capsule suspended high up above the ground, on the peripheries of a strange city. No reason to be here, except that the train which was ready to pull out of the station when she got there, had Marseilles as its final destination. It made as much sense as anywhere else. It is causeless, neutral, utterly arbitrary. It suits her fine. She thinks, maybe I'll spend the rest of my life here. Why not here. Why anywhere. She does not deserve the protection of a home. When she looks out the window, she sees other rectangular tower blocks, their glassy exteriors shimmering in the sun. She is on the thirty-ninth floor, and she feels groundless, gravity-less. A monk's cell, a rehabilitation cell, an isolation chamber. Here, the randomness of her life, her superfluous freedom, has come home to roost. The anonymous whiteness of the room reflects perfectly her condition. And anyway, aren't there millions like her, cutting across the globe without ever touching ground? Who has a whole life, any more, coherent and unbroken? Isn't she, in living like this, joining the common lot?

She tries, out of habit, to practice in the mornings, in a dingy studio she has rented for this purpose. After a few days, she realizes there is no point. How could she ever do it, hit one note after another, as if it mattered? As if it added up to something? She contemplates the black and white keys as if they were levers of some antique machine, the once malevolent teeth of an extinct animal. Her fingers still know how to run through an arpeggio or a melody, but the notes do not link up to make a melodic line, do not gel into sense or shape. Why is she sitting in front of that strange cumbersome piece of furniture, how could she ever think she could conjure up significance out of a piece of wood? After repeating a passage several times in the hope of discerning some meaning within it, she begins to feel that she is engaged in an activity from a Dadaist manual. The old upright, with its yellowed keys, bespeaks stale, shabby paltriness. The instrument of the petit bourgeoisie, which she used to think held the cosmos in its innards. She has been living in some kind of illusion, layers and layers of illusion, like layers of a dream from which you think you have awakened, only to realize you are still in it. Now she has been jolted out of it, that's for sure. Out of her misty longings and into some more naked reality. This is what Anzor did, this is what the explosion did: it has exposed some possibility in the world that makes the activity of stringing musical notes together absurd. The ugly thud, the broken chandeliers, the rubble-strewn sidewalk outside the concert hall: in the scheme of things, it is not a large event; but it means that she cannot make separate notes of the Chopin Ballade add up to music. I have fallen into despair, she thinks, isn't that supposed to be the greatest sin? Rose, thou art sick. She feels she is sickening from the inside. The worm of disenchantment has made its way into her innards, twisting, filling her with a contaminated leadenness. When the contamination reaches her arms, she looks briefly at the yellowing chipped teeth, and shuts the piano's lid.

Once a day, she descends in the soundless elevator to do her shopping and sit in a café. She takes her cart through the *supermarché* and then sits for an hour at a glass-topped table under a linen umbrella. She seems to have no need to eat these days, her body has stopped giving her those signals; but she consumes food out of some obligation to herself, some remnant hope, or rather inference, that some day she may actually want to eat again, that she might feel hunger, or appetite, or desire. On the street, the usual polyglot mix: blue jeans and turbans, gorgeous African prints and Muslim headscarves. Among the colorful costumes, the tanned Frenchwomen in their brilliant-white shirts and narrow pants look oddly old-fashioned. Creatures of another era, she thinks, passé, done for. Or at least done with, no longer the problem. No longer the subject. They have been dissected and described, their desires and affairs, their frustrations and their marriages. They have all read *Madame Bovary*. It is the others who look serious, who walk with gravitas, who are not completely knowable because they have a fate to accept or fight against, something to struggle for or figure out, about their condition. Or so Isabel conjectures. She suspects their lives have conditions, and choices and costs attached; and this gives them the vividness, the edge of tension and of interest. Though the Frenchwoman she's observing at a nearby table looks erotically confident and elegant in her soft sports pants and shirt, knees raised languidly on a chair as she talks briskly on her cell phone. This is not a place of misery, after all, just an ordinary neighborhood in Europe, where everything has been done to enhance the well-being of the inhabitants, to make the surfaces of life clement and comfortable. The people wearing the turbans and the headscarves shop at the *supermarché* too, though they rarely sit at the café.

In the afternoon, she tries to take a walk, toward the sea. The sunset is reputed to be beautiful. But Anzor has infiltrated even the sunset, his rage is like an ultrasound she hears within the quiet. The jagged high-rises, the laden coastline, the gigantic ships: why does it not explode from sheer compression, from the collision of so many lives, the crossing of so many purposes . . . Legitimate and illegitimate. She feels the city hurtling, vibrating, pressing against its borders, and she thinks, why doesn't it erupt, and what bitter lava would it release if it did.

In the evenings, she watches the news. Addictively, compulsively. She used to watch the news in order to find out more or less what was going on, out of some vague obligation to know. Isn't she, after all, one of the educated, the responsible, the well-intentioned classes? Now she watches for some other reason, more obscure, more twisted and twisting. The way we live now, she thinks. That's what she wants to understand. When she can't bear to see the repetition of the same item on CNN, she switches to BBC World or France 2. There, she hears with slight variations what she has already heard; but this doesn't slake her thirst for more. More what? More rage, more outrage, that's what, she thinks; a kind of unholy excitement. Images of famine, child soldiers with machetes, babies dying of AIDS, and bombs going off. Always the bombs going off, and the splintered, cut, maimed, mutilated bodies. The politicians with their sound bites and the journalists with their predictable biting questions: the rage she feels at each stage of this spectacle is violent, virulent, viscous. There seems to be more and more of it each evening, it is unstoppable. The world is contaminated, wrong, despoiled by madness. She wants someone to declare its entire bankruptcy. There is no resting place. In what, in whom can she rest, where could she find the frame to contain her, the enclosure for her own life . . . Her Own Life: she finds the idea risible, worthy of Mrs. Brownley. She has seen the surface of the world rent and cracked, and she knows she doesn't count. How could she ever have thought she did? The personal is over. The earth has been seamed through with violence and it will swallow them all, it cannot bear that much humanity. Her fury rises tidally, explosively. What borders will it burst? Only her own, only her own.

The anchor is interviewing an African strongman about a possible link between his militia—the footage shows a helter-skelter band of young men in fatigues, waving an array of guns triumphantly in the air—and a massacre in a small village.

"We have no connection with that unfortunate incident and we resent the insinuations directed at us so eagerly by the Western media," the strongman says in a confident, Americanized accent. Where did he do his studies? Indiana? Milwaukee? He is broad and rather handsome and impeccably dressed, in a well-cut jacket and tie. He fills the TV screen impressively. "Our government does not condone acts of random violence."

"And yet, your soldiers were recently reported to have committed other massacres in which many hundreds of civilians died. We have had reports of mass rapes," the anchor asserts, his voice registering a quaver of disapproval.

"Those events were widely misreported in the Western press," the strongman states calmly. "Our troops were engaged in acts of self-defense. I repeat, we resent the suggestions linking us to terrorist acts."

"And yet," the anchor persists, cutting in quickly, "we have had strong indications from reliable sources that yesterday's incident was committed by people linked to your militia." Clearly, he knows something, and clearly, he has no evidence with which to confront his interlocutor.

"Those allegations are entirely unproven," the strongman responds readily.

"Witnesses have come forth—" the anchor tries again.

"They are our enemies. They are entirely unreliable."

"Sorry, we have to stop there," the anchor says. "Thank you for being with us." Isabel thinks she sees the hint of a self-satisfied smile on the strongman's face. He's done well.

She turns off the television, and thinks no, this is impossible, you cannot say "Sorry" in a polite voice to a person known to have committed massacres. You cannot say "Thank you for being with us" to someone proclaiming murderous lies in your face. You cannot do this without some basic order being overturned. She feels nausea threatening again as she brushes her teeth, as she looks at her own pale face in the mirror. The interviewer should have raised his voice on her behalf. On everyone's behalf. He should have shouted with rage, banged his fist on the table. He should have called the strongman a bastard and a criminal, to his face, so she could see it crumple. She is being childish, she knows. She's misunderstanding something again: the rules. The rules of civilized discourse, for which she should be grateful. And yet, she thinks, you cannot remain civil to mass murderers on TV without something breaking down. Without uprightness yielding, integrity dissolving into hollowness. Without all honor being lost. Yes, honor, she repeats in her mind, throwing the word bitterly back at Anzor. In bed, she tosses and turns, unable to find a resolution, a resting place.

One evening, there is a report from Chechnya. Columns of refugees, carrying their bundles with mulish patience. Open trucks carrying loads of young soldiers. Then she sees him, on one of the trucks, or thinks she sees him: the man in the head-dress. It's a nanosecond of footage, but she's pretty sure she has recognized him, and instantly recognized his calm pose as that of a leader. Behind him, in camouflage fatigues, a man who might or might not be Anzor. She is almost sure it's him, though the man's face, in the brief image passing across the screen is gaunt and unshaven. She feels a brief pang of sympathy, then disgust at her own reflex. She must hate, must keep up her resolve to hate. As it is right to hate. As it is indecent not to. That much Anzor would understand.

The reporter refers to the men in the convoy as resistance fighters, but a Russian ambassador invited to comment on the situation, makes strong objection to the term. The men are terrorists, he says, pure and simple, and their tactics are getting more vicious by the day. "We have to defeat them entirely," he says, his vowels broad and sing-song, like Katrina's. "Or I'm afraid we will see more atrocities like the recent explosion in Moscow, in which hundreds of innocent people died." He sounds and looks the confident politician, not a leader, not a chieftain. This man is used to holding power rather than battling to the death for it, he is used to leather chairs and good clothing rather than rattling trucks and caves in the mountains. She doesn't know whom she should loathe more, him or the sheikh, which one has the true power or if it is power itself she should hate. She has let some of Anzor's vision seep into her mind, she knows what the Russians have done; but now it is Anzor who is holding them all hostage to his humiliations, he and his calm fanatic leader. Hostage to their violent whims, to their real and supposed slights. Who has the advantage over whom? Anzor's honor will not let him stop, she wants to tell the Russian politician. You might as well be prepared for long and bloody carnage. She knows Anzor's feelings on that score are punctilious.

She feels a vertigo of confusion again, and suddenly knows why: it is that Anzor will now always be with her. It is he who now holds center stage, not she, not her antique, precise art. It is he who is the coming man, the norm and the point of interest. Why didn't she understand earlier that she too is part of the grand historical museum? While he's the manifest present, present incarnate. He is the one who holds the world hostage and in thrall. His hurt honor can explode a thousand bodies, that is how much force it has. She can measure the force of hate, now that she knows what it feels like. She knows what it can do, if it's accompanied by the right instruments. Accompanied, augmented. The guns, the explosive devices, the bombs: fury squared. Her own instrument, her precious struggles to make it yield beauty . . . rendered null and void. One thudding sound has canceled them all. Beauty, where is thy sting. She paces up and down her white-carpeted room, as the lights in the apartment buildings come on, bringing into relief squares of windows, in their hundreds and thousands. Lives going on, as if they mattered. In her own space capsule, she knows she has ceased to matter. The worm of time is working its way through her body, her days, her microscopic portion of mortality. And that's all. And that's all.

*

And then, she's an item on the news herself. Not much of one, just a brief bulletin, a flicker of footage, noting the mysterious disappearance of Isabel Merton, a well-known pianist last seen in Barcelona, after the concert made famous for a bomb going off. Murder or kidnapping cannot be excluded, though there's been speculation about a mental breakdown. Of course, Isabel thinks, they would jump to that conclusion, there is a long history of breakdowns among pianists, a roll call of the over-sensitive, or the exhausted, or the disenchanted. Statistically, women pianists don't come off well, and she wonders what demon lovers were responsible for their despondency. Vladimir Horowitz, on the other hand, came up with the most perfect symptoms. In his distress, he became convinced that his fingers were made of glass, and would shatter if they touched the piano's keys. Love turning dangerous, perfection bringing him to break-ing point. The newsman briskly advises that anyone who has any information as to her whereabouts should notify the police. She wonders briefly if Anzor might watch such a program in his mountainous wilderness. She hopes not. He would understand that her disappearance has something to do with him; that she has been affected. She doesn't want him to have the satisfaction, she thinks furiously, and suddenly realizes that she hates him with the hatred of still fresh love. Personally, specifically, within all her vast, oceanic, indiscriminate rage. Him, with his intense eyes and delicate hands. With his turn of the torso, like a sculp-tured Greek boy throwing a javelin in a beautiful elongated line, and his willingness to throw the grenade, undoubtedly with the same gesture. His will indiscriminately to kill.

Who was Anzor, what turns of feeling have led him to the sheikh, to his truck . . . Then she realizes it doesn't matter. It doesn't matter who he is, what he feels, what exquisite tremors of love or anger have brought him to where he is. It is the instruments he uses, and the bloody convictions powering them that matter. The personal is over. It doesn't matter if Anzor disappears, if any of them disappear; there'll be others, powered by simple crude Ideas, just as it doesn't matter whom precisely they kill . . . The unique person is over. She paces up and down her room, groaning with anger. She wants him here in this white room, so that she can lash out at him, shake him, wreak violence upon him. Well, he'll probably see to that himself, she thinks, and then feels the inadequacy of anything that she could do to him. It is not violence she wants, no, not to destroy his body. She wants him to take back the power he has come to have over her, the power to skew the world with his injured pride and his hor- rifying certainties. She wants him to admit, again and again, that he is in the wrong. That he is wrongness itself. Otherwise, the world won't be righted. But of course it won't be, the world will never straighten itself out on its axis again.

Her fingers drum unconsciously on the café table. They're mov- ing through a Chopin Nocturne of their own will. She notices and tries to stop, but the melody, winding and elongating itself into an elegant, elegiac line, is too deeply encoded in her to be halted. It seems to follow some furrow in her mind that has been laid down through countless repetitions, a physical incorpora- tion. It is in her body, *in corpore*. She knows it by heart, that's what it used to be called, it is in her and cannot be easily extracted. Undoubtedly, the pathways of her brain have been altered by this somehow. The nocturne's gesture of wistful tenderness has attached itself to her inner cells. How utterly unsuited to everything around her, she thinks harshly, how redo- lent of parlors and young girls with heads bent over the key- board, while a suitor lingers nearby admiringly, hopefully. Redolent, yes, that's the word, even her vocabulary is ridiculous. Parlors and suitors, and later, the concert. The heroic artist. The hushed hall, the reverend audiences, the moist-eyed, moist-lipped fans. Sublimity and transport, a hysteria of transport. You can be ruined by sublimity just as much as by kitsch. How could she have fallen for it, when what's going on outside is screaming pain and violence? Screams, redolent of blood. That's the sound the world makes now. No longer armies clashing in the night, no longer rows of soldiers ranged in their terrible beauty, to declare their intention before proceeding to the business of killing. No terrible beauty at all, just the pure hatred, yes, pure, unmodified, made potent by its impotence, moving from rage directly to the act, the bloody act. Between the intention and the act, there falls no shadow. There falls no thought or pity. Beauty, where is thy power?

She nearly brings her fist down on the small table, then recoils out of instinct. The hand apparently still wants to protect itself. She gave herself over to the music in perfect faith, threw herself at beauty as at a sacrificial pyre, in which she could burn and become incandescent. She wanted to be consumed, because not to be consumed was to be only herself. Or to be less than herself. Some ancient instinct of self-sacrifice working its way in her, the need to burn so as to fully live. Isn't that how sacrifice is supposed to work, to take you up into Something Greater, isn't that what Anzor wanted as well, why he left her to ride on his thuggish truck, to hold his brutish gun, to throw himself at his sacrificial pyre? Except he is going to die, and take others with him . . . Carelessly, wantonly, with no thought for the forever mangled bodies or the scrambled limbs. Nothing personal. Nothing personal at all. She feels ill again, gut-sick, soul-sick, in some way she can't pinpoint or define. Fear, nausea, heartbreak, all intermixed. One could probably make a pharmacy of feelings, if one knew enough. One day, probably we will know enough, we'll take feeling pills in homeopathic doses. The business of simple humanity cannot go on much longer, it has done too much harm. But now she knows only that she feels ill, that the homeopathic dose she has taken in through Anzor has been of something perilous. A sickness unto death. Her fingers on the table are moving through a Bach Partita. She cuts the phrase off midway in her mind and calls the waiter over for the bill.

She goes down to the bar the next evening, and drinks without thinking. A man in a white jacket puts his tanned hand on hers, and she feels its heat. He asks if she would like to get some fresh air, and she says OK, why not, all right. It'll be a diversion, it'll distract her from her Thoughts. As they walk toward his apartment, he tells her he is a businessman, and works mostly in Africa. She asks him what he does, but he is evasive. Suddenly, she's sure: He's an arms dealer, he delivers precise instruments which shred the body to those unhinged-looking child soldiers she's seen on TV. She looks at the man's thick-featured face and his Rolex watch with revulsion. He indicates a pleasant villa, where he lives; does she want to come in for a drink? She peers at the house vaguely, and without a word turns round and begins to walk away.

"Hey," he says, grabbing her roughly by the shoulder. "This isn't fair."

"Don't you dare," she says, and something in her voice must convey its own menace, because he lets her go. "Don't you dare use that word, or I'll call the police." She means the word "fair." Now he must conclude she's not quite right in the head, because he shrugs and makes an exaggerated gesture with his arm, indicating she's quite free to go.

She goes back to her white room to watch the news. This is really what she wants to do, administer her own punishment to herself in her own monastic cell. Punishment for what? For her innocence, in excess of what is allowed, her need for Anzor, her need to believe in Anzor, her need for rapture in excess of what is allowed. For her insistence that there is something beyond the banal surfaces of things. For not getting it. That's the moral crime. She has had the presumption to want to live in beauty, to glide above the intractable concreteness of the world. She has wanted undue privileges.

On television, a debate about pension plans, then another about whether ethnic cleansing in Bosnia is equivalent to genocide. An obscure guerrilla group somewhere in Indonesia has conducted its very own massacre. There's an image of an armless body, and she turns away and tries to keep her stomach from lurching. But the group apparently has a good cause, a just cause, an excellent cause. Moreover, they are careful not to target women and children. These are the kinds of distinctions, she thinks, she must learn to make:

* Do they kill only others, or also their own.
* Do they kill only those who have done them harm, or anyone who is conveniently within range.
* Do they kill for reasons of state, or of statelessness.
* Do they kill for any reason at all, or just for the hell of it.
* Do they kill functionally, just to kill, or do they wish to inflict extra suffering and pain.
* Do they kill to provoke or to retaliate.
* Do they kill because they have too much power, or because they do not have enough.

She used to think that what mattered was the difference between piano and pianissimo, between a crescendo which ascends into triumph, and one which signals calm resolution. Instead, she should have been paying attention to the differences between a massacre and an act of war, mowing people down out of despair or out of conviction; mass killing perpetrated by deliberately marching armies, and carnage perpetrated in orgiastic mayhem. What use is her kind of knowledge, in the face of this? The exquisite nuances of Schubert, the hypertrophied involutions of Strauss, the whole super-subtle history of the soul? One thudding sound renders them null and void. Obsolete. No ideas but in music, that is what she has believed. She sees herself through the eyes of the camouflaged guerrilla in the Indonesian jungle, through the sights of his gun, the lens of his relentless, monotone Belief. From that perspective, she can be swatted like a fly, and maybe she deserves it, she's so hypertrophied, so . . . unnecessary. What does it matter if she, or another like her, is deleted from the face of the earth? She has spent her time examining the demi-quavers of her own perceptions, considering how to move from lyricism to storminess in a Chopin Scherzo without violating the integrity, the truth, the truthfulness, of the musical line. She has crossed the world at will, and has worried about whether it is sufficiently *interesting*. A late bloom of a luxurious time, a superfluous woman. From the perspective of the grenade. And she has no perspective from which to answer it. Her sickness unto death extends to herself. She has nothing with which to answer the guerrilla, or the terrorist. Or herself.

One afternoon, she turns on the radio, and the sounds of Brahms' Third Symphony startlingly reach her, in all their somber, stately beauty. She turns it off as if stung. This is danger, pain. She does not want such beauty to exist in the world. Let there be no more beauty. Let there be no more love. She'll never love again, how could she? She understands now that the world is pervaded by poisonous hatred, she has breathed the air of virulent ill will. Wolfe knew this, now she knows it too. She has seen the laughing faces of boy soldiers in Africa, the merry swagger of Serbia's henchmen, and she knows they're intoxicated. They're having the time of their lives. It is their laughter that is killing meaning, that injects the veins of the world with venom. The cold touch of mockery, under which all love and sense wither. Death administered with insouciance. If this can be done . . . No, let there be silence, at least; let there be no more music. Let there be no false consolation. Wolfe was right. She'll never love again, she'll hate coldly, as the world deserves to be hated. As it is right to hate.

About two weeks after her attempt to disappear herself—has it been only that long?—the phone she has failed to disconnect emits its startling rings. She looks round in confusion, before picking up. It is Anders, calling from New York. Apparently, someone spotted her in her Marseilles neighborhood after the television report, and contacted the local police, who in turn contacted Rougement, who in turn passed the problem on to Anders, where he apparently felt it properly belonged. Anders, who usually rides over all impediments placed in his way like a Caterpillar truck, sounds positively abashed. Is she all right? She isn't in some nasty kind of trouble, is she? There've been all kinds of rumors flying around. Briefly, she feels disconcerted at the thought of what these rumors might be, a twinge of embarrassment coming from some former self, which would have cared about such things. Which would have cared.

She tells Anders the rumors are likely to be all wrong. When he understands that she is not in danger and has come to no bodily harm, his voice regains its full pugilistic force. Isn't she being a bit of a prima donna, frankly? He wouldn't have thought this was her style. "I mean, I understand you were shaken," he shouts into the telephone. "Who wouldn't be? I probably would have been rattled too." She stays quiet by the telephone, as he rolls on. So OK, missing one concert would be perfectly understandable. But why not call him up? Why not talk to him—isn't that what he's there for? Why go to these . . . histrionic lengths, just because some detonating device was placed outside the concert hall? "It wasn't even inside the hall, was it?" he clinches his argument. Frankly, he thinks she's being a bit precious. Well, she thinks so too. When she doesn't respond, he changes his tone. "Who were these guys, anyway?" he asks, with some concern. "I mean, they sound like a really bad crowd. Evil. Are you worried they'll come after you again?"

She says no, but, nevertheless, there is no way she can perform right now. Or even play. Or practice. "I've tried," she tells him, dry-voiced. "And I can't."

He considers and swerves from his assertive course. "Are you depressed? Is that the problem?" he asks almost hopefully. Depression has plenty of precedents in the biographies of performers, it would provide a respectable explanation. "You can tell me, you know," he persists, more kindly. "I've had plenty of clients with problems, it's nothing to be ashamed of. Depression is an illness, and if that's what you have you need to get yourself some help. Meds, if you ask me, not that talking stuff. Never knew anyone who got any benefit from it."

She considers if he's right, if he has hit on the right diagnosis, and says no, she doesn't feel depressed, not really.

"Well then, what is it?" he demands impatiently. "How would you define what is going on?" Good question, she thinks. But she cannot tell him what she really believes: that she is having a crisis of meaning; and that it is this strange, outmoded condition that is weighting down her arms and paralyzing her fingers.

"But I need to be able to tell people something!" He's booming again into the receiver, and she flinches.

"I'm sorry," she says, and means it. She is behaving badly, and wishes she could behave otherwise.

"You know this has financial consequences, don't you?" he says. "I've had frantic calls from people all over Europe." She feels another twinge of anxiety, from the former self; then the indifference returns. Years of Zen meditation could not have achieved a detachment from matters concerning her ego as complete as this.

"Please handle this however you think is fair," she says, and means this too.

Anders breathes hard, as if stopped in the middle of a run. "Well, I can't say I understand what's going on," he says. "But call me if things change. I'm sure we could have you booked again in no time. Who knows, we might even be able to turn this to some kind of advantage . . . No such thing as bad publicity, eh?"

"Sure," she says, playing along. "I'll let you know if I feel I can play again . . ." But she's speaking to him as though through some filmy barrier, from the other side of some great divide. She is surprised herself at how remote she feels from the things that have been of utmost concern to her; from what she has called her life.

"Well, don't take too much time about it," he advises, the boom subsiding to a more friendly growl. "Publicity doesn't keep forever. Just don't forget, everyone has a sell-by date."

She opens Wolfe's *Journal* the next day, as to a forgotten conversation.

September 1, 1982

They're leaving, the youths of this summer; the briskness of fall is in the breeze, and in the trembling of leaves. Before she left, Isabel Merton looked at me shyly, as if wondering about everything that had been left unsaid. Then she came up delicately, as if I were some forest animal that might skid away, and gingerly, she embraced me. She said, "I wanted to thank you for everything you have taught me this summer." Her delicate, feminine body in my arms . . . her smooth skin, her almost audible heartbeat . . . I felt a keening, acute sensation in my chest.

The erotics of teaching. For although I do not know her body, I know something of her mind. I have listened to the tremors of her musical soul. What I feel for this young girl is not so much Eros as pure Agape.

I quoted Edwin Fischer to her, the purest of pianists: "To be a medium, a mediator between the divine, the eternal and the people." I told her it was my parting thought, for her to take away. I allowed myself to hold her for a moment before letting her go. She looked at me with her great green eyes as if hoping for an answer to a question. But of course I could not give it to her. I could not even acknowledge that a question had been asked.

But alas, I cannot avoid my own questions or my unfinished composition. I must keep distilling until it achieves absolute purity. And yet, I sometimes wonder whether it is that ambition which is the sin. Last night, after they left and the wind battered at the windows of my cottage, I felt a great anxiety come upon me, as if I had committed a fundamental error and must pay for it. As if the Devil would come to collect his dues . . . Or my very own demons. They call me the Great Refuser, apparently. They are not wrong.

The phone rings for the second time in several days, and she shudders in response. It is Peter.

"For God's sake," he says simply, after ascertaining it is she who has answered the phone.

"You've talked to Anders," she states.

"Do you know how worried . . . how utterly frantic everyone has been?!" Like Anders, he is shouting, though with a different sort of anger.

"I'm sorry," she says, and again, means it. "I just . . . had to have some time out."

"Time out?" he repeats incredulously. "Is that all?" She doesn't answer, and can almost sense, over the long-distance wires, his resentful bafflement. "Are you OK?" he finally asks.

"Yes," she says, though a note of sadness has crept into her voice. "I'm fine. Basically."

"Well then, could you tell me what's going on? If you still deign to talk to . . . people who care about you." His voice is thickened now with hurt reproach. She has not shown him much trust in these last weeks.

"Maybe I'm just being a capricious artist," she says, with false nonchalance. "You know, bourgeois heroism can get to be pretty exhausting sometimes. For a sensitive artist type."

"Oh come on," he says, suggesting that her flippancy doesn't merit a response. "We've known each other for a long time. Just talk to me, will you?"

She takes in his concern. Yes, they've known each other a long time.

"OK, I'll try," she says, and her voice cracks a little. She hasn't realized how abandoned she has felt; even though it is she who has done the abandoning, who has given herself to abandonment, who's been lost to herself. "But get ready for a longish story." She decides to make full disclosure, of a different kind than she offered to the Barcelona police. She owes him that much. She manages to speak evenly as she tells him about the first encounters with Anzor, the rooms in Warsaw and London, the sheikh; but her voice cracks again as she describes what happened in the concert hall.

"The bastards," Peter says when her account comes to its end. "Goddamn bastards."

"Yes," she says, resignedly. "But the thing is . . ." She stops herself, then decides to go on. "The thing is that . . . you know, I fell for him." That seems the right phrase. Love, fortunately, no longer seems to apply.

Peter's voice is taut with sarcasm. "Every woman adores a fascist, is that it?" He's quoting an impeccable source. "Or a fanatic. You fell for the tritest cliché in the book, kiddo."

"Oh, don't worry, I hate myself," she says breezily.

"That's not my point," he says, very carefully. He has forgotten himself briefly; and she is, in the midst of everything else, touched to realize how difficult this is for him. "I mean, surely the person you should hate is him."

"Oh, I hate him too," she says, her voice darkening with all the accumulated feeling of the past weeks.

"The thing about fanatics," Peter says, changing tack, "is that they have charisma. Like psychotics, or sociopaths. I've seen it when I was doing cases. They have no scruples, that's what makes them irresistible. They can charm you like a snake with their ruthlessness. You just got drawn by one of those fuckers. It's probably your . . . St. Teresa tendencies. You got yourself hypnotized."

"Yes," she says, almost humbly. "You're probably right. Though he was not a psychotic, no, that's not the right word . . ."

"I don't care what the right word is," Peter cuts in. "But I don't see why you should be punishing yourself like this," he presses on. "Why you should turn into some penitent anchorite. It's . . . irrational. Wouldn't stand up in court. I mean, you're not the guilty party."

"No, not guilty," she agrees. "But I am culpable." Again, she feels almost a sense of relief to have found the right word, the word that seems to apply to the case; to have pronounced the right sentence on herself.

"Please," Peter says impatiently. "Don't be so . . . histrionic. You haven't done anything *wrong*."

"Well then, what have I done?" she asks, resignedly. Maybe he'll define it for her.

"You haven't exercised your best judgment in regard to this . . . Chechen gentleman. This . . . jerk. You've been . . . oh you know,

223

not very smart. I'll give you that."

"Thanks," she says.

They fall silent for a while. "Have you contacted the government?" he finally asks. "We do have a government, they have to be good for something."

"What could they do about this?" she says. "Anyway, isn't it up to the Spaniards—"

"Well, if you won't, I'll call somebody," he cuts in decisively. "At least you need to know what you are required to do. I mean, by law. You've been involved in a crime. You probably have to file a report." He's speaking in his professional tone, and she can tell it's out of the need to take charge, to feel he can do something effective in this situation, which has rendered them all strangely ineffectual.

"I wish you wouldn't," she says. She wants time, more time, to deal with her illness. To lick her wounds in private. To sort things out in that place where laws don't count, which is untouchable by regulations. Where she'll know things she cannot yet tell even herself.

"Isabel," he says quietly, recalling her to him, to their intimacy. "I'm worried about you. This is . . . not good. Why don't you come home? Or why don't I come to wherever you are and bring you back."

She tries to figure out how to explain. "Because . . . I couldn't face it," she finally says. "Not yet. Because everything makes me ill. It doesn't matter where I am. But I can't bear . . . oh, at the moment, I can't bear much."

They stay silent for a while, and she imagines him in his leather chair, his graying hair falling over his forehead, his cup of coffee at hand.

"How are you, anyway?" she asks, feeling a surge of warmth at the thought of those details.

"Fine," he says flatly, refusing the inquiry. He is angry again, and she's almost glad of it, glad he isn't being too determinedly self-restrained, too willfully kind. She hears his breathing over the phone. "I think I may contact the government anyway," he states drily. "Without giving your name. Just to inform myself. Since you don't seem to be interested."

"You have the right to be angry at me," she says.

"I sure do," he says. "I have the right to be furious. But somehow that doesn't help."

His tone has turned wry, and she smiles at his implicit allusion to their old conversations. Reasonableness, in this case, doesn't seem to be the issue.

"I'm worried about you," he then repeats.

"Don't be," she says. "I haven't gone . . . mad, you know. I just need to . . . think some things out."

"Well, OK then," he says. "Just let me know when you're ready—"

"I will," she interjects quickly. "I will."

In Between

She packs her bags and gets on a flight to Los Angeles. She needs to find another kind of away. She reads the *Journal* on the long flight; she finds it is one of the few things which gets past her hypersensitive nerves, her bruised alert system.

September 3, 1982

I am left to my own devices, to my days and hours. My moments and my eternities. Left with nothing but time, my old antagonist, and the exertions through which I try to defeat it.

225

My experiments with time: in childhood, to make time stop. First, to stop the sound of my parents' quarrels. Then, as I sat in the basement, so the bombs wouldn't fall. Then, to stop the sound of my parents' silence. Their horrible, pickled silence. Mater and Pater. Heaven knows what they had done or seen.

Later, to arrest time in meditation, to hold it in its pure motionless state. To expand moments till they were as large as stillness.

September 4, 1982

Today, a few bars for the flute, the most elegiac of instruments. I wanted a melody that would be like Orpheus' song after he emerged from the underworld. A flute line, simple and direct, that would sing of what he had seen.

I am haunted by that Day, and all the Events which were my beginning. And by all I have failed, since then, to become. In my solitude, I do not know which is the deeper regret. I no longer know what I am atoning for, and whether the penance is also the sin.

Los Angeles

She rents an apartment in another tower block, sparsely furnished and luxuriously spartan, with a big picture window and a spectacular view of the ocean. She might as well be in Marseilles, except for the enlarged scale of what she beholds, and the highway visible from her bedroom window, with its never-ending stream of silent cars, dully glinting in the day, a glow of firefly lights in the night. The serpentine movement never stops, cannot stop; and the ceaselessness itself is filled with menace. It cannot stop. Something here is out of control. Once a day, she drifts through the Elysian aisles of the gigantic supermarket, extracting a few fresh things from among the supersize boxes and bottles. Fields of forgetfulness, she thinks, as she looks at the other drifters, with their blank faces, picking jars and cans from the shelves with surly apathy. Lethargy, the great evener, reducing everyone to desultory indifference. The awful phosphorescent lighting reinforces the dull hostile glare which a very large white woman directs at her, or rather at her cart, which apparently seems to be in the way. And if anything bothers you, the look prophylactically declares, then you can just shove it.

In the street, the snake of cars has snarled, and is writhing in agitation, horns honking, people emerging from their cars and slamming doors behind them, their postures pugilistic or limply, childishly fed up. In the snake's front, two men are pointing at a car and shouting at each other; as she is crossing, one of them grabs the other and is about to start hitting out. "Stop it!" she says, in an exhalation of rage; and there must be some authority in her voice, because they actually do stop and stare at her as she continues to cross. She has learned something about violence, apparently.

In the late afternoon, she walks along the beach, listening to the undertow of the water, the thud and suction of the waves blending with the ceaseless surf of the traffic, the setting of the pollution-dimmed sun, the never-ending tides. Apocalypse is in everything, in the late afternoons. On the news, hills bubble and slide with mud, and forests burn. People stand in front of their flattened houses, the habitual hostility of their bodies turned strangely passive, as if the forces they had witnessed had quieted them down, shocked them into a kind of calm.

Nothing, nothing enchants her. The breezes from the ocean do not make her think that it's nice weather. The glorious views of the coastline bring her the chill of *nature morte*. I have fallen into acedia, she thinks, the greatest sin . . . Such a quaint idea, sin, and yet there it is again, and the sensation to go with it in her gut, or is it her psyche, or even soul, as if she's been violated, or involved in a violation . . . Violation of what? Of whatever it was that made the world seem desirable, that gave it a horizon and made her want to move beyond it, made her *want*. In the Elysian supermarket, the whirr of air conditioning is like a loud insect drone, and she changes her mind about getting the food and walks along the sidewalk of the vacuous street, among the clapboard houses and the burger joints. She feels a solitude that is absolute, solitude made more gaping by the vast spaces which can be intuited just beyond the clusters of makeshift buildings, by the graceless clumsy movements of the passersby, as if they were unused to being out of their cars, by the lethargic postures which declare they don't care, that nobody cares. They seem as disposable, as provisional, as the warehouses and tacky transient businesses lying low along the sunny, mean street. Nobody cares, she thinks, nobody cared for; and the thought punctures her with such cold hopelessness that she feels as if she has understood another layer of hell.

She rents a car with no particular goal, and drives on to a highway and into the wavering smog. There are those who want to undo, she thinks, and those who want to be undone. As Kolya wanted to be undone, as Wolfe worked toward his own undoing. The great, the only, question is why not commit suicide. Who said that? Somebody did. In the slowly moving car next to her, a woman in a bright yellow jacket is pushing a child angrily back into its seat. Dolce & Gabbana, she thinks, the yellow jacket. On the news, a senator from somewhere talks in a toneless voice about the need to improve farm subsidies in his state. The vacuity of vast empty spaces. Nothing but this endlessly reiterative motion, the metallic glint of cars inching forward through the poisoned air. Somewhere, she now knows, soldiers are waking up in their barracks; somewhere, clusters of men are bending over local maps and putting together simple mechanisms which will explode. Somewhere, someone is keening because they have lost everything which was their life. Is that the only beyond there is. Violence and suffering, suffering and violence. My hate is my love, she hears Anzor saying, and sees his dark inward-turned eyes. I love my hate, she continues in his voice, I cling to it as I cling to my ancestors' memory, to my integrity, my faith. If we're not willing to die for something, she hears him say, then we do not really live. If we're not willing to kill, she adds for him. For she now grasps the implications. The old rites of sacrifice draw us on. Yes, she thinks, I begin to understand. Because what alternative is there to pointless motion? What other terminus to our condition, our utterly limited repertory? If you do not transcend yourself . . . Enclosed in her metallic capsule, she feels the anxiety of pointless movement, a metaphysical claustrophobia. She is just one creature, horribly arrested in the car, in concreteness, in the moment. In her mind and skull. Her very own black box. Nothing beyond, nothing to pitch herself toward. A downpour, sudden and cataclysmic, beats against the windshield. She gropes toward an exit from the highway, and half blindly drives back to her apartment, where she turns on the news and, afterward, luxuriates in her hate, her seemingly limitless rage.

September 6, 1982

My experiments with time, continued: to freeze Time
into solid state, into white expanses of ice. Thomas
Mann knew. His Faustus knew, with his icy visions and

229

his inhuman System. I have studied Faust's dark purposes and have seen his ghastly ends. I have seen the consequences of hubris, and they are as ugly as mass death. I want to sweep the decks clean, in one pure, encompassing sound. No more grandeur! No more pomp! Distill, reduce, compress. No folderol! Only what is true should remain. Only what is pure, without pomp or dross. The condensed dark-light kernel.

September 7, 1982

Falling into State X. Pure darkness, pure dread. Whereof one cannot speak. Wherein one cannot speak. The chaos of nothingness, which is also a current of pure energy. Pure, electric, pre-animate. I seem to be touching on a stratum at which life and death meet. I think the Chinese call it qi.

Only music. Or silence. Or music which gives full brief to silence.

Apocalypse is in everything; it's in her breakfast, in the silent elevator, the gilded lobby, the streets outside. She goes down to the beach, hoping for some peace, but the Apocalypse follows her there. It doesn't let her go as she lies down on the towel she has brought with her, and closes her eyes against the sun. There's no relief from it, now that she has seen the skin of the world peeled back, and the mayhem within. Sidewalks crumple from the heat; forests burn. Maybe that's as it should be, she thinks, it's all been going on too long. Let it be cleared away, let the decks be swept clean.

One afternoon, as she walks back from the supermarket, she feels that a large man walking behind her is adjusting his movements too closely to hers, and she begins to run in a suffusion of panic. He doesn't run after her, but that night, she plunges into nightmares of being lost. She doesn't know which city she's in, she's lost her passport, she has somehow given away her home, she's late for the plane and once she's in it, it will crash . . . In her turbulent dream state, she feels an acute longing for Lena, and then an acute anger. See, she says to her mother, what has happened to your daughter. See how lost and adrift I am. How can I understand the world I live in when you've never taken me by the hand and explained? When you've abandoned me, so that no one can ever make it safe.

As she stands at a street crossing, she hears a car horn honking, and her name being called out imperiously. She turns in the wrong direction first, then spots a woman waving energetically through an open window of a red convertible Saab. It's Jane, her tanned face half covered by a cascade of black curls and glamorous sunglasses, gesturing Isabel impatiently toward the car, and pointing at the lights, which are about to change. "Get in!" she shouts, in a way which brooks no contradiction, and Isabel does. Jane steps on the accelerator as Isabel shuts the door, and bowls on, amid urgent honking from the momentarily stalled cars.

"Well, old girl," Jane addresses her, once they are on a main thoroughfare, "fancy meeting you here! Who knew you were in LA of all places? You've been quite the sensation, you know. In your absence."

"I'm staying near here," Isabel says. "Do you want to come in? I'll give you a cup of coffee. I'm afraid I can't offer much more."

"Sure," Jane says, and Isabel guides her into the enormous parking lot with its reek of gasoline, and then to the elevator which takes them up to the thirtieth floor.

Jane's three-dimensional energy makes the apartment seem even more Warholian by contrast. She inspects it with mildly disapproving bemusement. "I see you've taken Wolfe's advice to heart after all these years," she says.

"What do you mean?"

"You know how he always said that to be a real artist, you have to be a monk. Or a nun. I mean, this is a convent cell, girl."

"It suits me," Isabel declares. "It suits me just fine."

"So are you going to tell me what's going on?" Jane asks, curving herself down into the sofa. "I only know a few things from Anders. He's been tearing his hair out. It's almost a satisfaction."

"That's not what I'm doing it for, believe me," Isabel says and stops.

"Of course not," Jane agrees merrily. "But then what on earth . . . I mean, you've never been a drama queen."

"Haven't you ever had the cello go dead on you?" Isabel asks.

Jane emits a brief, are-you-kidding sort of snort. "Sure, it happens sometimes. Happens to all of us. I mean, is that all?" She curls the phrase in elaborate incredulity.

"That's one way to put it," Isabel says. "I just can't . . . make the music come alive."

"Well then, play on automatic for a while," Jane retorts cheerfully. "Sometimes you've got to do that, it's what being a professional is about. Being able to do it on automatic."

"I suppose," Isabel says drily.

Jane lowers her voice to a parodied confidentiality. "And sometimes, frankly, if I may share a bit of wisdom with you, there's nothing like a little fuck. Before a concert. Or after. Or almost at any time. To stir things up. To get the juices going."

Isabel ignores the effort to cajole her into a better humor. "This is worse than usual," she says flatly. "Or rather, it's different."

"Oh honestly," Jane says impatiently. "Why, just because some guy you got involved with turned out to be a nasty?"

"I suppose that's one way to put it."

"Well, just forget it then, OK? I mean, he's gone, isn't he? Or is he still giving you trouble?"

"No," Isabel says. "Not really."

"Well then, relax a little, you know? I mean, what's the point of taking everything so seriously?"

Then she gives a kind of what-the-hell shrug and looks at Isabel more directly. "Not that I'm not serious, in my own way. My very own way. I'm dead serious, actually, if the truth be known. I play for real, that's my seriousness. I say fuck it all, and this is a matter of life and death. It amounts more or less to the same thing. You know?"

"I do," Isabel says. She has seen it, Jane's all-out fearlessness; playing as though she had nothing left to lose.

"That's what Wolfe couldn't understand." Jane sounds almost wistful. "He just didn't get it about me. Though he took me seriously too, in a way. Don't you think?" Her voice betrays a need to be reassured; apparently, not even her self-confidence is impermeable.

"Oh yes," Isabel says. "You were his challenge. His problem. His all-American problem."

Jane laughs. "Mad old Wolfe," she says. "Was it worth it, what he did to himself? Driving himself crazy over a composition. A big ghastly sound, as far as I can make out." She looks at Isabel with concern. "And now you're driving yourself crazy over some mad Chechen."

"Don't you think there was something heroic about what Wolfe tried to do?" Isabel asks, partly to keep Jane's perceptive attentions off herself.

"Oh, spare me such heroics," Jane says, energetically. "It was just masochism. He was kind of anorexic, don't you know that? I mean, didn't you see how thin he was?"

"I'm not sure that kind of word applies—"

"I mean, he had a sort of . . . spiritual anorexia. He couldn't stand all that . . . life around him."

Isabel looks at Jane, sitting in comfortable amplitude on the sofa, her eyes alive and impish. She's sparkling with affirmation, with good spirits, good health. "But the thing is," Jane continues, "that you mattered to him. Really mattered. To tell you the truth, I was almost envious when I was reading . . . those parts."

Isabel smiles. "Oh well, maybe we both meant something to him. He did take us on, in his way. You must give him that."

"Well, here's to him," Jane says, raising her coffee cup. "The great sourpuss. The Last Great Artist."

"What are you doing in LA, anyway?" Isabel asks. She suddenly realizes she doesn't even know where Jane lives nowadays, where her base is when she's not on the road.

"Having Fun," Jane pronounces sententiously, as if reminding Isabel of an important principle. Then she shrugs merrily and explains that she's been hired as a consultant for a film about a cellist. "It's going to be a certified piece of shit," she says. "But hey, they pay more than you'd believe. And you should see some of the guys around the set. They work out at the gym a lot. And they don't take anything too seriously, I can tell you that."

She looks at Isabel with her girlish complicity, even as she considers her carefully. "I'll see you soon," she says. "I'm going to come and get you *out* of here, show you round LA. We're going to have ourselves some fun."

September 9, 1982

. . . what Arthur Schnabel called "the second simplicity."
This is what I want to achieve. It is what every true
artist wants to achieve. But perhaps I have not been simple enough. I confess that I am forced to think about

that girl, Jane, who has provoked me all summer. Is it possible that this Jane from Iowa has achieved the simplicity I strive for?

But no, she only has the first simplicity: innocent, ignorant, unscrupulous. She just wants to get whatever she wants, with no conflict and no price. I want the resolution which comes after strife and darkness. I am still battling my way through the complications of my composition, and all my dread. But I know it is only after this struggle that I can hope to attain the true second simplicity.

She knows Peter will call now, and he does. "I guess I'm getting easier to find," she says, and is surprised by the lightness of her tone.

"Surely you didn't think Jane would be discreet," he returns. "She's worried about you."

"I can't imagine Jane worried."

"I don't mean she's tearing her hair out," he says wryly, and then sighs. "I don't suppose you're going to tell me why you're in LA."

"No," she confirms. She doesn't really know the answer herself.

"Right," he says briskly. "In that case, why don't you tell me how you spend your days?"

And so she tells him about the Elysian supermarket, her walks on the beach, the angry traffic.

"Ah yes, road rage," he says. "There was quite an example of it today at the Fairway."

"The Fairway?" she repeats. The idea of any kind of rage in her familiar old neighborhood supermarket seems very incongruous.

"Or rather, lane rage," Peter distinguishes. "A special subcategory. We'll probably have to make new laws for supermarket traffic, if this incident is any example."

"What happened?"

"Well, you know how crowded the place gets, especially in the late afternoon. So this guy, sort of self-important and obnoxious-looking, pushes his cart right into a little old lady who's taking too much time getting her stuff off the shelf. In the organic vegetable section. You know, the floor is quite slippery over there. He shoved her pretty hard, I think it was deliberate. Or semi-deliberate. It's not the kind of distinction the law is good at. Anyway, she sort of slid on the slippage, and then just fell. Straight on the floor. There was a thud."

"You saw it?"

"I was right there. I tried to help her up, but all of a sudden there was complete pandemonium. Scattered vegetables, someone screaming to call the police."

"Gosh."

"Wait, there's more. Because in the middle of all this, some runty kid snatches the guy's briefcase. I mean, the guy who pushed the old lady. The perp."

"All this in the Fairway?"

"Yup."

"OK, so then what?"

"So then the guy, I mean the perp, goes absolutely berserk. He's shouting, 'Get him! It's government documents! Classified!' And you know what? The runty kid hears this, and actually turns around and throws the briefcase back, while everyone watches with their mouths open."

"Just because it was government documents?"

"I guess some people are still awed . . . Or the kid just got scared. I mean, who knows what 'government documents' means these days. You know, all those movies where someone gets to know something, and the next thing you know he's dead."

"Yeah," she says. "All those movies."

"I didn't mean to suggest—" he begins.

"I can't stand it," she says.

"What? Can't stand what?"

"What we're getting used to. The meanness. The routine . . . aggression." Fury has flared up and is working its way through her chest.

"Hey, kiddo," Peter says briskly, as if speaking to a child, "this was a . . . non-significant incident. A shaggy-dog story. I was just trying to amuse you, for God's sake."

"Just," she says. "It's always just." She knows whom she's echoing.

"Well, what would you want to do about it, anyway? Declare a protest against the Fairway? Or its clientele? Or the current state of the world, as it actually manifests itself?" He sounds energized by exasperation.

She hears herself breathing in agitation, reins herself in. When will her rage subside, now that it has been awakened . . .

"I'm sure you're right," she finally says, and her voice is now small and discouraged. She can hear him listening to her, registering her tone; her mood.

They remain silent for a while. "Why don't you come home?" he then says, his voice dropping to another key, a reminder of their intimacy. The voice brushes against her like a touch, and she doesn't recoil.

She gauges her own reactions, and sees that something is changing. "I suppose I will, one of these days," she says. "I just don't know when."

"I don't mean come back to me, if that's not what you—"

"Oh, Peter," she interjects, the words emerging spontaneously out of her gratitude, and something else as well. "I love you, you know."

She hopes he won't misunderstand, and he doesn't.

"Well, I suppose we'll talk soon," he says, trying to sound

casual. But she knows all the gradations of his seemingly flat voice, and she knows he is moved.

"Yes," she says. "Soon."

The phone rings again in the evening, and she looks at it with some caution before deciding to pick up.

"You may not remember me," a woman's voice says, but she instantly recognizes the prolonged, lilting syllables. It's Katrina, the Russian poetess.

"How on earth did you find out where I am?" Isabel asks. She suspects Anders, Rougement.

"From McElvoy, actually," Katrina says. "If you remember him."

"I don't understand," Isabel says, though she now remembers that Anzor said something about McElvoy. What was it? How well do they all know each other?

"Well, you know, he's been concerned about you. We have both been. We've been . . . tracking your movements to some extent, ever since that embassy party in Sofia, where you got acquainted with our Anzorichka. Actually, ever since Margarita recommended him to you. That was stupid of her."

Isabel tries to think back to the reception in Paris. It seems to have taken place ages ago, and she remembers it as a placid event. "So you mean, you and McElvoy are colleagues."

"Oh, you know, we've worked together from time to time . . . nothing very big. I am sometimes able to offer some information. You know, we're all on the same side now."

Isabel now rewinds to the reception in Brussels, and Katrina's ubiquitous presence. Only connect, she thinks, though this is hardly what the moralists had in mind, these shadowy linkages, undertaken in the service of breaking up linkages which are more shadowy still. Shadowy and simple, if only she had been willing to see. To look at the obvious, rather than trying to discern something beyond, below, within.

"But this is outrageous," she says. She wonders how closely she's been watched, whether there are photographs somewhere.

"What is outrageous, darling?" Katrina asks calmly. "That we were concerned? That we were watching out for you?"

Isabel considers, and feels herself making another readjustment, to a more comic bemusement. She thought she'd fallen for the romantic sublime; instead, she'd been caught in some low international farce. The joke is definitely on her. "How much did you know?" she finally asks.

Katrina sighs again. "Not much, believe me, not as much as we would like to know. Anyway, it was one of those . . . borderline situations."

"Then why didn't you at least warn me."

"I tried, remember? As much as I felt I could. Given that the situation was . . . not yet clarified."

Isabel remembers some oblique signal, at the reception in Brussels. They all get these ideas in their heads, Katrina purred, in her sly suggestive tone. Not much of a warning, not enough for her to understand. At least not if she didn't want to.

"But you seemed . . . close to Anzor," she protests, remembering the reception.

"Well, what do you expect?" Katrina retorts. "I was supposed to watch him. Besides . . . to tell you the truth, I sort of liked Anzor. Before he got mixed up with that really odious gang."

"You liked him."

"Well, didn't you?" Katrina asks, in her impish lilt.

"But you knew what he was up to."

"Oh, don't get me wrong. I disliked him too, especially when he took up with those . . . gangsters. Believe me, I disapprove. I'm going to do everything in my power to help wipe them out."

"Now you frighten me."

"It's not a polite game," Katrina says tersely. "But you know, Anzor was one of our elusives. Very hard to make out. His allegiances—well, shall we say they shifted. By which I don't mean he was an opportunist. I mean the opposite, really. He was a sort of . . . idealist. He followed his ideas. His beliefs. He was highly intelligent, our Anzorichka, but also very stupid."

"He didn't seem stupid to me," Isabel says, helplessly.

"He was stupid with ideas," Katrina says. "A kind of moral idiot. You can read Dostoevsky, we have our very own tradition of these loonies. You know, madness is most dangerous when it's rational. There's this visceral madness, the kind you recognize from their eyes, where they go unhinged and out of control. But that kind of madness is . . . feeble. They don't know what they want, so they're prey to anyone who comes along and takes them in hand and gives them a Kalashnikov or an explosive belt to strap themselves to. They feel just great, being sent on a mission. They're the ones who get used as fodder by the big guys, the ones who think they have a grand strategy." She sighs. "You know, I've seen quite a few of them by now, I can tell the various types—"

"But Anzor—" Isabel interjects.

"Oh, Anzor was one of the *intelligents*," Katrina answers, and launches into her flow of explanation again. "That was what made him so susceptible. You know, there's no one like an intellectual to become fanatical with ideas. They think there's nothing outside them. Anzor . . . he wasn't deranged, just deluded. He got fooled by his beliefs. He was a purist, that was his problem." She has been sounding very impassioned, by Katrina standards. "Once he fell for this stuff . . . I mean, I can understand how you fell for him. I know these characters, they become kind of . . . incandescent with conviction. And ice cold with it, too. After a while, there is no human scale of feeling."

"But he seemed—"

"Oh seemed. It's such an old story. We're idiots too, we just lap this stuff up, the man looking into the middle distance and seeing the Cause. It's so romantic, so . . . charismatic. Especially if you live in a nice democratic country where nothing much happens. It's very exciting. But you know what, these guys are actually not very exciting. Or interesting. I mean, maybe your Anzor was an exception, but for the most part . . . They're fanatics, but they're also boys with toys. It's easy for them now, that's the problem. They get upset about something, they get some ideas, and bingo, the Kalashnikovs are right there, or something worse. There's nothing to it, that's the problem. They get very drunk, or they pray a lot, or somebody gives them drugs, and they think they're going to change the world. By blowing it up, of course, because what other kind of revolution is there. Bring down Mother Russia. Or the Wicked West. Or whoever they happen to hate. It's easy. Much too easy."

Isabel realizes that something has been out of kilter while they've talked. "Why are you speaking about Anzor in the past tense?" she asks.

There is an audible sigh on the other end of the receiver. "We've lost track of him," Katrina says. "Which is really too bad."

"Do you think . . ." Isabel begins.

"Possibly," Katrina answers. "You know, they do more of those suicide missions these days. The heroes." She pronounces the last word with definitive sarcasm. "Sometimes we don't know exactly . . . who was involved."

They don't speak for a moment. "Anyway, darling, you should take care of yourself, all right?" Katrina says, and there is no irony in her voice this time. Her tone is almost maternal, but then, she is the older one in this conversation, the one who has known for a long time that the world is murky and impure, and that behind its facades there is no beyond, only more shadowy links, more conflict, more of the same.

"Are you going to try to find him?" Isabel asks tonelessly.

"Sure," Katrina says. "But we may not." She sighs again. "Anyway, this is not a reason for mourning. Or for feeling sorry.

He knew exactly what he was doing. It's the others . . . the ones who get blown up for no good reason. There're too many of them. Too many."

It's easy, that's the revelation she has to contend with. She's driving on automatic, hardly paying attention to where she's going. By the time they decide to pull the trigger or the switch, or detonate the device, or throw it, there is nothing to it, except performing the maneuver deftly and hoping to escape under the cover of the big brute noise. Or in some cases, to vanish in it.

"You just don't get it," Larry had said to her, in another epoch. "You don't get it."

Now it all seems connected, the things she didn't get. She didn't get how *uncomplicated* the world is, how simple human purposes, how transparent. How most things are put together from component parts, like the bombs that Anzor or his buddies may be putting together right now. Constructing. Deconstructing. No vatic spirit interfused with things. Only a few Ideas, bestriding the world like ancient beasts, like clumsy mastodons. Only the doing and undoing. She remembers Anzor's long, mobile fingers, his easily ignited pride. But she now knows: it doesn't matter who Anzor is, or was, or what sort of character he has. Or had. Character: another word from another era. Anzor's easily kindled sensitivities, the way he traveled the gradient from loyalty to hate . . . Irrelevant. Character melts at a certain degree of heat, or extremity. His hate would have been as finite as his love without the detonating devices in his hands. He might have kicked in the door, gotten drunk at the local pub. Might have raised his fist too violently at the football match. Without his devices and his Beliefs. It is those that augment rage to the nth power. She thinks of the man in the kaffiyeh and his hand on Anzor's shoulder, summoning him, sealing a compact. That was what really mattered, the serious thing; the gesture which left the imprint, which prepared Anzor for his deeds. He was readying himself to become an instrument, pure and streamlined. No interferences allowed. In such a state, detonating the device would have been logical. Easy. A simple QED. The mauled bodies, the fragmented limbs—a necessary result. A little deconstruction wreaked in the flesh. Probably, Anzor never imagined that part. But then, he didn't need to. He had his iron-clad reasons. Killing the enemy: it's a very old business, the oldest profession. We're in the business of life and death, she thinks; we've always been in it, and it is such a finite proposition. You live once, you die once. Amid collective carnage, that, at least, is a consolation. At least death cannot be augmented beyond itself. She steps hard on the pedal as the traffic begins to move. There is no vastness into which the smoke of Anzor's sacrifice ascended, nothing beyond the asphalt of the highway and the smoggy air. Nothing to take her beyond the flatness of the world, its bitter banality.

Then it is McElvoy himself on the phone. "I feel awful about what happened," he says, after the throat-clearing preliminaries. "Even though I had no way of knowing that anything would happen, of course. I was an unwitting agent of events."

"But you knew Anzor," she states.

"Oh not well, not well."

"Not well enough to warn me, I suppose," she says, and some resentment steals into her voice.

"I'm not sure that would have been appropriate," McElvoy asserts firmly. "It was all pretty haphazard. Our meeting, your meeting with him. I didn't want to overinterpret. This was below the radar. Not the kind of thing we can figure into our equations." He pauses, before going on. "Anyway, frankly, I couldn't have predicted that you would—"

"Yes, I know," she interrupts drily. "I suppose I couldn't have predicted it myself." Despite everything, she feels a sort of regret at how altered she must seem in his eyes, how tarnished her image. She wonders what will happen to his admiration for her, whether he'll still listen to her CDs.

"Well, maybe I should have been more prudent. Or more prescient," McElvoy concedes soothingly. He's letting her off the hook by suggesting the errors have been partly his. "I suppose I should have taken his passion for music into account."

"In the equations."

"We need to make our calculations more sensitive, that's for sure. Not that they can ever be completely reliable. There are limits to our control over events, I'm afraid." He sighs again. "Are you all right, though? This must have been a shock."

"Yes. It was a shock."

"I'm just sorry we didn't catch on to how deep he was in this new Chechen stuff," McElvoy is saying. "If we had known, I'd have warned you, of course. I'd have come to Sofia, or Brussels, if necessary."

"So it was all just a bunch of coincidences," she says.

"Pretty much," McElvoy confirms, and then corrects himself. "As far as we know. Certainly meeting you was. He couldn't have arranged that. No, that was just . . . something that happened."

"Is it all random, then?" she restates, unhappily. The Rotterdam incident floats up in her mind, from an epoch ago.

"Up to a point," he distinguishes. "We can see what's happening on a large scale. But in micro, we're dealing with unknowns. Our forecasts can damn well tell you that there'll be more of this stuff around, but we have no idea where it will flare up next. That's the advantage these guys have, random aggression. Or maybe it's just aggressive randomness, maybe they're just profiting from the way things are."

He's speaking zestfully, and there's no trace of that emollient respect in his voice which marked their earlier conversations. He's on his own ground now, and he's enjoying his authority.

"Who's 'we' exactly," she asks, because she's irritated at him. Then she feels irritated at the sanctimoniousness of her own question.

"Oh, there isn't much of a we, unfortunately," he responds breezily. "I've been following this on an ad hoc sort of basis. Frankly, I had to persuade my old pals at the State Department to take any interest in this stuff at all. Not our sphere of influence, really. Except insofar as everything is interconnected."

"Interconnected and random," she points out.

"Yeah, that's about right. Not an easy equation to work with, you must admit. Hard to nail the specifics down."

"Do you know what they're up to now?" she asks. "In Anzor's country? Or God knows where? What they're planning to do next?"

McElvoy sighs. "If I'm going to be completely honest with you," he says, "I'd have to say no. We don't. These characters come into our view and then recede. We have them in our cross hairs, and then all of a sudden they've vanished. They are like amoebae, that's the problem. Or like these clusters of cells which sometimes coagulate into sort of . . . blood clots. And which then explode or dissolve." He's clearly enlivened by the metaphors his analysis is throwing up. "Yeah, that's a better analogy. They're not so much random as . . . protean, these guys. As well as brutal. As well as . . . evil."

He almost spits out the last phrase, as if he's reached the acme of revulsion. There's a pause. "But we're going to get the better of them," he picks up, as if the notion of protean evil energized him with a new sense of purpose. "We're going to stamp them out. They have no chance in the long run. We're going to beat them back, whatever it takes." He speaks calmly now, but his voice is metallic with determination, with the hard energy of power. More power, she thinks, than she ever heard in Anzor's voice, in his inflamed pride, or his flaming certainties.

September 13, 1982

"In art as in everything else, one can build only upon a resisting foundation: whatever constantly gives way to pressure, constantly renders movement impossible . . . Whatever diminishes constraint diminishes strength."
—Igor Stravinsky.

The resisting foundation: time itself. The basic element from which music is made. I have tried to ignore its surface flow, and to pierce through it to its true nature, its underlying structure. To that place where it is immovable, where motion blends with stillness. Is that hubris? Was I just piercing into my own, strained self? Is the world knowable in itself, or do we only sense it through our always subjective minds, our distorting senses? What can I know of time, except how I live in it, its sheer dread which is the dread of my own end. I cannot defeat time, no matter how much I struggle. I am merely a conduit for it, a reed through which it passes. Sometimes, it sings within me. Sometimes I can hear its obscure message.

September 15, 1982

Music of the spheres, it is not for us. We no longer hear those eternal, elliptical harmonies. We cannot hear them because we cannot believe in them.

September 17, 1982

Left to my own devices, I only know the blankness of
daylight, and the blank regrets within me. Sometimes,
the face of Renata blends with that of Isabel Merton, as
if they existed in the same moment. As if the interval of
years between them did not matter. As the passage of
time does not matter in my mind, where all memories
are juxtaposed, and all lines lead always back to the day I
began my composition; the condensed point where time
stopped and began. That day, with its blackness and
beauty, its two epiphanies. How to do justice to both in
one musical language—

Isabel closes the *Journal* and paces around her deluxe cell.
Occasionally, she pauses in front of the picture window to
contemplate the beating of the ocean against the narrow shore,
eerily silent, way down below. Across the passage of time, across
the irrevocable movement from the past to the present, she
caresses Wolfe's cheek, and stays pressed against him a fraction
of a moment longer as she says good-bye . . . Yes, there was
agape between them, amid the erotics of teaching, an exchange
across their shared medium as close as if their minds touched
each other.

She remembers some of his sharp aphorisms: "All art is in
the resistance." "No theory without praxis, no praxis without
theory." "No objectivity without subjectivity. And vice versa.
You can only know the world through yourself. But if you don't
know the world outside yourself, you will have no self." He
believed in condensation, Wolfe did; but he was right about
many things, she knows that now . . .

She pauses at the picture window again, and sees some miniature figures of surfers gliding in and out of the waves, their

tanned torsos sprayed by white foam. Through this measure, Wolfe's diary comes from an archaic age. What are his contortions, in comparison to these healthy, agile bodies? A lurid medieval form of self-torment, tinged with traces of religious rites, with the stigmata of irredeemable history, and the need to atone for sins not one's own. The ambition of it, or the arrogance . . . Perhaps Jane is right to pour the brisk water of ridicule on the whole enterprise. And yet no, she cannot muster Jane's light-hearted disdain. The business of art has been going on for so long, she thinks, only because it is necessary to us . . . As necessary, apparently, as the business of killing. She thinks of Wolfe's sculpted face and his concave chest, and his attempt to whittle away at himself till he was nothing but a conduit for music, the inner music of the world he wanted to hear at the heart of things. Without his kind of struggle, she thinks, what are we but bodies surfing the foamy surfaces, bodies which live and die. But as she looks through the windowpane at the toylike figures below, at their straining to keep balance within their graceful glides, she thinks, perhaps even they are questing for something; for the Perfect Wave. We apparently cannot do without this, we must strain and strive . . . must mold ourselves and the elements we live in, our humanity and our inhumanity. Wolfe should have forgiven himself, should have found someone to forgive him. She should have put up her hand to his cheek when they said good-bye. Across the distance of time, she feels the brush of something against her mind, as of a wing . . . Wolfe's mind against her own; her own angel of the past, passing across a certain kind of knowledge.

Walking along the sandy strip of beach, she notices a woman wearing a gauzy mauve scarf, and looks away instantly, as if the flimsy piece of silk had stabbed at her eyes. Mauve scarf, Kolya's sign. His stylish signature. Then she forces herself to look at the woman, who has stopped to examine a seashell, and to follow the delicate fall of mauve material over a billowing white shirt. It's only a piece of silk fabric, she admonishes herself, worn by somebody else . . . It's not a symbol, we do not live in a forest of symbols, or the sea of allegory. Or the empyrean of extra meanings. But it comes back to her, or at her anyway, as she stands on the white sand: the very heart of pity. She sees Kolya being lifted on the stretcher, his body supine and helpless, but still glowing with taut, graceful youth. It was the look he directed at her, as he was about to be carried out of the dingy room, that has bored itself into the center of her soul. The look, simply and eloquently, said, so you see, my sister, I have wanted love, and now I am dying. I am young and full of vigor, and I am capable of death. His face, with its smooth skin over high cheekbones, was oddly purified, almost transparent; he extended his hand toward her, and then he closed his eyes.

The pity of it. The pity. The membrane between life and death is very thin, she knows that for a fact now, and Kolya slipped through it almost unwittingly. But he took nobody else with him, she thinks, the comparison hitting her with chilling clarity. A beautiful death, Anzor said, all that time ago—it seems an epoch now—as they were lying back among comfortable pillows, in their erotic lassitude. He wanted to go toward death as toward a misty vastness, wanted vast justification to enlarge his acts; instead, he created a tangle of destroyed flesh in which all space collapses. Whereas Kolya died only for himself and through himself; not from hate, but from the lack of love.

It is so hard to traverse our trajectories the whole way, she thinks yet again, so much easier to hurtle toward oblivion. Perhaps that is the secret we cannot bear. The membrane between life and death is paper-thin and easily, oh-so-easily crossed. And also, she adds to herself, between Kolya and

Anzor, Wolfe and Anzor, Anzor and herself . . . Between making meaning and destroying human flesh. A hair's breadth difference, the thinnest line, a quaver between one turn of the soul and another. And yet, the membrane mustn't be pierced, the line mustn't be crossed; everything depends on it. Perhaps that is the only choice, she thinks, the minute choice leading to enormous consequences.

The woman in the mauve scarf straightens out, and looks quizzically at Isabel, whose concentrated gaze she doesn't quite understand. Isabel waves at her reassuringly, and begins to walk along the ocean's edge.

It is upon her again, the return of meaning. She buys herself a small radio and finds she can listen to music. One afternoon, she happens upon the Mozart Requiem, which Wolfe had heard on his crucial day. It is not easily bearable, its beauty. Who was Mozart, what was he? Unless one posits a most capricious god, implanting the plasma of divinity in a scatologically inclined imp, he was one singular person, endowed with an unerring attunement to the motions of the human heart, and with a musical language which increased his genius to the nth power. His impalpable, all-potent instrument.

The applause—this is a live broadcast—jolts her like some small trauma; through it, she hears the sound of the detonation, as if it were right there in the room. The thud, the screams, the menace. She walks about, calms herself down, and thinks, but it is nothing to the force of Mozart, the immensity he traverses, the Herculean effort to shape the energies which course through us and sometimes tear us apart. The struggle to contain our rage and yearning in lucid form till they become eloquent with meaning. There, she says to Anzor, actually enunciating the words in her agitation, there is the beginning of purpose: in the molding of our forces till they are no longer brutal. Not in your rage, or even your Cause . . . or your crude instruments. In comparison to the music she's just heard, the detonation was cramped, stupid . . . literal. A short cut, quick and easy, and without pity . . . Sometimes it's right to hate the rightful objects of hate, she continues her argument; but not with such wanton ease. Not without mercy for our human smallness, our vulnerable flesh. For the trembling pity of it all, our utter transience. She thinks she can hear, through the still audible Requiem, some vibrating, delicate, radiating energy at the heart of things. It is that which is my answer to you, she thinks, speaking, still, to Anzor. For she will now always have to speak to him, she will always have to rise to his challenge. She knows she cannot hold on to her reply for long; she knows it will come and go. But for the first time in weeks, she feels something like peace.

Tenderness; it's upon her again. Tendrils of tenderness, entirely unjustified, entirely unreasonable, uncurling toward arbitrary objects, haphazard faces she encounters, the tiny terns drawn by the tide, the cries of seagulls in the late afternoon. The small courtyard in the back of a café she has discovered, suddenly seems to her poignant with loveliness, with the lushness of the cascading bougainvillea against the trellised enclosure. She looks about, savoring the gentle sway of the breeze, the low hum of conversation, and smiles with bemusement at a pretty girl in a Muslim hijab, saying, into her cellphone, "So yeah, so I'm going to chill out for a while." Chill out, yes, what a good idea. A very old lady, bent and with scarce white hair, shuffles in on her walker, and Isabel feels a twist at her heart, yes, it is her heart, at the frailty, the need to bear the knowledge of our own passing. Ordinary human pain, of which there is enough.

She listens to the stilled moment, playing its counterpoint with the sharp diagonal shadows of the setting sun, the low clinking of the forks and spoons, the occasional burst of rap from a portable radio. Images come to her unbidden, fragments moving through her mind with only their own rhyme and reason. An anonymous street in Buenos Aires . . . Why does she remember that so vividly, as if it were the most important thing? A dusty street, empty with a Sunday vacuity, hot and bored. And then, the Étude, streaming suddenly out of a window. A cascade of peerless sound thrown across the emptiness. Chopin, No. 23. She was stopped, as if shot through by a bolted arrow. Stopped in her tracks, in a street now suffused with Chopin's liquid light. It was nothing but a stream of sound, and it had the force to arrest her and make her gasp. Blitz of beauty.

She has tried to take her own short cuts, to elation; to exaltation, to Chopin's synoptic wholeness; and now she feels again an obscure guilt. She should have paid attention to the ordinary moments in between, the unfinished provisional prose of life. She goes down to the beach, and the flow of memory continues. The concert in Kenya, and then a trip to a village school. The children listening wide-eyed, and then beginning to sway to Bartók, as to an African drumbeat. The Bartók Suite came off her fingers electrically, as if powered by a magic motor. The savannah; the sun-baked glow of earth and grass; that's still in her skin, as the packed sand of the beach is under her bare feet. She remembers animal eyes through the tall grass, fixed and fixing hers. An exchange, silent and gnomic. Something had been communicated, so she was sure she should walk on, quietly.

The charm of her meetings with Peter, near Columbia and Juilliard, the movies, *Jules et Jim*, *Chinatown*, being young and smart, best and brightest, the new bohemians, the adventure of it, the excitement . . . The first concert, her nervousness, sharp and new, sending febrile currents down her arms. Then a calm, miraculous, as if she were faced with her own end and had accepted it; and the stage, bathed in dazzling light.

And Kolya, listening to her play Schubert's Impromptu, his face rapt and serene. The wheel of Ixion's torture stops for the duration of Orpheus' song.

In the slow dusk, the moments come back to her with an acuteness that is almost melodious. Her own collection of motifs, arbitrary and cherishable. Something has accumulated in her nomadic life, her own private repertory. It is only tenderness which gives these frail fragments meaning, which surrounds its objects with enchantment. Otherwise, the world is barren and unbearable. She feels her breath come in and out, the basic beat, the measure of the body. What else is there to feel for the world, except tenderness? For its adventitious loveliness, its soft tissue, its utter fragility? It is what's left after the fear and rage are gone. Always justified rage, always unjustified tenderness. She begins to hear, in her mind, something like a motif, an intimation of a sound coming both from within and from somewhere else. It's nothing she has heard before, and it summons her attention, like a faraway bird cry or a bugle call. Then it begins to mingle with the deeper textures of her memories, with the swish of the sea and the urban surf of the traffic. She doesn't know what it is, but she senses, with a kind of certainty, that what she's hearing is the beginning of a composition.

The news from Anzor's country is of random violence and slaughter. It seems his lot is now on the losing side, although it is beginning to seem remote again, the battle fought in that part of the world; the name of the country no longer throbs for her with pain and relief as if it were the name of a human being. But it has entered her dreams now, the imagery summoned by the news and by Anzor; jagged hoary ruins, severe stone towers; a child's dead body; processions of scarved Shades moving with an uncanny steadiness. Our time's inferno, waiting to reveal its instruction.

In other dreams, plane trees from Budapest rustle her on to some dark cul-de-sac, the warm brick of Amsterdam presses up with a libidinal richness against a blurry suburban railroad, where she discovers with a vague and boundless fear that she has lost her suitcases and nobody will help her . . . That curve in the street beyond which she tried to peer as a child, and that will always stand for enigma. A path in the Paris park that leads, each time, to the unfolding of light. Her own metropolitan poetry, made from fortuitous fragments.

Through her dream, or reverie, she winds her way back to an image, so lovely and so ungraspable that she feels a line of longing arching back toward it, as expressive as a most lyrical melody. It must have been in the hacienda where they spent their summers when she was a child, and she can remember—feel—a white muslin curtain fluttering in a gentle breeze, and her mother's face, warm to the touch, bending over her, looking at her aslant, the curve of her neck bent by tenderness. Someone opening the white curtains, and then the breeze coming in with the new-morning light (Schubertian, Schumannesque). Going out on the balcony of the long, low house, to find her father standing there already, in his pajamas, looking out at the early sun and the dew. She ran into the garden in her bare feet, with the expanse of the pampas just beyond, into that all-encompassing sensation of happiness, happiness and beauty all combined, the rolling grasses and the breezes which combed and ruffled them like waves over changing water. She was breathless with the living beauty of it, with wanting somehow to leap into the harmonious motion rushing through the open space, so that she could be part of it, part of its great utterance. And now she thinks, perhaps this is one of the deep old sources too; the urge to give homage to the world not for its goodness, but for its Being; to give voice to it in all its permutations.

And just beyond these memories, beyond the reach of any

images, there are the inchoate spaces of the imagination, with their intimations of as yet unsung melodies, as yet unknown tones. She listens to something burgeoning within those spaces, to strange new textures and timbers, a premonition of aural shapes and motions, which she will have to transform, by whatever effort, into intelligible structure and articulate sound.

She knows she'll be leaving her isolation cell soon; but before she does, she has an unexpected visitor: Marcel. He is in California to conduct some important negotiations, having to do with the wine trade between France and the U.S. She still can't follow this kind of thing in detail, but perhaps she isn't obliged to. He has tracked her down through Peter in New York, and he quickly tells her that he knows all about the recent drama. "Or is it melodrama, my dear Isabel?" he asks. He casts his skeptical eye over her apartment, and she is once again surprised to see how pleased she is to see him, how much she likes the effect of his unfailing, unflappable poise.

"What exactly do you *do* with yourself here?" he asks after concluding his inspection.

"Isn't it you who told me that no one does anything exactly anymore?" she counters.

"Ah yes," he says. "But you've been one of the honest exceptions, didn't we agree on that? That's what is admirable about your profession. You have your exact, honest craft."

"That sounds nice and humble," she observes. He gives a little shrug, as if to say he can't help that.

"Nothing humble about what you got mixed up in, though," he picks up. "I didn't know you were a woman of such . . . romantic extremes." It's her turn to shrug.

Marcel insists on walking down Sunset Strip before dinner. He finds the idea of Hollywood fantastically amusing, fantastically *mythique*. He finds the reality perhaps a little disappointing; but in a way that has mythical connotations too. "Ah, I am so reminded of Gertrude Stein," he says, as they walk down the Boulevard, among its low, provisional-looking structures. "There's no there there. She was so right, was she not? There is not, now that we are here." His soft voice is seductively unhurried, his intonations amused and precise. "I suppose this is what there is," she says. "Ah, now you are getting properly philosophical, my dear Isabel," he says approvingly. "Now you're catching the drift."

They pause in front of a shop displaying a haphazard assortment of Western clothes. "You know," Marcel continues, looking at the ramshackle goods, the low, tacky buildings around them, "sometimes it's hard to know whether this country is the center of world power, or a banana republic." "Which is preferable?" she asks. "Neither, of course," he answers amiably. "But look, that's a very nice item." He points out a denim blouse with some red embroidery. "From cowboy films. It would suit you very well, don't you think? You'd be a sort of cowboy moll, isn't that what they call them? Ah, how I used to love those movies."

They decide to have dinner at a tacky-chic restaurant that Marcel believes he also recognizes from a movie. Its interior is deliberately plain, but not beyond his powers of interpretation. "Ah, this is so . . . unpretentious. So West Coast. I find it positively exotic," he avers, as they sit down. He scans the menu and allows himself to raise his eyebrows at the prices. "Yes, that's exactly what I find so interesting about being here," he goes on, mildly. "This . . . special kind of decadence. Kind of voice-of-the-people decadence, don't you think?" She takes it in too, the *faux-naïf* interior, the sauce of crushed raspberries with goat's cheese being offered with the beef carpaccio on the menu, the very tall woman at the next table putting on lipstick with an expression of high anxiety on her high-gloss face, the group of deeply tanned men at another table, shouting over each other with aggressive conviviality. She looks back at Marcel.

"You know," she says, "sometimes I think we're in an endgame. That we've blown it. To quote a famous line from a famous movie."

He looks up from the menu with quick, bemused interest. "*Easy Rider*, is it not?" She confirms and he looks pleased with himself. "But of course, there is no doubt," he continues, "that we're living in a declining empire. We're not ascending anymore. Of course, you Americans . . . well, you may be a little behind us in that respect. You can still do some harm. A considerable amount, I'd say. But perhaps you can also do some good. Though that, of course, is much more difficult."

"Does nothing matter to you?" she asks, as she did once before. But now she's asking the question through Anzor. She's still looking for ways to answer him.

"You know, when things begin to matter too much," Marcel says, "then we begin to kill each other. That's one thing I believe I have learned from studying our, shall we say, very long history. That's why I prefer to stay a little bit neutral."

"You think one shouldn't care," she states, half reproachfully. Marcel's eyes fill with a fine mischief. "Only as much as necessary," he says. "Only as much as cannot be avoided." He attends to the wine list, quite intensely. "Also, one should remain flexible in what one cares about," he resumes, having made his decision. "One should avoid too much . . . dedication. Because, you know, once you are in this game of power, things change very quickly. The cowboys and the Indians just don't stay in character, like they do in the movies. They exchange places all the time. So you have to be very supple. You have to adjust."

"So you think it's pointless to take sides," she states.

"Ah, sides," he repeats mildly. "There're so many of them nowadays. Now that we've had our end of history, I believe we are once again in a Great Game. No sides, just lots of players. And probably lots of mayhem. That's exactly why it's important to stay flexible," he concludes with satisfaction, "and to enjoy yourself."

The waiter brings their first course, and Marcel gives a prolonged moment to the contemplation of his exquisite piece of flaky cod, adorned with a cream sauce and a whole fennel. He raises his wine glass to her. "Now, the wine treaty," he declares gravely, "that's very serious. Wine is extremely important in times of decline. Wine and music, you will be glad to know. At least such is my theory."

"Should I be glad?" she inquires.

"Of course," he assures her. "We should take our pleasures where we can."

The waiter has brought their dessert, a small marvel of creamy vertical balance, which Marcel savors with appreciative noises. "Well, you can gag me with a spoon," he pronounces, with languid precision. "Isn't that how you say it?"

Isabel laughs. "It's not when you'd say it," she tells him. "It's not quite the context. But your English is certainly becoming very colloquial."

"Well, you know, I want to communicate with my American hosts," he says amiably. "Or at least, I don't want to be misunderstood by them. Officially, they're still the center of world power."

"But not for long?"

"Ah, I'm not a soothsayer, dear Isabel," he says. "I'm just having a nice time talking to you. But perhaps you would like to go to a disco? I think there is a famous one near here . . . you know, from that movie about Hollywood." For some reason— maybe it's Marcel's accent—they get past the bouncer without being quizzed. Once inside, she yields briefly to the music's insistent, repetitive, simplistic beat. She watches Marcel's precise and cool maneuvers with some amusement. They seem a bit out of context too.

"Ah well, enough," he says after a while. "I have seen it. Been there, done that, got that T-shirt."

As they part, he takes her hand in his, with some of their old camaraderie. "The thing about living in a declining empire," he says, "is that you can have a lot of fun. Is that not so?"

"As long as you don't care too much, is that it?"

"Exactly," he says. "I think you are understanding my wisdom. Finally."

On television, some end-of-century, this-is-your-history footage of the first moon walk, and she remembers seeing it the first time, remembers the bulky television set from which the images were emitted, at somebody's country house in Italy, where Lena had wandered with her and Kolya that summer. The children were allowed to stay up late for the occasion, and she remembers the inflated figures of the astronauts and the incongruous bounciness of their walk. Kolya was momentarily diverted, in a boy-child way, into utter enthusiasm and curiosity. How did they get there?! he shouted in his high voice, pointing his finger at the television screen. And, Can I go there? Can I walk like that?! The memory of his childish joyfulness no less a shroud on her soul than of his childish grief. The insufficiency of love . . . such an ordinary suffering, and his child self wanted so much to feel pleasure instead. After his death, she found a note in his desk drawer, scrawled in his jagged hand. It said, *"I've reached the end of pretend, and it is a dead end. Reality is not on TV. Too bad."* A more innocent time, the commentator on the program is saying, but then they've been saying that for a long time. She suddenly hates the notion, the conversion of the past into something wan and lyrical, almost as soon as it has happened. As if someone, somewhere were not suffering ordinary pain, or having their body pierced with bullets that day, as if armies somewhere were not forming their ranks in preparation for a just or unjust war, as if we were ever allowed not to know that, or not to choose. No, she thinks, she no longer wants to disappear into the past, or the future. She no longer wants to leap outside herself and to be held ecstatically within perfect forms. She feels a gathering of her own forces, an ingathering. Whatever she gives forth from now on, will be from within. She suddenly feels the return of an appetite, the need to move through her time, whatever it is; to come up against the unpredictable, edgy sharpness of the present.

And then the hunger for beauty comes upon her again, a need that's as tangible as the need for food. She listens to Beethoven's late quartets, and she hears them this time as a form of defiance. Defiance of the hard mercilessness of the world, the stony hate, the hurling of stones. Not solace, but antidote. Here's mercy which comes after anger, here's tenderness which transforms rage. Here is human force, contained in patterns so intricate and at the same time pure that they intimate a knowledge yet unknown. She spends whole days now listening, and sometimes letting herself cry, from the sheer wonderment of what she hears, or from the tension of trying to grasp, to contain, so much complexity. At other times, she makes clear or elliptical notes on various pieces, catching bits of insight on the fly, as they come. The music within comes back, in response and counterpoint; in phrases and rhythmic gestures, sharp fragments, melodic motifs. They're surprising, these snatches; odd turns of rhythm, timbers coalescing into chords, jagged progressions implying some irregular structure. She hears gorgeous cascades of Liszt's *Transcendental Études*, but also sounds of Jimi Hendrix and the blues, rumbles that may be of ocean water; or maybe of soldier-laden trucks . . . Different from Wolfe's singular, hypercondensed Sound. But then, she comes after the After. She buys some score paper and begins to make jottings of these phrases, as best she can; she needs a piano on which to try them out.

She rents a practice room and begins the laborious process of transcribing the emergent sounds in her head into marks and signs. She makes a mental gesture of gratitude to Wolfe, who taught her this. She tries to catch the faint, unearthly motif which first announced itself to her as an oscillating timbre, a summons from afar. But simultaneously, she senses, more than hears, a compressed mass of multilayered sounds, pressing in on her with an urgency that is almost libidinal. That *is* libidinal. No beauty without the libido, without desire. The sounds must out, they must get disentangled, must be transposed into intelligible music. She'll pull out the lines from the clustered aural masses and follow them as they unfold themselves, accumulating into larger sonorities, into groups of instruments and angled pitches. As she tries to write down the first motif for the appropriate instrument (clarinet, which is not quite right; but then nothing would be quite right), she already feels the intimations of hurtling, expanding forces behind it, jangling with imperious dissonance, building into tiered masses. Sometimes she hears herself groan with the effort of it. All art is in the resistance, and the resistance is mostly in the self. Can she sustain the musical materials she intuits, can she contain them, can she make sense of them? She doesn't know where this composition is going, how the aural pressures within her will range themselves into intelligible formations; but she hears beginnings of long sinuous lines, and the micro-rhythms of speeded-up time, passages of tender fragility, and of fierce, dancelike affirmation. She senses that this will be a large composition, and that it will contain instruments filled with the moistness of the human voice, and the hard sexual pounding of drums, and electronic sounds without any human breath at all. It will be her "Appassionata." She cannot burst the limits of her skin nor the bounds of time; but she can give herself forth, use herself as an instrument for what has passed and is passing through her. That is what will make it new. A difficult beauty is being born, she thinks, with a kind of wonder. She is being neither modest nor immodest; she simply wants to do justice to her task. For all the clamor and rush of its life within her, it will take time and strength to complete the piece; and she will know its meaning only when it will have emerged fully; when it is done.

She calls Peter, and tells him she's ready to come back.

"I'll pick you up at the airport," he says simply.

"Thank you," she says. She feels grateful for his not saying, or asking, more.

She tells him she has begun composing, and he's curious, wants to know what it is about. But of course, there is almost nothing she can say. It is really not about anything, and she hopes it will contain . . . as much as she truly knows. She says she'll play him bits of it when she gets home. She'll need some time to live with it, could she possibly use her old piano room . . .

"Sure," he says, and this time, she feels no chafing impatience at his tolerance. She hears a largess in it, a kind of strength. He has a very long fuse, Peter; but only because he knows his limits. He knows he will not, ultimately, betray himself.

She takes a brisk walk along the beach after they hang up, feeling a new sense of lightness. She hasn't realized how unhappy she has been, ordinarily unhappy as well as extraordinarily so. And how she wants an ordinary happiness, or at least contentment. She wants to lay her head on Peter's chest, and stay silent for a while. She wants to go to the Fairway, whatever may have happened there, and cook a simple dinner for herself and some friends, after emerging from her cave. She wants a pause from questions, and from having to know answers. Peter will let her have it, she can trust him for that; he won't ask anything, until she's ready to speak. She is deeply glad she can count on that. Eventually, they'll talk and talk.

In Between

See her there, walking through the airport in her jeans and leather jacket, her hair, tied back in a ponytail. Her eyes are still wide and pale, but her gaze is less inturned, directed at her surroundings with a different alertness.

In the airplane, she opens Wolfe's *Journal*, but the composition interferes. It's always with her now, its emerging patterns demanding her attention, a silent effort. For a while, she watches a documentary about nature preservation on her tiny screen. A young man, resembling a replicant in his miniaturized size, dives into a tropical seabed and then swims alongside stretches of coral reef, which have been damaged in the latest Very Big Disaster. Later, he is interviewed on a small boat. Palm trees in the background; traces of cataclysmic damage for the moment gone. He looks relaxed, pleased with himself. A few bits of the coral reef have been saved by his team. The heads of young people bob up out of the water, cheerful, healthy, earnest faces. They're doing something Good. The larger futility . . . it seems not to matter. Suddenly, she is almost moved. This is the world she happens to live in, of mediated images, meretricious motives and these touching, inadequate good intentions. This also is the current version of the human lot. It is hers to accept, to swim in. No other sea but this, for her lifetime, no matter what she can imagine, no matter what she wants. No matter how hard she wants it.

The long swoop of Long Island Sound, the pointillistic glow

of Manhattan's jeweled lights, like the glittering points of a hard-drive disk in her computer. Or is it the other way round. She's coming home; touching base. She has called Anders, and has told him she will be ready to take up her responsibilities soon. He growled at her at first, for the sake of form, but called back in triumph to tell her he rescheduled all the concerts she's missed for the next fall. In a few months, she's going to go to China and Japan. And onwards, almost all the way back, to Europe. If "back" is the appropriate word. In her kind of life, directionality no longer follows simple laws. She must get used to that too. She thinks of a Chinese pianist she heard in New York a while ago, absurdly young, and extravagantly flamboyant in technique and persona. A synthesis of Liszt, punk rocker, and all-purpose poet, with a flat body, turbulent hair and a long velvet jacket. Not even Jane could manage such an image, but then Jane is nearly two decades older than this virtuosic child. He makes MTV shorts in Hong Kong, apparently; and Isabel wonders why he doesn't do the obvious and play in a heavy metal band, or whatever it is that has replaced it since she last looked. But then, for sheer sexiness, Chopin still packs a punch. And in addition he is—romantic. The young pianist's "Spianato" and "Grand Polonaise" at Carnegie Hall was all ferocious elegance and pyrotechnic speed; and at the final gesture—that grand, abandoned sweep of the arm, as if he were giving himself over to triumphal ecstasy—the young Chinese girls who were there in flocks, got up and screamed in high voices, as if he were one of the Beatles. Or Franz Liszt himself. So she's curious about China, and about all the variations on her familiar art it can deliver. First, though, she will finish her composition, will pull it out of the roiling, unsort-ed sounds, the multilayered condensed information that is press-ing upon her, from within and without.

The plane is descending now, and she braces herself for the shock of landing. She feels the overpowering speed of the downward glide, and then the force of the plane braking. She listens to the machine's whistling hum, which she knows contains superhuman power, and her arms instinctively hold on to the arms of her chair as they hit ground. Hit earth. She thinks that Peter is probably parking his car at this very moment, and prepares for the trek through immigration, luggage, customs. The next stage.